# Absent Fathers

# Absent Fathers

## Sean Thomas

ANDRE DEUTSCH

First published in 1996 by
André Deutsch Limited
106 Great Russell Street
London WC1B 3LJ

CIP data for this title is available
from the British Library

ISBN 0 233 99003 8

Printed and bound in Great Britain by
WBC Bridgend

For Caitlin, Gareth and Alex

# Acknowledgments

The quotations on pages 229–30 derive, in a paraphrased form, from three books: *Paediatric Neurology* by Ingrid Gamstorp (Butterworth, 1985), *An Introduction to Paediatric Neurology* by Gwilym Hosking (Faber, 1982) and *Paediatric Neurology*, edited by Clifford Rose (Blackwell, 1982).

I would like to thank Tim Cumming, Catherine Schofield, Lizzie Coffen and David Newman for their invaluable help and advice.

*Ein jeder Engel ist schrecklich*
Every angel is terrible


*The Duino Elegies,* Rainer Maria Rilke

# 1. London Wall

'Fifteen Twenty!'
'Fifteen Twenty!'
'Fifteen Twenty!'
'*Cunt* —'

Juggling three phones and a pencil I bark at my intercom, very loudly. Since arriving at the dealing room at seven this morning I have had three cups of coffee, smoked five clandestine Turkish cigarettes, stared out of the window from a multitude of angles and completed the *Financial Times* crossword by filling it in with arcane swear-words. Swive. Tup. Coun. Merkin. For long stretches of the day I have done very little – very little has been happening – and now this sudden action.

'Two!'
'Twenty —'
'You twat —'
'Thirty. THIRTY —'

Flashing fingers in the air, like a bookie at a racecourse, I remonstrate with one of my colleagues; then I wink across my dealing desk at another friend and colleague, Andy Mackay. We are working as one this morning, trying to undermine confidence in the European Exchange Rate Mechanism. Today he is spanking the franc, while I am caning the peseta.

1

'EIGHT!' says a broker over my intercom. Instantly, I flick the intercom switch, and bellow back: 'Yes. Mine! My Amount!'

'Three million?'

'Three quid!'

'You got it —'

'Yeah!'

Lowering the volume on my intercom I start adding figures up. From my right I hear Andy's wry voice. 'Told you the recession was over.'

'Sorry?'

'I knew it when I saw those scrubbers down the Cross last night.'

'What the fuck are you on about?'

He fingers his purple, silk-knot cufflinks. 'There were these whores, right? Outside the Casey Jones burger bar. You should have seen them. Real slappers, real dogs. Tits like half-full Hoover bags. Track marks all over their arms. Weeping scabs on their scrawny white thighs. The ugliest bunch of sluts you've ever seen in your life.'

I nod, intelligently: 'And that means the recession is over?'

'Right.' He chuckles. 'It's obvious. If the prettier birds aren't being obliged to go on the game any more, that must mean the economy is picking up. You see? It's the GNP Growth/Fucked Up Old Scrubbers Index.'

Hand-combing his dark hair, he grins. I chuck a ball of screwed up paper in his direction. Then I flick the switch of my intercom to Off. The skirmish is over, the cannon smoke is hanging. I shall retire behind friendly lines to water my horse.

Across the vast, humming, grey-carpeted arena that is the Bank of Osaka Dealing Rooms, high up here on the thirteenth floor of London Wall, I take a left and a right and press a plate glass door and enter into the

2

backroom area. This large, air-conditioned, library-like space is known to the dealers as The Cloakroom, because this is where the anoraks hang. The train-spotters. Here one can find the market analysts and corporate economists and socio-industrial experts, and all the other boffins that spend their time auditing statistics and spotting trends and advising the rest of us how to gamble. At one desk I see Dave Barlow, head of Osaka Bank's European team. He is about twenty-three and has taken advantage of the company's Friday wear-what-you-like scheme to come to work dressed in deck shoes, white chinos and an acid-blue blazer. He is obviously going yachting in his coffee-break.

'Dave!'

'Guy . . .' he repeats, unenthusiastically, like the swot greeting the bully in the corner of the schoolyard. 'How can I help?'

'Just wondered if you've got any figures on the Spanish labour market. Think I spotted something.'

'Really?' His face is bleak and wintry. He hates all of us dealers; he hates our camaraderie, our *esprit de corps*. 'I suggest you ask Kash.'

'Kashmir? Why?'

'She's working in here, temporarily—'

'What?'

He smiles, this time smugly: 'They moved her from reception because she was causing problems.'

'Such as?'

'Bike messengers refusing to leave, board members having heart attacks, you know . . .'

Kash Anderson is the most attractive young woman in the company. She is a sort of the first water. Following Dave Barlow's nod I turn and see that the girl in question is sitting directly behind, taking calls. The way she handles the telephone receiver is unworldly. She is using her lips and her hands. The

3

concept makes me swoon. The idea of Miss Kashmir Anderson using her *lips* and her *hands*.

Reluctantly traversing the room I go to Kash's desk. Now I feel like Dave Barlow feels when he sees me. Kash Anderson is a bully; she bullies with her looks. In all probability she will tease and flirt and pout, and I will be left a pulp of jellified hormones. Every man in the company, from the meanest broker to the fattest Vice President, is witlessly scared of this girl. Scared of this teenie. They are scared of her yellow hair. Of that stripe of pelt between her legs.

'Uh, Kash . . .' She twists her lips from the phone. The air around her seems to shimmer.

'Yes, Guy?'

'Um, I . . . just . . . well, need some stuff. On the Spanish labour market. Cyclicals.'

She nods at the wall behind me. Then she gets up, and as she emerges from behind her desk I see that she has taken advantage of the company's casual Friday policy to wear a leather mini skirt.

'Fucking A—'

'Sorry?'

'Nothing.'

'I think the Spanish data is in here.'

She is reaching up to a filing cabinet. Top drawer. As she is quite medium-sized, she has to climb on to a chair. To this end she removes her shoes and ascends the chair in her bare feet. I notice that her heels are quite dirty, and her ankles slightly scuffed. The sluttishness of this makes me ache even more. I can't help it: I love sluts: those *dirty-ankled* girls . . .

Now, as I watch, rapt and expectant, like a Sicilian peasant gazing at the miraculous Madonna, the view up Kash's skirt improves. From this angle I can see the sweet curve of her buttocks, and the white crotch of her knickers, scarcely concealing her pubic hair.

Gulping, I try to think of something else. No good. As Kash bends into the drawer and blindly hands me down the right data, I look deeper and harder and closer, and – Kash turns around. Her face is knowing.

Gazing down at me she says, in her weird, drawled, slightly West Country accent: 'Is that enough? Have I given you enough?'

It is now obvious she was doing it all deliberately: admiring her beauty in the mirror of my gaze. Despite the knowledge, I am helpless. What can a man do? Swallowing I think, to hell with it: I ask the girl a question:

'Kash?'

'Yeah?'

'Why are you called Kashmir?'

Climbing down from her chair the girl kicks back a heel, to slip on a shoe. As she does the same with the second, she replies: 'My parents were hippies. Real Somerset hippies. Living in teepees, eating twigs, schlepping round the country in buses. All that malarkey . . .' Her eyes meet mine. 'Give me Dior and a Docklands flat any day. Have you got what you want?'

'Sorry?'

Her sly face tilts at the computer printouts in my hand. 'Is that OK?'

'Oh, sure . . .'

And I stroll off towards the coffee-machine.

Later I lean over to Andy and tell him about the epiphany that transpired between Kashmir and myself. His face goes from fear, to envy, to exultation, and ends up at incredulity.

'So you're telling me she's actually got a brain?'

'Seems so.'

'She's not just a simple invertebrate? With a

5

rudimentary nervous system?'

'No.'

'Jesus Christ. Jesus shagging Christ . . .'

Slumped in his chair, Andy sighs. Then he picks up a pencil and doodles. Beyond his expensive haircut I can see sunshine slanting through the glass and airplanes chalking vapour trails across the sky. It is one-fifteen: lunchtime. Thinking about this makes me feel happy. Soon I will be out there in the late spring sunshine. Soon I will be outside in my shirt-sleeves, lolling in the plaza, munching my M&S sandwiches, relishing the first micro-skirts of May. Setting my pencil flat on the desk, I clasp my hands behind my head and smile, at no one in particular.

## 2. Portobello Gold

Raising his glass, my friend says: 'Toast?'

'Toast.'

'Absent fathers—'

Chinkingly, I repeat the phrase. Then I return to the topic in hand: 'So you were saying, Si. About cockroaches?'

'Yesss,' he slurs. 'Cockroaches. Atheists are just like cockroaches.'

'Er, right.'

My friend shakes his head: 'No, it's true. Think about the way they scuttle around. The way they scuttle across the floor, unaware of the splendour up above . . .' He shrugs, swayingly. 'They're just like roaches in a cathedral, and that's why I feel sorry for them.'

Looking across the table, I shake my head. I'm not quite sure how to reply. Simon Reeves and I have been having this argument – about God and atheism – since we were students together at the Bartlett School of Architecture, ten years ago. In which time I have never been able to refute his faith, nor he derail my disbelief. But I have never heard him speak with such surreal assurance. He is now banging on about theologians: comparing them to circus clowns.

'Right,' I say. 'So you're saying Karl Barth is basically

the same as Ronald MacDonald?'

Simon nods: 'Theologians are the only true atheists. They're the only ones who can say for sure that God does not exist and that it's all a load of rubbish. Because their study makes them see the contradictions of the Bible, and the illogicality of church teaching.' Downing his fourth G&T, Simon wipes his lips, and goes on: 'And the perfect metaphor for *that* predicament is the sad circus clown who spends his life making people laugh.'

'But if that's what you think, why do you believe?'

Simon smiles. 'Because I'm not a theologian. Thank God.'

We are chatting across a pint-stained wooden table, outside Finch's pub, on the Portobello Road. It is a Friday night in May and the streets of W11 are thronged with film students, scriptwriters, photographers, graphic designers and TV people. Viewing this parade of gonnabes it occurs to me these so-called creative people are so creative that they flock to the same part of town and drink in the same bars and wear the same clothes and sleep with the same people.

But maybe I'm just jealous – I'm just a Foreign Exchange dealer, after all. And the girls *are* pretty cute. There is one in particular, standing across the street. This girl is exceptionally pretty. She has tumbling curls of uncut golden hair that lie like epaulettes on her cashmere shoulders. Sitting here staring at the girl I am seized with a sudden desire to make the girl perspire. To make her *sweat*. To feel her soft skin cling against mine, like a silk-shirt in a rainstorm.

'Make it obvious, why don't you?'

I swerve. 'Well, look at her. She's tidy, man —'

'Really . . . Gosh . . .'

Upending my glass, I say: 'She's no pints.'

'Sorry?'

8

'I wouldn't have to drink any pints before sleeping with her.'

Not looking, Simon sighs and doesn't laugh. I do not mind this. Standing here, next to my old chum, I feel a sudden, strange, drink-fuelled flush of comradeship, a headrush of gratitude. Years ago I did something very bad to Simon – perhaps the worst thing a man can do to a friend. Years later he replied – by doing the best thing a man can do to a friend for me. And these facts amaze me. As I stand here, drink in hand, these facts amaze me, for the millionth time.

But enough: I don't want to get sentimental. Slapping Simon's back I say: 'How's the architecture?'

'Oh, OK. Underpaid.'

'And Sarah?' I am referring to my sister: Simon's wife.

Extracting his lemon slice, Simon sucks it masochistically. 'Not bad. She's coping . . .'

'How about my niece?'

He brightens: 'Alice is fine. She's great.'

'But,' I say, 'last time I came round you were screaming for the jailer. You couldn't see the TV for dirty nappies.'

He nods happily: 'Yes, well, parenting does have the odd pitfall. But you've just got to remember the good bits. The satisfactions.'

'Satisfactions?'

'When you hold up your first-born and you show them the world and you say, one day all this will be yours —'

'Come again?'

'It is amazing. Honestly.' Gazing at my sceptical face, he smiles. 'Sarah's meeting me here with Alice in a minute, actually. So you'll be able to see.'

'What?'

'Her latest achievement. She can almost tie her shoelace . . .'

9

I make a *gosh, how interesting* face. He continues: 'She's my daughter, Guy. My child. You can't put it any other way . . . It's profound. It's like God's love for humankind —'

That's it: that's enough. Awkwardly extricating my legs from under the wooden table, I step inside Finch's and press through the Friday night hubbub. At the bar I lean over the beer-splashed veneer and check out the Kiwi barmaid's sunbronzed thighs.

'G'day, Guy. A Youngs and a G&T, right?'

I nod. Lisa tuts as she pumps: 'Everything OK?'

'Sure. My best friend's wittering on about the joys of fatherhood. Again.' Handing the money over, I grin. 'Cheers.'

Burdened by the pint and the gin, I head back to our pavement table where I discover that everything has changed: my seat has been usurped by my sister and my niece. On seeing her uncle emerge from the pub, two-and-a-half-year-old Alice Reeves jumps from her mother's lap, runs over and puts her arms in the air.

'Uncle Guy! Uncle Guy!'

What the hell . . . Bursting into a big dopey smile, I set the glasses on the table, grab the little girl around the chest, and lift her to my side as I kiss her beerily on the forehead.

Understandably, Alice makes a *yuk* expression, and smears her face with a fist. Then she blurts: 'Uncle Guy, I had bagetti!'

'What?'

My sister intervenes, looking at her daughter: 'She had spaghetti for tea, didn't you?'

'Mmmm. Bagetti! Bomato! Bagetti-bomato!' Turning to me, Alice smiles and laughs and shuts her blue-green eyes, then opens them wide. This close to my niece's face, I can see a purplish stain on her tongue, presumably the result of some lollipop she has been licking.

Noticing me noticing this, Simon inputs: 'Your grandad bought them for you, didn't he? Didn't grandad buy you some lollipops?'

Nodding, Alice looks downcast. Then gleeful again. Then sad again. Sarah tuts.

'Simon, I think she's tired.'

Standing up, my sister extends her chubby, motherly arms and collects her daughter. Thus transferred, Alice buries her sleepy face into her mother's cardigan.

At this point, Sarah and Simon exchange glances. I reckon he wants to carry on drinking with me; as usual, the husband accedes to his wife. After a flurry of good-byes and a teasing kiss on my cheek from Alice, the three Reeveses disappear towards Simon's car, parked outside the Portobello Gold; as they go I spot Alice waving to me over her mother's shoulder. Painfully aware that I am being watched by half the coolest people in London, I wave back.

Once the three of them are out of sight I re-think the evening. There are a few acquaintances of mine inside the pub but the person I most want to speak to is that girl: the blonde one. Downing my warm pint of bitter, I prepare my expression and purposefully cross the road. This is it. This is the moment. I am inexpressibly confident. I am the quintessence of wit. I am pissed.

The blonde-haired girl is surrounded by grungey white boys, attired in baseball hats and flapping tee-shirts. The boys all look high. As I approach – neatly tripping over the gutter-strewn bottles of Moravian beer – I change my mind: the boys look happy and excited not because they are on drugs, but because they are with the blonde: with the best-looking girl in the pub.

In truth this girl is too much. Nearer to the group I begin to realize, with a sinking feeling, that this girl is just too damn pretty to front up, to cold call. She has an inhibiting beauty; she is a *sort*. Despairingly, I make for the bar. A voice calls me back.

'Guy!'

It is Patrick Randall, an old friend. Patch has just joined the selfsame group of white soul boys, and he is inviting me over. Sweet: this gives me the perfect intro. Retracing my steps, I begin listening to Patch and his friends, and to the blonde-haired beauty, whom Patch introduces as Nicola. The group's conversation is all about the Yugoslavian civil war. They are talking about how Sarajevan mothers have reportedly been delivering stillborn babies because of the Serbian shelling.

Absorbing this, Nicola nods and pipes up, opening her red mouth: 'You know, that's like a really weird coincidence. My *boyfriend* was stillborn . . .'

With a cough, I stall for time. Two significant facts can be inferred from this remark. The first is that Nicola is a retard; the second is that she has got a boyfriend. Of the two, the latter disturbs me the most. It irks. Standing here on the periphery of the gang I find myself suppressing a laugh as I simultaneously get angry about Nicola's boyfriend. Controlling myself, I turn and start talking to the second girl.

The new girl is called Eva Speisser. Pretty soon I elucidate that she is of Swiss-German provenance, that she is intelligent, and that she is, in her own way, very pretty, if not quite as pretty as No-Pints. Time passes; we chat.

'So what do you do?' I say.

Brightly Eva tells me she is an art student. This is no shock: I have already deduced from the spatters of paint on her barrack-boots that she is one of those I-Go-To-Art-College exhibitionists. Concentrating on Eva's breasts I try to contain my cynicism. The next thing I know I'm offering to crush through the crowds and buy some more drinks.

Eva contradicts. 'Let me go. You do want another?'

'Sure, why not . . .'

'What sort?'

'Gin and tonic . . . No lemon. No ice. No tonic.'

She squints. 'I'm sorry . . . I don't get you . . .'

'It's nothing. I'm a bit out of it. A bit drunk.'

'Also,' she says, uncertainly. 'Do you always get like this?'

'Only when I'm with *exceptionally* beautiful women.'

This is pretty obvious, but she buys it. Cutely tilting her head, Eva smiles. Instantly my heart goes out: to her sad little smile and her hopeful little squint and her mildly German accent. And to her suntanned young shoulders, so fetchingly set off by her orange cotton singlet. Observing these dimpled brown arms as they disappear into the pub I get a strange urge to protect this young woman; I want to be her man; I want to be her man standing by her side with my arm around her bare, slender, belt-cinched midriff. I want to be taller and bigger and stronger than her, and yet to be enslaved by her.

By the time Eva comes back from the bar I am totally persuaded. She has already told me she is an art student and has a Teutonic background. This is information enough for me to try and seduce her; question is, what precise angle? Taking a gamble I move the conversation on to the Viennese Expressionists. To my gratification, it works. The girl's green eyes start to shine and her red cheeks get redder; she looks like a child at a bonfire party. Calculatingly I ask her if she likes Egon Schiele and she nods enthusiastically and tells me about her first visit to the Kunsthistoriches in Vienna. After this it flows: we chat about Gustav Klimt and I ask her if she has seen those drawings he made of *women masturbating?* I do this with a totally straight face and she doesn't quite know how to take it. Then I alter tack a little and mention the girl in Klimt's *The Kiss* and how she reminds me, slightly, of Eva. 'Those endless legs of yours, you know.' Again she flutters. Afterwards I ask her about her home and the most unhappy day of her life: which in turn gives me a chance to tell her about one of my unhappiest days, the day I heard of my parents' divorce.

'Yeah,' I say. 'It was terrible. But I don't *blame* them for it. They were just too similar, like two trees that were planted too close together. You know? By the end they had grown *into* each other. Every move they made reopened the wound, the cut in the bark —' Discomfited, she squints, again.

Ignoring this, I say: 'Maybe it *was* my mum's fault, though. She wanted to be free, and all that. I think women should stick to the kitchen. Don't they say something like that in Germany – *Küche, Kirche, Kinder?*'

Now there's another silence. A silence while my eyes twinkle and Eva giggles. She is shocked, amused and intrigued: as I intended. Presently we set off again: talking of Michelangelo and Leonardo, and Schiele, and their mysterious sexualities: whereby I enquire, naturally, about her first sexual experience. When she tells me I say uh-*huh*, then admit my own daft romanticism: how I long to be in love, to be really, truly, deeply in love, to be properly in love just for once —

Then I stop.

At the height of my pitch, I have stopped – and taken Eva's hand. It's a gamble, but not a big one: as I press Eva's damp palm between my fingers and put my lips mere inches from her coyly smiling face, I confess to Eva that I want to . . . *kiss* her. That I can't help it. That if she won't let me *kiss* her then I'm going to walk away and forget her, forever.

And Eva is so drunk, so drunk on the drink and the words and the warm sweet air of this balmy May

evening . . . I can see her doubting. I can see her confusing. I can see her entertaining the fatal suspicion: for
a second she has doubted the certainty that she will not
fall in love, not here, not tonight, not with me.

We have kissed.

# 3. Broadgate Six

US Payroll day. Stepping out of the lift I cross the hall that leads into the Bank of Osaka dealing room and I see Andrew Mackay.

'Hi, shag.'

'Hi, shag . . .' I grin. 'What's new?'

Rolling his eyes, Andy shrugs. 'Not a lot. Deirdre's put some stuff on your desk. The usual crap.'

'Sure . . .' Sidling round the bay I take my seat at my dealing desk. This comprises six intercoms, two telephones, a Reuters touchscreen, a fat computer, three Telerate monitors and reams of Tuffs reports on the implications of today's US Payroll data. Lifting the Tuffs reports I uncover a copy of *Viz* and a half-eaten *pain au chocolat.*

Across the way Andrew is smirking.

'OK, Mackay. What's the problem?' He continues smirking, while I retort: 'Still living in London W Fuckwit?'

'Guy?'

'Sorry?'

Directly behind me is my boss: Deirdre Lavelle. Aged thirty-three-and-a-third, blonde-haired, sharp-tongued Deirdre earns £350,000, plus a six-figure bonus, and has got more bollocks than most of Great Britain. Today she looks slightly peeved.

'Good morning, Deirdre,' I shrug. 'Just . . . shooting the breeze.'

'Evidently,' she says, and sits down. As she does this I admire the shapeliness of her thighs. They remind me that I like having a young female boss, inasmuch as it gives you something nice to look at when you are staring at the boss with contempt.

The morning proceeds. Everybody in Spot is waiting for those US Payroll figures. These will tell us if the US economy is pulling out of recession as fast as it ought. Leafing through the data on my desk I scan Dave Barlow's précis of the various latest currency market ramifications. Then I seek a better and second opinion by glancing at the Knight Ridder section of my Telerate screen. The KR text informs me that *DA to propose Folic Acid for grain products* and *Canadian cheddar cheese futures: subdued.* Right. Knocking back the rest of my coffee I glance at one of the TVs suspended over the dealing room. It is showing Skysport: Aussie Rules football . . .

The hours pass; I try to learn something, to gain something from the day. But none of it avails: all I glean is that Aussie Rules is a punch-up in vests, that Deirdre *is* wearing knickers and that the *Dutch Labour Chief says Flemish tyre industry needs more investment.*

Several coffees later, I resolve to do *something.* Sitting up I make a couple of tentative cable transactions with the broker from Marshalls.

His intercommed voice is mateily sarcastic: 'You sound like you had a hard night, Guy. What's her name?'

'Eva Speisser.'

'Come again?'

'Her name's Eva Speisser.'

'New bird is she? Goes a bit, right?'

'Bangs like a barn door —'

'Ha ha ha,' he says. 'Ha ha ha ha ha ha ha ha ha ha ha —'

Idiot. I switch him off. As I turn to add my figures, I am distracted by a low whistle from Andrew.

'It's her,' he says, kicking my left shin, hard.

'Who?'

His head tilts to the Financial Futures Dealing Desks. Between the bays there glides, as if on castors, a vision of Oriental loveliness.

'Christ, she's pukka . . .'

'Interest Rates Futures?'

'Yep.'

Deirdre disagrees: 'She's in Swiss Francs. And her name is Beatrice.'

'Beatrice?' I am mystified. The girl appears kind of Asian.

Deirdre tuts. 'She's half-French, half-Vietnamese – if you're really interested . . .'

'French, eh? Guess that would explain the stylish blue blouse and the silk Chanel neckscarf —'

'And the filthy little arse.'

Deirdre flashes Andy a warning glance. Before their stand-to can flare, a buzz goes round the dealing room: it's one-thirty – time for the Payroll Data.

Hushed, we wait. Almost coyly, it flashes up: 150,000.

As soon as this figure has sunk in, we realise that it is much as expected and therefore anti-climactic. For several minutes several of us make a pretence about dealing on the Payroll data, but it's pointless. After half an hour of not doing much dealing, Andrew whistles and yawns, and fingers his silver university cufflinks.

'Might as well go home.'

I am inclined to agree. Sometimes dealing Foreign Exchange on the Spot Market can be grand. At times

18

dealing Spot can be the best job on earth; the nicest gamble in town. There are occasions, indeed, when I get positively giddy with the sense of being where it's at: at the centre of the nexus, the fibre optic web, the chic new freemasonry that is the transglobal money market. Not now.

Rising from my desk I grab some silver coins and wander over to the coffee machine; once coffeed-up, I gaze down out of our thirteenth-floor windows. From this vantage I can appreciate the architectural beauty of the Barbican Centre: the algae-green lake, the whizzy steel fountains, the perpendicularity of St Giles Cripplegate so pleasingly set off by the Corbusieresque Aldersgate Housing. Visoring my eyes against the sun, I survey the rest of the lakeside esplanade. I have just spotted a trio of tourists consulting a map. These people are lost; two hours ago I saw them in the very same place, consulting the very same map.

'Guy —'

My reverie is revoked. Deirdre is tapping me on the shoulder.

'Phone call.'

Crossing to my desk I pick up my receiver. It is a girl; she is saying, amongst other things: 'I want you to meet me.'

'Meet you?'

'Yes. Meet me. *Now.*'

'But – Belinda . . . I . . . where?'

'Anywhere. Use your *noddle.* I'm at Liverpool Street Station, I haven't got all day.'

'OK, OK. I'll . . . just a sec —' Mildly panicked, I put Belinda on hold and turn to Andrew.

'*Andy!*'

Distractedly, Andy drawls: 'What?'

'Quick. Think of somewhere discreet where I can meet an ex-girlfriend.'

'Why would you want to meet an ex-girlfriend?'

'I don't. She's just rung out of the blue and said I've got to meet *her*, right now.'

Andrew whistles.

'She's probably preggers. You naughty boy.'

This awful possibility hadn't occurred to me. Until now. Groaning at the prospect, I flick a switch and immediately I can hear Belinda's agitated voice.

'*Well?*'

'Yes — I'll meet you . . . In the café at the back of Broadgate Arena. It's called Benito's.'

'Benito's? When?'

Checking my watch and estimating the taxi-time and the traffic, I muse: 'How about two-thirty? In twenty minutes?'

'Fine. *Don't* be late.' Her telephone clicks.

Pulling my jacket from the back of my chair I go to the lift and descend to the ground floor and step out-side my huge, unlovely building – Alban Gate, on London Wall – and lazily wait for an empty taxi to swing by. It doesn't take long. Hopping into the empty cab, I slide down the window and feel the easy June air on my face, meanwhile recalling recent afternoons spent with Belinda. With the girl on the phone.

Belinda was/is a trainee doctor, a trainee oncologist, at Queen Mary's Hospital. I went out with her for a month, during which time I got to love her doctor-liness. It was so unusual. So different. It was so nice to go round to her rooms at QMH and fuck her without letting her take off her white coat and stethoscope. The only drawback to this arrangement was that, being attached to the oncology ward, Belinda was constantly on call. Therefore our coitus was all-too-frequently interruptus: one moment I'd be taking her roughly from behind, rhythmically banging her head against the wall-

20

paper – the next moment her pager would go *bleep*. Then I'd have to withdraw, while she threw her coat around her nudity and disappeared down the corridor to Cancer Ward. There she would prescribe some pethidine, or authorise a morphine pump, or take a family aside and explain that Dad died very peacefully: all the while smelling of our recent fuck, underneath that flapping white coat.

In retrospect, it seems sweetly Freudian; a delicious juxtaposition of Eros and Thanatos. It was not. She was too aggressive, too bossy: when we were making love, Belinda liked best of all to go on top, to saddle up and ride. *Really* ride: there were times I felt that what Belinda truly wanted was to rape me – if only our relative anatomies and bodyweights had permitted. She was a sexual tomboy, and her proclivity turned me off. When it comes down, *I* have to dominate. Can't help it: I like a woman down and dirty and squealing like a manhandled sow.

The cab is stuck in traffic. Impulsively I decide to get out and continue on foot up Chiswell Street. I like Chiswell Street – it has a number of decent buildings, like the converted Georgian terrace that is the Whitbread HQ, and the cuboid-esque chunk of emerald glass cladding that is Number 1 Moor Street. Chiswell is also rather agreeable because it turns with suddenness into the big, rich, cool, travertine-and-steel urbanity of the Broadgate Centre.

There was another reason why I couldn't hack it with Doctor Belinda Gibbon. She insisted on condoms. It was a fetish with her: a symptom of her medically-honed mentality: and one which she took to unhelpful extremes. There were times when we'd be gripped by sudden passion in the temporarily disused children's ward, start grappling on a Formica table – spilling toys and teddies – when she'd calmly sit up and say: OK, stop now, put on a condom. Naturally I'd balk. But she'd insist. Then I'd stall and claim I didn't have any. So she'd get huffy and start pulling on her knickers, and finally I'd surrender: saying OK, OK, *Okay*, reaching into my pocket and unwrapping the thing. By the time I'd got one of the condoms on, after a good deal of manly cursing, our ardour would have become less urgent and we would end up doing it in bed. Which was particularly galling, as one of the things that has always turned me on is spontaneity. That *right now, right here* stuff: I love it. I love a girl who likes it, too. But so few do, in these dull days of Aids-consciousness.

As of now I am leaving the vicinity of Broadgate 9 and approaching Broadgate 3. While I gaze at the modernist waterfall, I realise that three things are bugging me: 1. That the government has so crassly painted itself into a corner on the question of interest rates and the ERM; 2. That most of the eighties' rebuilding of London isn't of the same architectural quality as the Broadgate Development; 3. Aids.

Taking a seat opposite my ex, in the crowded Benito's Coffee Bar, I suppress my annoyance and smile. 'Hi, Belinda.'

Soberly, she replies: 'I'm pregnant.'

'You're what?'

'I said: I'm pregnant. And don't ask.'

'Ask what?'

Tilting her head, sardonically: 'Whose it *is*, idiot. Take it from me. I'm a doctor, remember?' Her eyebrows lift. 'It's *yours*, Guy.'

Now, I suppose a normal reaction to the news of an unexpected and unwanted pregnancy would be anxiety,

22

consternation, anger, even grief. Not me. The first thing I feel like doing is leaping in the air and shouting *yippee*, before darting round the corner to order a crate of Bollinger. The reason I want to do this is because Belinda has just unwittingly informed me that, despite my darkest fears, I am fertile. Despite all those teenage years of too-tight jeans and hallucinogenic drugs and never-ending masturbation: I'm fertile. I've got what it takes. Yee-hah! Fortunately, I have the sensitivity not to ask for a special cake with sparklers to be brought to our table. Instead, I lean forward, with worry and concern faked across my brow: 'When? How? I don't . . . quite see —'

'You don't see how it's possible, mm? Don't you remember then?'

'What?'

'The third time we did it, that last Saturday? When the condom broke? I've had it dated. I've been pregnant six weeks. It's *six weeks precisely*, since that Saturday.' She shrugs: QED.

Hearing this latest news I have to further restrain myself from singing the *Internationale*. Not only am I fertile, I'm super fertile! The third shag of the day! Talk about sperm count!

'What . . .' I stammer. 'What . . .'

'What are we going to do?'

For once I am grateful for Belinda's habit of completing my sentences.

'Right . . .' I say. 'Yyyes . . . What have you . . . decided to do? You don't . . .'

'Want you to propose? Don't be stupid. Why would I want to marry a selfish bastard like *you*?'

If I wasn't so sure, I might forget that *I* finished with *Belinda*.

'I've decided, anyway,' she continues. 'I'm going to have it terminated. I just thought I should let you know.

And that maybe . . .'

Untypically, Belinda lets her statement dwindle away. She has suddenly lost it. Nervously, she starts toying with her silver necklace. I notice she is wearing chunky black loafers. White socks, beige slacks. An expensive white shirt. In truth she looks quite chic, attractive and in control. But I can tell she is not really on top of things. Sipping my coffee I stall for time, until I work out why Belinda is so anxiously fishing.

'You'd like me to pay?'

'Well . . .'

*Well yes*, obviously. And *well, fuck off* is what I feel like replying. Why should I? It occurs to me, as I sit at this table and suck spoonfuls of chocolate-covered cappuccino froth, that this is all rather unfair. If Belinda decides to keep our baby I have no say in the matter but I am legally expected to pay for its upbringing. Then again, if Belinda decides to kill our baby I still have no say in the matter but I am socially expected to support her decision, pay for the operation and feel a bit guilty to boot. Thus my instinct is to smile, slap Belinda on the back, and reply '*Our Bodies, Our Selves?* – Your Body, Your Problem, sweetheart.'

However, I don't. As I look across the sugar bowl into Belinda's averagely pretty face, as I take in that tightly coiffed hair under that neat velvet Alice band, I am suffused with affection and sympathy. The nice me wins out, for once. Here is a girl about whom I once cared, with whom I once made love: all too effectively, it seems. She needs my pity, my masculine protection.

Getting up, I go round and take the seat next to hers. Belinda lifts her brown eyes to mine and I can see that she is nearly crying. All that hard, modern, career-person-with-attitude stuff is falling away, is crumbling, and suddenly she is a frightened young woman in a frightening world, who is frighteningly in thrall to the

24

hormones already coursing through her body.

'Come on,' I say, embracing the girliness of Belinda's shoulders. She responds by hiding her face in my shirt and blubbing. She is crying so much she makes my own throat choke, just a little.

'Hey,' I repeat. 'C'mon. It'll be OK.' By which statement I do not know what I mean. Maybe I mean: if only the world was a better place and I were a better person then maybe this baby inside you would have a better chance of life. But of course it isn't; I'm not; it hasn't.

Taking Belinda's hand I pay for the cappuccinos, lead her through the door, exiting into Broadgate Arena.

Outside, all is sunshine and cheeriness. Office ladies are lying along the benches, their skirts hitched up for the purpose of tanning – and of attracting male admiration. In their second aim, at least, the girls are successful: twenty yards away a dozen males are standing around and gawping at the girls over their pints of fizzy-gold lager. Some of the men have shed their jackets, and their shirtsleeves look completely dazzling in the bright sunlight, pure and spruce and white against the pink maroon of Broadgate Six.

Watching this pleasantly textured scene I realise, with a start, that for a long time Belinda has said nothing. Perhaps because there is nothing to say. She is holding my hand, gently, and in that gentle press is all the articulacy that she needs, as we gaze across the flower-hung concrete esplanade of the Broadgate Arena. Incongruously it occurs to me that we must look like one of those old couples you see sitting in cars, at resorts, staring wordless out to sea.

# 4. The Bartlett School of Architecture

Waking up, I look at the ceiling, then turn my head to the window, to check the sky. The sky is grey and promises rain. Covering myself with the duvet I sigh and check my mental state. It is grey and promises rain.

Just as I am beginning to wonder quite what crimes I committed last night – to induce such a *bitch* of a hangover – I hear a girlish little snore. Peeping under the duvet, I see Eva; this serves to remind me. Last night I went out drinking with Eva Speisser: to Covent Garden and Soho, Mayfair and Notting Hill. That much I can piece together. But then what? From my side of the pillow I gaze at Eva's sleeping form. She has three bruises on her neck, a violet trefoil. The sight of these bruises jogs my memory further: last night, after we finished drinking, Eva and I rolled on to Oxford Street, hailed a black cab and came here to my place. Once home we didn't even bother to make coffee: as soon as we crossed the threshold we grabbed each other and kissed each other and pushed each other's clothes to the floor . . .

Eva wakes.

Propping my head on my hand, I say: 'You awake?'

She looks at me: '*Ja*. Are you?'

'Yes . . .'

'OK.'

'Me too.'

'Mmm . . .'

So far, so nice. I like the untaxing nature of our conversation; I am happy for it to continue in the same vein for the next few hours. Such a low-level dialogue would enable me to think about other stuff; however, another, less welcome memory has gatecrashed my consciousness. Late last night Eva and I had sex: and she completely failed to climax. She failed to orgasm, just as she has so far failed to orgasm whenever we have slept together. Up to now I have ascribed this failure to drink, or tiredness, or the embryonic nature of our sexual relationship; this morning I'm not so sure. The normal despondency of a hangover is uniting with worries about my sexual prowess to create a nasty and untypical feeling of self-dislike; happily, before I can get into a really serious mope, I am interrupted. Eva wants to be about her business. After asking me the time, she climbs from the bed, goes to the chair, rummages in her bag, and starts dealing with her contact lens holder.

'Steady,' I say, wincing at the sight of fresh bitemarks on her bare arse. Obviously I had a good time, even if she didn't. 'It's only eight o'clock, Evie.'

Eva continues her preparations. Black brassière, faded jeans, cool tee-shirt, Doc Martens. Attired, she turns: 'Should you not be at work?'

This is a pretty standard remark for my new girlfriend: to make me feel guilty with her diligence. Hauling myself up, so that I'm sitting against the pillows like a convalescent about to receive chicken soup, I shrug.

'Too hungover. Think I'll take a sickie.'

The girl tuts: 'You will never be a rich man if you do not work. They will sack you, no?'

'Nope. I'm the best.' I smile, tranquilly. 'Besides, maybe if they sack me I'll go and do something arty and worthwhile, just like you? Mm?'

Tilting her head, as she clips on her second earring, Eva mutters 'that will be the day', after which she leans over the bed and ruffles my hair with a sad, indulgent smile. This warm gesture makes me glow: it also depresses me. The gesture makes me feel ungrateful, because I know I will never be able to reciprocate Eva's evidently growing devotion. Even if she and I surmount our sexual teething problems, I am too frightened to fall in love with this girl: to climb the snowclad peaks of passion. Perhaps I am too frightened to fall in love, period. As I clearly recall, being in love is like being in a foreign country with one other person. Everything is fine if you are getting on – the language is strange but alluring, the food is weird but enticing, the sights and the smells are racy and gamey and seductive. But when it goes wrong, when you fall out with your sole fellow-traveller, then it's a nightmare of loneliness. Suddenly you are lost, and bewildered, and helplessly estranged from your friends, and the only person who can speak your language isn't speaking to *you*.

With a peck on my forehead, unaware of the dark thoughts within, Eva stoops to the chair and collects her bag. Seconds later she is at the bedroom door, saying: 'Next Wednesday, *ja?*'

'*Jawohl*, darling . . .'

After she's gone, I lie there.

Then I go back to sleep.


Waking up two hours hence, I realise I am feeling a little better. Stumbling downstairs into the bathroom I gulp some tap water and take a leak. Then I think about masturbating: reliving last night's endeavours. But the effort is too much so I have a shower, find

28

some clothes, and descend to the kitchen.

Lying flat on the kitchen table is a note from one of my flatmates saying, simply: 'Yours?' with a scrawled arrow pointing to a pair of black lacy knickers.

Pocketing Eva's panties, I turn on the radio and open a couple of bank statements and gloat over my massive income, sipping coffee the while. On the radio Mrs Thatcher's old economics guru Alan Walters is bemoaning the stupidity of the present government's monetary policy. He is saying that the government is stuck: that because of the recession they are obliged to drop interest rates, to prevent a slump – yet they can't because they are handcuffed to the almighty Deutschmark, courtesy of the Exchange Rate Mechanism. Ranting, a little, Walters goes on to say that this situation gives the government two choices: revalue within the ERM, or quit the System completely.

Nodding, I swig more coffee. He is right. He is absolutely right, and everybody knows it: the highflyers at the Treasury, the editorial board of *The Economist*, the old tramp on the Caledonian Road who has arguments with pigeons . . .

Folding my *Times* I switch the radio off. Five minutes later I put on my desirable front-quarter-horsehide leather jacket and exit the front door. I have decided to spend some of my huge income. It is time.

In The Square a few boys are skateboarding: they are wearing baggy, souped-up, acid house fashion. Stopping to look at them for a second it occurs to me that kids never used to be this trendy. I know I wasn't.

Attempting to maintain my dignity, as one black boy nearly knocks me over, and another nearly brains me with a football, I pass the public library and enter into the streetlife of the Cally. There isn't a whole lot of activity on the Cally today. The overcast and drizzly

June weather seems to have chased everybody away: all I can see are two diminutive Asian women in saris, a drunken old tosser shouting at pigeons and a number of buses obliviously shooting past.

I opt to walk into town: it is about forty minutes from here but the walk will help to clear the vestiges of my hangover, if nothing else. Down the Cally, turning right onto the Euston Road, I pass the perfectly proportioned, absurdly small Wellcome Institute building, after chucking a quick glance at the asymmetric massif that is the New British Library. Every time I walk this route the new BL never fails to intrigue. Sometimes I think it is nervous and timid, other times I revile its Sainsbury's vernacular, still other times I think it has a complex, discreet, understated beauty when set against the joyous Byzanto-Gothic of St Pancras Station. Considering these contradictions I get to feel I would welcome Simon Reeves's opinion on the subject: it might warm me on this unusually chilly summer day. Our discussions were always so heated. The very first time we spoke, we argued.

I was sitting in the Bartlett common room. It was only the first term of my freshman year at the Bartlett but I already knew I wasn't destined for a fellowship, or even a degree: I did not fit in. When I had applied, I had fondly imagined that it would be a place of intellectual dare-devilry, of theoretical cut and thrust. These ideas were swiftly quashed. The Bartlett was a church with one creed: modernism. Classicism did not exist. Gothic was virtually a swear-word. Post-modernism evoked the same irritated disgust one affords a turd that's too big to flush down the lavatory.

In keeping with this monotheism, the Bartlett lecturers were completely doctrinaire – especially the ones who revered Le Corbusier. They were the worst. When

30

they – or their keener students – talked about Le Corb, they had a disturbing light in their eyes. A religiose glow. They were disciples, initiates, fruitloops.

My disgruntlement came to a head in the Bartlett JCR, that autumn afternoon. Skiving off a particularly dull lecture on Mies van der Rohe, I had slipped into the common room to grab a coffee laced with hip-flask whisky, and read *The Sun*. After an hour or two my *Sun*-reading was disturbed when some first year prick in a Tattersal check waistcoat started pontificating to his friend about Le Corb. Very loudly. Having had a term of this already, I groaned and got up to go. As I walked to the door this wanker continued: he started talking about South London barrier blocks and their *muscular beauty*, and about how it was a shame the Nash Terraces weren't bulldozed, as suggested, after the war because then they could have really built *le Ville Radieuse*. The sentiments were, even by the standards of the Bartlett, offensive and absurd. Nevertheless, I was still making my way out of the common room when the waistcoated idiot made one idiotic statement too many. With momentous pomposity he started saying that the only problem with modernist public housing was that the Corbusierist vision wasn't pursued with sufficient rigour. As I stood there, *Sun* in hand, it struck my ardent, teenage, whisky-and-testosterone-fuelled brain that I knew where I had heard this kind of *apologia* before: from socialists. This was the equivalent of a socialist saying about the failed Marxist Utopia: yes, well, it just wasn't done properly.

Enough. Roused and angered, I decided to have some fun; or at least a fight. Shoving my way through the students, like a doctor at a road accident, I confronted the speaker, asking him to retract. He shook his head.

'You're wrong,' I told him.

'Oh really?'

'Yeah,' I belched. 'Fucking Le Corbusier is respons-ible for ruining millions of lives. I'd call that wrong, wouldn't you?'

My fellow-freshman shook his head: 'No. Actually, I wouldn't.' I went to counter; he continued: 'You're barking up the wrong tree. The reason most British housing schemes are a failure is simply because they were built on the cheap. That's all. It's nothing to do with the essential principles.'

Stepping nearer, I jabbed a finger: 'So you don't think putting small children in high rises is a tiny bit dim?'

'No.'

'Why not? Why the fuck not?'

Recoiling from the whisky on my breath, the waist-coat shrugged: 'It's not a case of high rise or low rise. That's got nothing to do with social problems. Look at South Central Los Angeles. Lots of nice one-storey houses with private gardens and fences and everything else the community architects want – and what is South Central famous for?' I demurred. He smiled, smugly: 'The worst crime rate in California.'

Nasty. I was quite into my role of being righteously angry, but being angry and *wrong* —

'You're still a cunt.'

'What?'

'I said,' I snarled, 'you are still a cunt.'

'Well, thanks —'

'— I bet you drive a Citroën DS, as well, don't you?'

'Sorry?'

'You're all the fucking same. It's amazing. Like fuck-ing sheep. You're all sheep.'

'And you're drunk.'

'Right. Sure. *Course.*'

Swaying backwards, I tripped over a pile of books, stumbled left, then whirled around; as I did so I barged

32

into The Waistcoat, nearly knocking him over. For a long second he looked at me, then diplomatically retreated. But I was over the edge now; clenching a fist I made my threat: 'Right. If you don't say Mies van der Rohe is a scrote I'll punch your lights out.'

I was standing off the man by about a yard; he glanced nervously at my clenched fist, and at some girls who were looking on. I could see the thought process whirring in his head: save face, or *save face?*

'Say it,' I burped. 'You dismal CUNT. *Say it!*'

'Say that Miles van der Rohe . . .?'

'That's right.' I picked up a milk bottle from the table – I had no intention of using it; I just liked the way it made him tremble. 'Go on ——'

'Mies . . .'

'Is?'

'Mies . . . van der Rohe . . .' He was blushing, hugely. His eyes were flickering around the room and at the milk bottle in my hand. 'Mies van der Rohe . . . is . . . a . . . scrote . . . um.'

'Thank you,' I said. 'Thank you . . .' I was beginning to sober up: the whisky and testosterone were starting to wear off.

'What's your name anyway?'

Waistcoat shook his head. 'Simon. Simon Reeves.'

'Really. Right. Simon.' By now I was almost blushing. 'Thanks for the debate.' Picking up my *Sun* newspaper and my hip-flask I fled.

I am here: Oxford Street. Ridding my mind of any remaining memories, I opt to concentrate on the task in hand. Spending money is not an easy business, it has to be done with the right gleeful insouciance, with a certain vulgar abandon. Taking out my credit card, I furrow my brow, gird my loins, steel my will, and step inside the Virgin Megastore.

# 5. EuroStar

'Nympholepsy.'

'What?'

'Nympholepsy,' Simon repeats. 'That's what you've got. I read it – NO, ALICE! DON'T DO THAT!'

At the other end of the line Simon is chastising his daughter. At this end of the line I am thanking Fate for not blessing me with children. Today it sounds like anarchy *chez* Reeves: Sarah, my sister, is in the telephonic distance shouting for extra nappies; nearer the receiver Simon is trying to prevent Alice from painting his trousers.

'We're decorating,' he explains. 'We've got all the pots and brushes out and she keeps trying to paint everything.' A melancholy chuckle. 'The bloody cat got striped yesterday.'

Smiling at the image, I hear my niece creating more mayhem, then more nappy backchat from my sister.

'Go on, anyway —' I say, trying to steer the conversation away from Peaudouce, and Pampers. 'You were about to solve all my problems.'

'Uh, right. I was reading some magazine of Sarah's, and it said that there is an actual term – nympholepsy – that applies to your condition.'

'What condition?'

'The condition that is symptomised by a desperate

34

yearning for the intellectually unsuitable.'

'Oh . . . that one.'

'Yeah —' I hear Simon chide his daughter again. Then he continues: 'I'm talking about your penchant for nineteen-year-olds.'

'I guessed.'

'I'm just trying to point out to you that it's medically classified. You're actually sick.'

'Really.'

He confirms: 'Apparently this nympholepsy is, essentially, one up from paedophilia.'

'Gosh, thanks.'

'You know what I'm trying to say. Why do you keep going for these krill-brained bimbos?'

I go to interrupt; he gets in first.

'It's no surprise your relationships never last more than an hour, is it, when you think about it?'

'An hour? I wish.'

'They don't understand you, Guy. So you get bored of them and find another. On and on and on and on. Why do you do it?'

'You know the answer. It's not some weird obsession. It's just because I fancy the hell out of nineteen-year-olds.'

'And why is that?'

'God, I don't know. That's a poser, isn't it?' I pretend to reflect. 'Do you think it could be because they're incredibly beautiful?'

'No.'

'Well . . .' I stall. 'You're wrong, anyway. I like all women. All of them. I love the way they talk about emotions and ironing, and stuff. Bless 'em.' My friend is trying not to snigger, as I continue: 'What's this to you, anyway? Why are you suddenly so concerned about my love life?'

'Since you asked me my opinion.'

'Oh yeah?'

'It's ridiculous. You complain about your lack of involvement. Then you take out women who can't actually speak English.'

'You mean that American girl?'

'Amongst others. It's sad. You're . . . sad.'

'Thanks. At least I'm not some dull, fat, chinless, pussy-whipped fuckwit . . . No offence.'

Thankfully, Simon remembers how my humour functions. At this insult he merely laughs. He is happy: Sarah has evidently taken little Alice off his hands; the sound of his family is a pleasantly distant babble. Hearing this, I envy Simon his marital *gemütlichkeit*. Again.

'But you are lonely, aren't you?'

A significant silence. Then I reply: 'Of course I'm lonely. It's called the human condition.'

'Right. But you do wish you had someone truly special, don't you?'

'Maybe —'

'Come on.'

'OK. Yes . . . On Sundays.'

'It's Sunday today.'

'I know. Fancy a drink?'

The idea obviously appeals; in my mind I can see him looking at my sister in the kitchen as he considers his escape plan. 'Perhaps. I've got to visit the site.'

'What, today?'

'Unfortunately. But there's a decent pub right by the station —'

'The Hole in the Wall?'

'That's the one. I could meet you there, at . . . twelve?'

I salute the idea: 'Done.'


Putting the phone down, I go across to one of the long

sash windows of my first floor living room, and stare out over The Square. The church that sits in the centre of our Square has just done its thing, and now the large black women who worship there – the only people who *do* worship there – are filing out into the mid-July sunshine. This church does get used by other people, but for other reasons: on Tuesdays it's a middle-class nursery school, where horribly confident children are decanted by suntanned mothers out of brand new Range Rovers; on Saturdays it's a venue for old-style criminal funerals, where the lives of local villains are celebrated by a procession of toughs with pony-tails, carrying garishly elaborate wreaths inscribed: 'All our love, dear Dad.'

The sociological texture of my square appeals. Likewise its architectural texture: it is an appealing jumble. The church is a not bad example of late neo-Gothic; the local library is a whimsical example of Beresford Pite; the surrounding houses are a fair example of early Victorian Georgian. In short The Square is an exemplar of that tolerant and humane eclecticism that makes London the greatest city in Europe – and, so often, the ugliest.

On the Cally Road, I queue for a bus. Miraculously, one appears in less than a minute. It is a 17 to London Bridge. Listening to some Purcell, on my Walkman, I leap up the stairs to the top deck, where I count the numbers stamped in the bottom left corner of my bus ticket. They add up to thirty-two. Scrunching the ticket and dropping it in my pocket, I gaze contentedly out of the window, quietly laughing at the helplessly hideous new Holiday Inn on King's Cross Road. At Bank Station I descend to the Tube, taking the Northern Line to Waterloo. On my Walkman I can hear Dido Lamenting.

I switch off.

\*

We are in the Hole in the Wall, a pub under one of the Waterloo railway arches that serves decent beer: a rarity in this no-luck neighbourhood. Simon is looking sartorially OK-ish, for once. 501s and a navy-blue jumper.

As I hungrily gulp my first pint of beer, he eyes me. 'You look like you needed that.'

'I'm feeling a bit . . . iffy.'

'What's the problem?'

'Nothing much —'

'Come on, what is it?'

Setting my half-empty pint glass on the bar, I say: 'Remember that doctor I was shagging?'

'Belinda Gibbon?'

'Yeah.' Picking up my pint again, I neck some more bitter. 'She's pregnant.'

Thoughtfully, Simon sups from his own pint. 'How do you know?'

'She told me. How do you think?'

'Well, you might have had a visit from the Child Support Agency. Or she might have asked you to the baby shower. Who knows?'

'She's having an abortion.'

'Truly?'

'Yep. I posted the cheque yesterday.'

Standing back, Simon opens his mouth.

I go first: 'I know what you're about to say . . .' Draining the suds of my beer, I gulp and go on. 'Look – it's not a fully-fledged human with a soul, OK? It's just a blob. Don't download your Catholic guilt.'

'I wasn't.' He was, I could tell. 'I was just going to ask you if you've thought it all through?'

'Yes. Yes we have.' I am sighing. 'She seems pretty keen to get rid of the thing, anyway. So it's not like I've got much say in the matter.'

'And you go along with that?'

'Why not. It makes a lot of financial sense. Three hundred pounds to abort the foetus. A hundred thousand to put it through school —'

My humour isn't happening. Simon smiles but doesn't mean it. 'Sure, Guy. I'm sorry I can't see it quite as lightheartedly. With such . . . flippancy.'

'Don't get heavy, please —'

'But it's bloody important. The most important thing.'

'The Test Match?'

'No, it's even more serious than that.' He is refusing to lighten up. 'It's a sin. It is. We have to believe that. Otherwise where do we draw the line? Why not expose crippled children? Or bash the brains out of retarded three-year-olds?' Patiently, I await the rest of his tirade. Sure enough: 'What is the difference between a seven-month-old embryo and a two-month-old baby?' I shrug. He answers himself: 'Nothing. There isn't a difference, is there? Apart from the fact that we're allowed to suck one out of the womb and incinerate it. And the other gets the full protection of law.'

'OK, OK.' Simon is obviously not going to blow himself out; I have to call a halt. Abortion is one of Simon's pet arguments; it used to be one of *our* pet arguments, until I tired of driving into the concrete lamppost of his Catholic Faith.

'I know you care about all this stuff, Si. And I respect your beliefs.' Against my better judgement, I am drawn to the debate, just one more time: 'But – look at it like this: what if Sarah was raped by a psychopath and got pregnant? Wouldn't you be a tiny bit tempted to abort?'

'No.' He is fibbing, but it's a special kind of irrefutable fib. 'I hope we would have the courage to have the child. It is our human duty.'

'Right—' Pointlessly, I thrust again: 'But what if a couple who had two handicapped children found that

39

the third foetus the wife was carrying was severely brain-damaged?'

His eyes do not avoid me. He means what he is saying. 'The same. Of course it is utterly terrible. Nonetheless abortion is worse, Guy. A worse crime. Just because women would probably have backstreet terminations if the law didn't allow them, does not mean we should just give up and legalise the operation. That's a specious argument. I mean – racism is endemic, but that does not mean it's correct, or that society should not take steps to outlaw it.'

'You're absolutely fucking right,' I say, picking up my second drink. 'It would be nice to see Australia using their spinners.'

'Perhaps you should treat this more seriously. You should try and treat something more seriously.'

'Life is too important to be serious about. Oscar Wilde.'

'Ah.' Simon nods, soberly. 'But he was an anguished homosexual dealing with a world that refused to accept his kind. He had no choice but to approach life from a facetious and satirical angle. Whereas you are a wanker. A difference, I think.'

Despite myself, I laugh: 'Oh, funny. Very funny. You twat. What's wrong with being a wanker, anyway? Why should I care about anything, what's the point in getting worked up about anything?'

Collecting his new pint glass from the bar, Simon drinks as he says: 'Is it because of . . . the past? Or because of your childhood, or something?'

'You what?'

'Is that why you're so determined to be shallow?'

'Jesus.'

'Is it?'

'Look.' I am glaring. 'Get over yourself, Reeves. I just choose not to care, to not worry about something I can't affect. Why on earth should I? I earn a decent wedge, I've got a nice squeeze —'

'Eva?'

'Who else?'

'Have you told her about Belinda? That she's pregnant?'

'Of course not,' I snort, collecting another pint and white-moustaching myself. 'What would it serve?'

'She's falling in love with you? Isn't she?'

'Keeps putting her head on my shoulder and staring up at me adoringly and saying I love you. Yeah, I'd say she's pretty keen.'

'And it doesn't worry you that you can never properly love her back? Or love anyone any more? Not even yourself?'

'Don't worry. I love myself. I love myself so much I even let myself sleep *around*.'

For all his keenness to argue, Simon chuckles, and subsides. This means the air has been cleared and the argument is forgotten. Which is only right. Through the years our friendship has withstood some pretty nasty set-tos; about football, about rugby, about the architectural merits of pre-war German turbine halls; it is therefore unseemly that we should fall out over the sanctity of human life.

Three pints later we waddle out into the Sunday afternoon sunshine, after a quick debate about etymology. I have informed him that the word cretin is derived from the French *chrétien* – a Christian; he has said I ought to get therapy.

We have agreed, lightheartedly.

Now Simon leads me down a sidestreet, round the back of Waterloo Station, to a wire-walled building site. This is the site of the new Channel Tunnel Terminal; this is Simon's building site: his place of work.

Snapping a pass at some foremen, Simon takes me into a Portakabin where he gives me a plastic yellow helmet; once we are suitably protected he leads me out into a maze of bricks and dust and workers and shouts and noise, up some steps and out onto a concourse that faces the gently curving steel-and-glass wall of the EuroStar Terminal, proper. Then he asks me the question, the only question, the single question I have been dreading all day: 'What do you think?'

What I think is that it is truly beautiful. That it is utterly ravishing. That I love the grey-and-granite colour scheme, and the A frame corner struts, and the innovative gasketing, and the neoprene tongues that link the obloid ceiling panes, and the blue steel bow-string trusses, and the serrated glass canopy, and the silicate fins and the scarlet Eames chairs and the metal halide luminaires and the shiny steel decking softly dappled by scattered rays of summer sun.

'What do you think?' he repeats.

'Not bad,' I say.

# 6. Battersea Power Station

For two months now I have been trying to bring Eva to orgasm. It has proved exceptionally difficult: either she lies there like a frigified pudding, or flinches from my hand like a dog that's been whipped once too often. Today, however, there is hope.

It is nine am on Sunday and I am crouching over Eva's body like a boy sitting by a rock pool – probing under stony overhangs, blindly feeling for anemones, watching the seaweed waft in the sunwarmed water – and I am strangely optimistic. Today Eva's big eyes are wet and green: green as emeralds in a Kashgar stream. She is nearly crying, and this evidence of her loving submission is, in turn, persuading me to greater patience. So: as my tired third finger once again coaxes the reluctant sea creature, Eva twists and bends, and contraflexes her physique, and yes! She is rumbling, she is stirring. The sensation that I am an oil prospector, breaking through the final crust of rock, is unavoidable: the ground is trembling, the hills are shuddering, the workmen are scattering into ditches – and suddenly it happens: the drillbit pierces the cavern's ceiling and instantly a subterranean reservoir of gas expands, and bloats, and hurtles to the surface: 'Shit shit shit – Jesus fucking CHRIST ——'

Startled, I gape. In the two months I have known Eva

I have never heard her swear – not a *merde* or a *scheisse*. Now she is emitting a mindspinning stream of obscenities, such that it can only mean one thing. When a relatively demure young woman like Eva comes up with an outburst of coprolalia like *this*, she must be close to climax. Sure enough: after grabbing a fistful of my dressing gown Eva holds me and moans and swears some more; then she reaches round my waist and starts slapping my back. Such is her rocking and grabbing it is difficult for me to stay in digital contact with her clitoris; nevertheless I manage; we lock mouths; she bites my chin; I strum – and then she does the business: seeping samples of herself onto the bedsheet.

'Are you happy?' she says, after it is all over, when we are lying there, panting and exhausted, on the further shore of love. 'Are you?'

This is tricky. I do not quite know what to say to this remark, so I say nothing: sitting up I ignite and smoke a Turkish cigarette, and look away, in the hope that she will desist.

She doesn't. After she has babywiped herself with Kleenex, and binned the gunky ball of tissues, Eva lies back on her side and stares at me, and repeats: 'Really, Guy. Tell me. Are you happy?'

What to reply? I have always abhorred post-coital cross-examinations: maybe I should plead the right to silence. Propping myself on an elbow I sigh and gaze down into Eva's trusting face, playing with a lank lock of her yellow hair. Looking at the wet porcelain of her eyes, at those delicately flecked green irises, sends me: I get to feeling the vertigo, like I am toppling, like I shouldn't look down. Refocusing, I stammer: 'Yeah . . . 'Course . . . That was great . . .' Then I rise from the bed and fight my way into a tee-shirt and walk, naked from the waist down, to the window, where I throw open the curtains.

Outside it is high summertime. Through the window I can see sparkling cars parked in Chalcot Square, the golden green trees of Primrose Hill and a series of fluffy white clouds yachting across a big blue sky. At the top of the Hill fathers are wrestling with purple kites that tail long streamers in the wind and I am thrilled with a sense of something. Is it the sense of time, standing still? Of this being a certain moment to relish? Or is it just because I've finally made my glacier of a girlfriend thaw out, and my ego is consequently dilating?

'It's eleven,' says Eva, looking at her wristwatch. 'You're going to be late for Winchester.'

'Eleven! Jesus!' Jumping into some shorts I find my jeans and boots and soft leather jacket and – following a valedictory kiss on my girlfriend's forehead – skip outside into the August air, where I jump into my little car.

It is Sunday. It is eleven. I am still in London and I am due at my father's house near Winchester in about an hour for Sunday lunch with my dad and my step-mum, and my sister and Simon and Alice. It is going to be a real family get-together – if I can get it together. Thrusting my foot to the floor I skid out onto Regent's Park Road and steer a semi-conscious course through Marylebone, and Mayfair, around Hyde Park Corner and down the King's Road.

The first time I really wake up is as I scoot my Alfa across Battersea Bridge and see the hollow shell of Gilbert Scott's Battersea Power Station. This building looks noble, and ravaged, and useless. This upsets me, so I avert my eyes and look due south, towards the grey slate rooftops of the South London terraces that stretch away towards Brixton and Peckham.

At least I think it's Brixton and Peckham. Rubbing my bitten chin, I wonder . . . It could be Dulwich and

45

Southwark. Or Morden and Earlsfield. I never did understand South London – how it fits together, how you get from Tooting, say, to Balham. Or how Wandsworth relates to Lewisham. Or why the fuck anyone lives there.

Turning from this unlovely sight, I sigh and switch on the car radio. It is playing old tunes: chart-songs from the mid-seventies, that era when most hit singles were by Pickety Witch. The sound of this old bollocks depresses me further, until I am not sure *why* I am suddenly feeling so down this glorious morning; it could be slightly delayed post-coital *tristesse*, it could be because I am leaving London. Exiting London always makes me sad, always makes me think about death. Maybe it's because leaving London is like growing old: you start off in the middle of youth, amongst the nightclubs and the cinemas, then you move into middle-age, to the suburbs and the semis and the garden centres, and finally, right at the edge, everything signifies mortality: it's all cemeteries and nursing homes, and crematoria.

If this is the case, if quitting cities is like getting old and dying, then at the moment I am motoring through the early-to-mid thirties, where socially aspirant Clapham finally gives up the ghost and settles for a semi in Wimbledon.

Once I reach the open country my mood lifts. We are speeding up; that's good. I love speed. I love driving. I love.

Turning off the motorway at Andover I hurtle down some country lanes. In a fit of impulse, I have decided to take the short cut to my father's; partly because I am late, partly because it is more scenic. Roaring through a sleepy village I see a heron hovering above a silvery river and a deer breaking cover. And a church being English. Putting my radio on again, and dialling

46

through FM, I settle for Mozart.

'Guy!'

It is Simon, standing at the porch of my father's big detached sixties house, the bell of which I have just rung.

'Wotcha cock,' I say, stepping inside. 'Where's the old man? Down the pub?'

'No . . .' Simon shakes his head. 'Guy . . . I don't know how to tell you this, but he's gone off with some . . . *floozy*.'

'Really? *Really?*' This is news to me. This is bizarre. Ever since my father and mother divorced and she returned – with us – to Cornwall, he's lived here in my semi-rural childhood home with a pleasant and attractive lady – my stepmum – who could never remotely be described as a *floozy*.

Halting in the large, sunlit, lavishly parqueted hall, I ask: 'Who is she?'

Over-nonchalantly, Simon shrugs: 'I think she said she was from his firm. Something about a golf match.'

'Dad doesn't play golf.'

'She had a fast car, too. Morgan.'

This decides it: 'He's shagging her! The old goat.'

Quietly nodding, Simon leads me towards the stripped pine kitchen. 'Could be. She was quite sexy in a horrible, fat, ugly, repulsive kind of way. Isn't he . . . into your stepmother any more then?'

'I don't know. I thought she was going to be having lunch with us. Isn't she?'

'No. She had to go up to London yesterday. Back tomorrow, I think.'

'So he took the chance to ship in his *fancy woman*!'

'Perhaps, perhaps.' Opening the kitchen door, Simon skates his socks across the shiny wooden floor, to the French windows that open out onto the large back garden that overlooks distant Lexley Wood. 'Of course, all this does mean it's just me, you and Sarah, not to mention the children.'

'No problem,' I say, walking onto the lawn and taking lung-size breaths of warm country air. 'It's nice just to get out of London. Jesus! What's that noise?!'

Here in the back garden I have been engulfed by the sound of squadrons of Stuka bombers flattening the centre of Minsk. That is: three under-fives around a swimming pool.

'Three?'

My sister, who has just emerged from the kitchen, wipes her hands on an apron in a mumsyish way, as she comes over and kisses me. 'The other two are next door's. We said we'd look after them for the day. God knows why –' She rolls her eyes in Simon's direction.

I take issue: 'Come on sis, you know you love it.' And to give her credit, she agrees – because she does love it: the whole shebang. My sister actually likes the cleaning and the cooking and the fussing and the budgeting. Maybe this is because she is so good at it – and because she was so bad at doing everything else, at being a student or pursuing a career or hanging out in nightclubs. I cannot blame her for these failings: it was she who took the emotional rap of our parents' divorce.

'How's Mum?' I ask. 'Is she OK?'

Distractedly, Sarah says: 'Oh fine, fine, I rang her yesterday.' But I can tell her attention is elsewhere. She is concentrating on the sight of my two-year-old niece nearly falling into the pool.

'William, watch Alice, please!'

'Alice is so active,' Simon explains, as my sister rushes out to comfort my niece and chastise the neighbour's eldest, and deal with the general chaos. 'Sarah's paranoid that she'll fall in, or something. Come on, let's have a beer.'

48

Three beers later the bedlam of the children has become an attractive hubbub. I am slumped in a white plastic poolside chair, enjoying the sunshine and the garden and the trees at the end. These impressive trees are blue cedars; they have always hypnotized me. I have always loved and prized their shape and scent and colour, and their lofty serenity.

When my parents were divorcing, and my sister was getting horribly involved in the concomitant arguments, my response was to run away, to run out of the house and stand under this stand of blue cedars. Here, as I recall, I would gain some strange comfort from the trees' existence. Despite my tender years, I was smart enough to have worked out that, as the actual name of our house was Blue Cedars, they'd built the house around the trees. Which in turn meant that long before sadness, and anger, and arguments, and *parents*, these five trees must have been standing here: loftily observing the human comedy: like ambassadors from a superior civilization; like kindly aliens in a 50s film.

Lunch is a mess. The children are appalling. Right at the beginning of the meal Alice tips her Ribena down William's tee-shirt, and crows triumphantly at the huge stain, then William runs wailing into the front garden, towards the village High Street, and consequently has to be rescued and pacified. This takes half-an-hour of my time, just enough for David to steal a slice of strawberry roulade and squeeze it into my jacket pocket. But I do not really mind: the afternoon is gloriously warm and I am getting slowly drunk and the day is passing in a pleasantly analgesic haze, and soon Sunday will be over and life will begin again.

As I replace an empty bottle of Rioja on the big white garden table, sighing appreciatively at the peace that has finally descended, I feel a tug at my hand and, tilt-

49

ing my sunhat, I look down and see that it is Alice. She is imploring me: 'Come and push me! On the swing! Please Uncle Guy! Pleeeeezzzz!'

Given that I have just decided on a post-lunch snooze, Alice's idea does not go down too well. Pathetically I try and argue that I am too drunk, too tired, and uninsured. She starts raucously singing, anyway:

> Postman Pat! Postman PAT!
> Batter my CAT!
> Early in the mor-nin'
> As the . . . day is . . . DAW-NIN'

Sitting here in my comfortable chair I wonder why Alice is singing so exuberantly, why she is grinning determinedly and saying 'HA HA HA HA!' right in my ear. A little thought explains. She is going to keep annoying me until I do my duty and give her a push on the swing.

> Bah bah black sheep
> 'Ave you any WOOL!
> YES Sir – NO SIR -

'I know,' I suggest. 'Shall we have a go on the swing?'

'Yeahhhhh!!!!' Alice says, trying to drag me by my hand from my chair.

When we reach the swings I dutifully load my niece into one of the yellow plastic seats; as Alice is installed, she sings a little tune to herself, then she keeps trying to twist in her seat to look at me.

'Be careful, you'll fall out —'

'I'm gonna marry James when my hair is long,' she says. 'I am. Do you think he loves me?'

'I don't know,' I reply, distracted by the danger. As

her swing swings back, her face nears mine again and she pouts outrageously.

'Uncle Guy, I'm not going to go to heaven.'

'Aren't you?'

'Nah, I'm gonna go to . . . Southampton. With all the people.'

'Right.' I chuckle.

'Push me 'igher!' she says. 'Do you luvs me!?'

As her swing arcs and returns, and her little legs kick out at the cloudless blue sky, I query this remark: 'What?'

'Do you fink you luvs me. I love yoo, Uncle Guy!'

'Yes,' I say. 'Yes, I love you.'

'Are we going to heaven? For longer and longer and longer and longer and longer and don't come back again. HA!'

As Alice says this she twists in her yellow plastic swing seat a little too much and: it happens. She falls out of the seat onto the grass. This is not a big drop, but still a frightening one for a small child; rushing over to the girl's side I pick her up and put her back on her feet and stare into her eyes that are already filling with water. As I do this I notice that her eyes have a strange, piercing, mineral blueness. For some reason this saddens me.

'Are you going to be brave?' I say.

The girl sighs hugely. 'Yes . . .' she murmurs. 'Did I fall over and bop myself?'

'You did,' I say, holding onto her shoulders like I am lecturing her. 'But you're not going to cry, are you?'

'No,' she says, but as she does so her face twists into a sob and she starts emitting a sharp keening sound that immediately has her mother scampering towards us, dropping tea-towels on the way. Deftly Sarah picks Alice up and hoists the child to her capacious maternal bosom.

'What happened?'

'She fell off the swing,' I reply, feeling hugely and inexplicably guilty. 'She just . . . climbed out . . .'

'Mm,' says Sarah, flashing me a significant glance. 'She is so bloody adventurous. Aren't you, darling?'

Shutting her eyes, Alice sinks her face onto her mother's shoulder and starts sucking her thumb; thereafter the two of them disappear towards the kitchen – towards Elastoplasts and TCP and chocolate biscuits and Thomas the Tank Engine.

Their presence is replaced by Simon. From the terrace of the house he has witnessed this little drama; now he has strolled over, keen to chat. I do not mind chatting. As the day passes we find ourselves ambling blokeishly towards the end of the garden, where we stand and survey the sun that is sinking into a pink and grey sky, behind the Forestry Commission conifers of Lexley Wood. In turn, our conversation touches the usual bases: cricket, architecture, money, football, religion. At religion the debate pauses, and takes on fresh supplies. Simon has a pet new theory about religion and science.

'It's like,' he says, enthusiastically, 'it's like – imagine there are two clocks. The first clock is five minutes slow. Always. It's never totally accurate, but it's still just about close enough for us to happily use, on a day-to-day basis.' He is beaming. 'The second clock is much worse. It's totally broken. Totally stopped. Which means it is exactly right twice every twenty-four hours – more right than the other one can ever be. So, do you see what I mean? The first clock is Science and the second one Religion. One is OK for day-to-day use, even though it's slow, but only the other one, even though it's completely stopped, can ever be truly, precisely accurate. And that's religion. Right?'

Looking at Simon, at his worn corduroys and his

weak-chinned young face, I decide there is only one reply: 'You're not trying to steer this on to Belinda's abortion again, are you?'

Abashed, he frowns. 'Well . . .' He is deliberating over his words. 'Have you told Eva yet?'

'There's no need. Really —'

'But what about the doctor – Belinda? Maybe you should talk it through with her. I mean, properly.'

'Why?'

'Because you might even find you want the baby. Or love Belinda.'

'Yeah, right —'

Approaching me from an angle Simon places a fraternal hand on my shoulder. 'All I'm saying is – love is a dangerous game, Guy. It has a funny way of . . . panning out.'

'You what?'

Manoeuvring, Simon looks into my eyes: 'I'm not trying to drag up the past. Absolutely, I'm not. But you and I more than anyone should know what a combustible thing it is. One mustn't treat love and sex lightly. They have a habit of blowing up in one's face.'

Rattled by this remark, I go quiet. I know my friend is referring to the blemishes of the past, to the dark history that lies between him and me. The question is: why? Usually the memory of what happened back then – of what I did to him and to his girlfriend – is as painful for him as it is for me.

Finally, I reply: 'But that's a bit different. That's something we sorted out, a long time ago, no?'

'Of course. Of course . . .'

For a moment I fear he is going to pursue the subject; he doesn't. Widening his eyes he starts enthusing about some of the more interesting churches in the countryside hereabouts: East Meon, and Avington, and Breamore, and Northington . . .

53

I am not listening; I am observing. In the field beyond the end of the garden, I can see a hovering kestrel. Its tawny-white wing feathers are trembling, almost imperceptibly, as it floats and soars over the cornfield. Transfixed, I watch as it buffets and rides on the warm summer thermals – until it drops, like a stone, down into the golden, ripening barley.

I am thinking about Simon. And me. About the way, the time, the place it all began.

# 7. The Oranjeboom Pub

A few months after the fracas in the Bartlett Common Room, after the undignified altercation with the guy in the Tattersal waistcoat, I was drinking with some fellow first-year time-wasters in the basement bar of Carr-Saunders Hall. This was a London School of Economics residence that lay right across Maple Street from Ramsay Hall, my own student digs. We members of Ramsay often did our drinking over the road: our Hall had no cheap bar of its own and Carr-Saunders was the nearest subsidised venue. The problem with this otherwise convenient arrangement was that the students at Carr-Saunders resented our rivalrous presence. They were at the London School of Economics, we were at University College London; they were at the best school of political science in the world, we were at the oldest atheist university in the world. And none of us had got into Oxbridge. A provocative mixture.

The animosity was particularly bad that night. We had been carousing for an hour: already there had been several hard stares. Nonetheless we chose to ignore it. Three rounds went by: it was my turn. After collating the orders of my friends, I ambled to the bar; next to me was another student.

'Hello,' he said. Turning to my right, I clocked a young, weak-chinned face – and beneath that, a frayed, stained, Tattersall-check waistcoat. Embarrassed and mortified I tried to pretend I hadn't heard. The waistcoat persisted.

'Hello,' he said, quite shyly. 'It's Simon. Simon Reeves.'

'Uh, hi . . . Simon,' I replied, feeling like a crap actor, cornered in the dressing room. 'I know you, don't I? You're the guy who . . . the guy who . . .'

He helped me out. 'I'm the chap you attacked, last term, in the Bartlett JCR.'

'Yeah,' I stumbled, nervously. 'Well, I . . . er . . . I am sorry about . . . winding you up like that. I don't know what came over me.'

'Don't apologise. There's no need.'

I flinched: 'Sorry?'

'You needn't be sorry . . .' He was tugging at his woollen tie. 'It was partially my fault.'

'Don't understand.'

Staring at the bar, Simon fingered a spillage of beer, making scribbles of liquid. 'You see . . . it's intellectual. I get carried away by Utopian systems. Catholicism. Communism. Corbusierism. I admire their internal logic. Their rigorous consistency. To a fault, perhaps.'

'Right, right —'

'I should have probably stood up to you but . . . what does it matter, really? Actually I was pleased to meet someone who feels so keenly about these things. Most of the other students just want to build office blocks and make a million.'

This was a bit *too* fair; swallowing some of my new pint, I had to confess: 'To be honest, Simon, I can't say my actions were exactly . . . ideologically driven. I'm just a bit of an aggressive bastard. Comprehensive school background, you know.'

'Really.'

'Yeah.'

56

'So you don't care that they've thrown you out?'

'Nah. I didn't want to do the course anyway. I never wanted to do the course. I couldn't give a toss about the bloody course —'

He raised his eyebrows at me: 'Then why did you choose to do architecture, if you didn't *want* to do architecture?'

'Had to get into Uni somehow. Make my dear mum happy.'

Twisting the corner of a bar-top spill-rug, Simon shook his head: 'Well . . . I don't believe you. I reckon you're just saying that to justify your actions, after the event. I remember your expression. You were genuinely angry. Genuinely wound up by the argument.'

'No I wasn't.'

'Yes you were. You were —'

'Bollocks.' I said. 'Bollocks bollocks bollocks bollocks bollocks —'

'You don't totally concur then?'

'No. I don't.' Scrutinizing Simon, I tried to assess him. For all his appalling taste in architects and ties, he appeared to possess a certain dry kind of wit. So dry I wasn't sure if it was there at all. 'I'm doing philosophy now, anyway. I've transferred.'

'Really? That's quick work.'

'Uh-huh. It's an improvement on the Bartlett. More birds. There's this one girl, Julia . . .'

'Lloyd Davies.' He smiled. 'I've heard about her. Isn't she the pretty brunette with the enormous . . .

'Tits?'

'I was going to say -ly rich parents. But yes.'

Both of us were laughing, now. As we laughed, something in me clicked; I decided to invite Simon to drink at our table. This wasn't because I needed friends; it was because he intrigued me. Yet I couldn't tell why. Even from this brief acquaintance, I could see

57

Simon Reeves was the kind of student I had already decided to revile: the sort of keenie who would spend his university days getting into politics, or starting small magazines, or attending a number of lectures, or wearing overlong scarves. And yet: there *was* something about him.

'Fancy a beer?' I said, raising an imaginary pint-glass. Simon looked bemused: 'What, with you?'

'Fuck no, I meant do you fancy having a beer in the corner of the room, on your own. *Christ.*' Guiding Simon over to the wreckage of our table I introduced him to my drinking buddies; within minutes we were chatting away, animatedly.

Then there was a scene. I was downing my fifth bottle of Museum Bitter, when one of the drunker LSE students wandered over and started making loud, anti-UC remarks. Dismissing these insults as horseplay, we carried on talking. The man got uglier; I went to the Gents. When I emerged things had got worse: everybody was standing up and talking to each other, too loudly. Finally some LSE trendy went over the top and called my new acquaintance Simon Reeves a 'public school twit in bicycle clips'. Instantly I reacted. Not because I disagreed with the general thrust of the remark – Simon was indeed wearing bicycle clips – but because Simon was my brand new chum, and I had just drunk five pints in an hour. So I reacted. With comic slowness I poured a bottle of bitter over the LSE student's head.

The effect was instant. The beer-soaked LSE guy spluttered and swore and swung a punch: I ducked; in classic fashion the blow clobbered the man behind. Slowly this second giant rose and round-housed a massive fist, that in turn floored the first punch-thrower. As if on cue, everything exploded: glasses flew, bottles smashed, chairs got chucked. A few seconds were enough to show us that LSE had the edge on UC. We were heavily outnumbered: those of us that weren't being chinned were being thrown over tables.

Appraising the situation I made a nifty decision to do a total runner: kicking some doors open I sprinted up the nearest stairs, closely followed by Simon and my Ramsay Hall comrades – the whole drunken dozen of us tearing down the corridor, slamming into swing doors and falling out into the chilly winter air of Maple Street.

Here one of the girls who had been drinking with us – her name was Jenny – had the brilliant idea of barricading the LSE students inside their own building. Manfully we pressed the swing doors shut and held them solid, against the scrum of would-be economists within, while Simon and another friend went off and returned with a plank which we slid between the doorhandles. After this we nonchalantly dispersed, clapping the dust off our hands in a calm, brisk, job-well-done kind of way. We'd got about seven yards down Charlotte Street, when it was brought to our attention that the London School of Economics was now pouring out of a second exit, brandishing chair-legs.

This time we properly scattered – me, Simon and Jenny and some others running down Rathbone Place, past the Post Office and over Oxford Street, where we figured we had finally lost our pursuers, and consequently piled into the Oranjeboom pub, off Shaftesbury Avenue. Inside the pub we celebrated. Ordering quarts of Dutch beer we drank and laughed and slapped each other on the back and relived the entirely miraculous and already legendary ten minutes again and again. After half-an-hour everybody was inebriated and chanting anti-LSE slogans. I was the only one still drinking. Trying to stay erect, I reached for the table to find my pint and instead found myself stumbling into Simon.

Holding me up and handing me the pint, Simon looked almost bashfully into my eyes.

'You know, this has been the best night of my whole term. Of my whole first year.'

Slapping Simon on the back, I slurred agreement: 'Yeah, yeah. I know. Don't you LOVE being a student?'

We were friends.

# 8. John Trindle Highwalk

Along the bay of the dealing desk. Andrew Mackay is holding aloft a phone: 'Got the Kraut on the line. What do you want me to say?'

'Tell her . . . Tell her I love her and I want her to have my children.'

Curtly, Andy returns to the receiver.

"Fraid Guy is in a meeting, Eva. Any message?'

I am in the strangest mood this morning. Switching off one of my speakerphones, I say: 'Andy, do you ever miss your ex-girlfriends? I mean really miss them – miss them so much it hurts, in your stomach?'

'You mean like you had a Chicken Madras the night before?'

'Yeah —'

Andrew shakes his head. 'Nah . . . Biryani maybe. Never Madras . . . Why?'

'Well.' I say. 'There was this . . . one girl . . . who makes me feel like that.'

'Christ,' he says. 'That's *fascinating*. What happened?'

'Nothing . . . I've just been thinking about things.' He makes another sarcastic face. I go on, anyway: 'I've been thinking about my love life and my past and all that. You know. And it shocked me that . . . when I miss her, I miss certain aspects more —'

'You're going to tell me?'

'I miss her laugh, and her smile —'

'So?'

'And I miss her sense of humour and her intuition – and her femininity and her elegance and her consummate musicality.'

'And?'

'Most of all, I miss her *cunt*.'

Now he laughs. 'So that's what's been chewing you out?'

Picking up my pen, I drum it against this morning's *FT*. 'Right. In spite of all her . . . cleverness and culture, and all that stuff, it's her tits and her snatch that I really miss. Isn't that terrible?'

'Nope,' Andy snaps. 'It's always the real sluts who make you sad. It's always the girls who really cooked in bed who make you want to cry, years later.' He muses. 'It's like mates. It's always the old friends who made you laugh who you really want to see again.'

'You reckon?'

'Def.'

'I guess you're right . . .'

Distracted by my scrolling Telerate screen, I check out some prices. Nothing doing. The day is quiet. Swivelling my chair, I re-engage. 'Don't know what I'm talking about, anyway. I guess I'm worried about the irredeemable shallowness of my banal and fatuous existence. What kind of sarny do you want?'

'Pastrami and mustard. Stilton and grape.' Casually he chucks a scrunched up fiver in my direction. 'Cheers.'

Outside, my weird mood of the morning is soon a memory. Jamie Tasker, a broker from Godsalls, is passing the front door of my corporate HQ, en route to the Crowder's Well pub. With a grin, he eyebrows the direction of the pub.

'Pint?'

Eagerly, I agree. Moments later I am downstairs in the basement of the Crowder's Well, playing pool and smoking cigars and generally enjoying being male. After the third game of pool, I glance at my watch and jump: I have just wasted forty minutes of what was intended to be a forty-five minute lunch break. Swiftly I down the dregs of my pint of Bass and slap Jamie Tasker on the back, then I run out onto Moor Lane, onto Moorfields, which leads onto Moorgate.

Here I purchase the requisite sandwiches – then I slip out into the bustle of Fore Street. From here I take a short cut along the John Trindle Highwalk, past Lever House, right into the heart of the modernist, multilevel, concrete and steel Barbican Centre. Sitting down at the edge of the lilypadded artificial lake in the middle of the Barbican, I take out my sandwiches and my quarter-litre carton of orange juice, and eat. Directly opposite me, around an alfresco pub table, are a couple of office girls and two older men. The men are trying to impress the girls with talk of deals; the girls appear distinctly unimpressed. For some reason I wink at one of the females – she is no better than a five or six pinter, but I do it anyway. Instantly she starts, and blushes; smiling, contentedly, I stare into the soupy green waters of the lake. Skimming across the surface of the water is a silvery waterfly. A pondskater. Watching the insect collide with another, then go free-booting across the water, my mind wanders. I am wondering about my own pondskating existence, the shallowness of my life – again. Maybe I should get married ... to someone. To anyone. This strange thought has been bubbling under, for ages. Am I, in staying single, avoiding my inevitable destiny? Is it time to give the freedom up? Am I like an athlete or a footballer, who always think they have two seasons

63

left in them, when in reality their career is over?

I trust not. I *like* being unmarried. I *like* the fact that, unlike many of my friends, I have avoided the marital fate. There are times when I even picture myself as the last British soldier at the Somme: still plodding his way through no-man's-land, still whistling to keep his spirits up, when all his other comrades have been machine-gunned to the ground.

OK. Vigorously balling my sandwich wrapper I stand and suck the last of my orange juice and stroll across the hot concrete plaza, en route to my corporate HQ. Locating a rubbish bin I jettison my litter and moment-arily stop to look at the distant view of those buildings: Alban Gate. From this distance these twin, pink-and-grey, postmodern colossi, posed by the motorway of London Wall, look like two children squabbling over their Scalectrix. And their passé postmodernity un-settles me. They remind me of the slightly passé nature of my job, my pseudo-vocation, my oh-so-eighties career.

Once again I am seized by that strange, quixotic mood. The lovelorn mindset of the morning has returned. Taking out my portable phone I dial a num-ber and I ask the telephonist at Queen Mary's Hospital to connect me to Belinda Gibbon, MD. A minute passes. Over the phone I can hear Belinda being paged. Two more minutes pass. This is an expensive call; surely worth it. Finally I hear a noise and a voice and a phone receiver being clumsily handled – Belinda Gibbon comes on line:

'Hello. Who is it?'

'Guy.'

'Guy *Simpson?*'

'Yes.' I am insulted. 'Belinda —'

She interrupts me: 'This better be important. I've got some granny conking out as we speak.'

64

'Belinda . . .' I repeat. Her vehemence has thrown me. I don't know how to say this. 'Belinda —'

'*Spit it out*—'

'Have you had the operation yet?'

She stalls. 'No. Actually, I haven't. Why?'

'Well . . .'

'*Well, what?*'

'I don't want you to do it.'

'Sorry?'

'Just that. I want the baby.'

A strange silence. Then her voice crackles out: 'Where are you, in the pub? Had a good lunch?'

'No. I haven't. I mean . . .' I am thrown. 'Listen, Belinda, I don't expect to convince you over the phone —'

'Glad to hear it —'

'Look . . . When's your next break?'

'In about twenty minutes. Why Guy? What *is* going on?'

'Nothing. Stay there. I'm on my way.'

With that I run to the roadside, hail a cab and direct the driver to Queen Mary's. It takes forty long minutes. As soon as we pull up outside the redbrick East Wing of the West End hospital I tip the driver, sprint across the car park, nip in through a little known portal, leg it down a corridor, fly up some stairs, and bang on the door of my ex-girlfriend's rooms. The door opens. It is Belinda.

'Can I come in?'

'Suppose so.'

Inside I lean on my knees to catch my breath; then, before Belinda can insult me or eject me or dampen my enthusiasm with the acid rain of her sarcasm, I open my mouth and say: 'Belinda, I want you to have the child. I don't want you to have the abortion.'

A long pause.

'Really.'

'I want you to have the baby. I don't want you to terminate it.'

'I see. Mind me asking why?'

'No. It's because,' I say, 'because I've been thinking about my life and about everything . . .'

Her eyebrow arches.

'. . . and I think that I need to do . . . something good. For once. Something unselfish. Altruistic —'

'Sorry?'

'It's true. I just want to do something that isn't completely self-centred and shallow.'

She has folded her white coated arms. A bad sign.

'So what do you say?'

She shrugs. 'I say this sounds like a mid-life crisis.' Leaning nearer to my face, she pretends to scrutinize my hairline. 'Bit young, though —'

'I'm serious, Belinda.'

'*You?*'

'Yes.'

Her arms fold even tighter: 'OK. For the sake of argument, let's just *suppose*. Where exactly do I fit in, in all of this? What's my role? To simply say yes? Say OK? Say I'll happily give up my career so I can . . . gestate the precious embryo?'

I hadn't thought about this. Not deeply, anyway.

'Well, er . . . of course I need you to want the child, as much as me. I want us both to want it. I think it is right. Because,' I am really busking now, 'how long can we go on putting off the end of youth? Mm? That's what I mean.' I think about this, and say: 'You know . . . sometimes I feel like I've been waiting at the luggage carousel . . . The luggage carousel of love. You see what I mean? I feel like I've been waiting for luggage that may never arrive. Whereas all my friends have smiled and picked up their own cases and are

66

already leaving the airport.'

'Nice image.'

'I mean it, Belinda. I really truly mean it as much as I have meant anything.' As of now, this is true. Right at this moment: this is the case. So what next? Taking a mighty breath, I plunge: 'I think we should get married.' She widens her eyes. Carried away by myself, I go on: 'That's what I reckon. That's what I believe. Really. Truly. I want you to have the child and I think we'd have a good and a better relationship if we were married . . . and well . . . we always got on OK, right?'

Slightly flustered, she shrugs: 'Yes . . .'

'And we always were kind to each other. And I'm earning loads of money. So I want us to be a family. I want to love you and the child and be unselfish. I'm bored of getting drunk and sleeping around and going to clubs. I want to be bored at home with my wife and my children . . . and my cardigans.'

'I'm not sure a distaste for Stringfellows is a proper basis for starting a family.' I look pained as she goes on: 'Anyway. How do I know this isn't just some whim, just another of your *impulses?*'

'It isn't —'

'But how can I be *sure*? You're always going off at a tangent. It's one of the reasons I was attracted to you. As a lover. But as a husband? As a *father*. . .?'

The air is empty. She turns and walks across to the window, which has been thrown open on to Praed Street. The traffic is heavy; beyond Belinda's white-coated shoulder I can see a man stepping out of a cab and another buying armfuls of flowers. Now Belinda turns and I see that there are tears brimming in her eyes and I feel like maybe I am doing the right thing. Maybe.

'I don't know what to say.' She says. 'I need some time . . .' Letting go, she sinks into a plain wooden chair – a chair that matches the plain wooden cabinet and the plain wooden wardrobe and the plain wooden bunkbed. Keenly I recall that narrow bed; that was where we did it; where this child, our child, was conceived. The idea of it makes me giddy. Seating myself on the hard edge of the bed I watch as Belinda examines the pattern in the carpet. Outside I can hear buses ticking over, and the wheezing hydraulics of lorries, and I can feel the mild lunchtime air breezing in through the open window.

Raising her red eyes Belinda looks at me. 'Look, do you mind pissing off?'

'Sorry?'

She has regained her composure. 'I want you to go. Please. I've had a long day. You don't expect an answer right now, do you?'

'No, of course not.'

'I haven't even had lunch yet. Or breakfast.'

'Tough week, right?'

She nods, and stretches her long, shapely legs. Dismissing some unsuitable thoughts I gaze at Belinda's face. Without even rising, my ex-girlfriend jerks her head; sideways. At the door.

# 9. Trellick Tower

Driving through the early September rain I gaze across my car at Eva. I don't know about this strange girl. Just don't know her enough. Could I ever love her? Can I love anyone, any more? Have I already had my share of love? Does love get weaker and weaker as you get older? Is love, in fact, like a tea-bag – something you can use once, or twice, or three times – *if you're lucky*?

It is uncertain. I know very little. I know that if I am thinking of falling in love with Eva I should disabuse Belinda of the idea that we are to wed; conversely, if I really *am* about to marry Belinda, I probably ought to tell my girlfriend, Eva. I wonder. I wonder about everything. Why are girls so difficult: so *different*? They are a miracle of otherness: they are a miracle, *per se*: looking at Eva crossing her legs gets me thinking about what lies between – that wound of hers that seeps like the stigmata of Padre Pio, that weeps like the Madonna of Syracuse, that melts every month like the blood of Saint Januarius.

'What are you thinking?' says Eva.

'About the Exchange Rate Mechanism.'

'The what?'

'The currency snake. The European Monetary System. The whole thing's about to collapse.'

'Oh, right,' she nods, sagely. 'I saw it on TV. I guess

69

it is exciting, yes?'

'Yeah —'

'And it is all Germany's fault. No?'

Taking a sweet from a dashboard tin, I pop and suck, and say: 'The Bundesbank have certainly got to take a lot of the blame. No offence.'

'None taken. I don't feel . . . truly German, anyway.'

'No?'

'I told you. I was brought up here, mainly. So . . . even though my dad is a Swiss, you know? — I feel more . . . British.'

This answer does not please: I like having a foreign girlfriend. I don't want her to start shedding her exciting attributes. Nevertheless I let it pass. I am letting everything pass, today: even as I suck another sweet and chuck the wrapper out of the window onto the Westway, I am being overtaken by a huge French lorry that is slewing rain water either side of its radials. Usually such a road-enraging insult would galvanise me; today is different. Today is Saturday and I am relaxed. Eva and I and Alice, who is at present happily asleep in the back seat, are on the way to Stourhead in Wiltshire, to look at the famous gardens. This whole trip was Eva's notion, that we should treat my sister and Simon to a free Saturday by taking Alice off their hands. It must be said that Eva's proposal does not seem to be turning out too well. Leaning forward to check the sky through the windscreen I look at the raindrops bouncing off the glass and I say: 'Should have brought a picnic.'

'Do you want to go back?'

After stretching to turn on the tape-player, I shrug: 'Nah . . . might as well go for it now. Look, there's Trellick Tower.'

Following the line of my arm Eva looks across the wind-and-rainswept housing of West London as far as

70

the famous tower block.

'That's the biggest tower block in Western Europe.'

'Fascinating.'

'Isn't it. Pevsner reckoned it was one of the most sophisticated and handsome monuments to modernism in London. Stupid git. Look at it. Why were they ever allowed to build things like that? They aren't just great big fuck off buildings. They're great big *fuck off I'm the architect* buildings. Aren't they?'

Amused by my outburst, Eva smiles. Meanwhile I accelerate us away from Trellick Tower, towards Perivale and the Hoover Factory, my mind spinning in time with the aquaplaning wheels: 'I've never understood it, Eves. The arrogance of architects, you know? All they care about is winning prizes for ruining the London skyline, or finding radical ways of making roofs leak. Wankers.'

Leaning across the car, Eva takes a sweet, and slips it in my gaping mouth. 'Shut up.'

'OK, OK . . . You know you are looking very pretty.'

She is. Eva is looking very pretty today: in hope of good weather, rather than expectation, she is wearing a short summer dress which accentuates the length of her thighs, and sets off the fragility of her neck. Everything about Eva is frail, I think. Her slender ankles, the breakable spine, the skinny arms, the thin wrists scarred with what I suspect are razor marks. There is something terribly sad and yet very feminine about Eva; and the combination of sadness and cheek-boned beauty keeps me keen, even though I know she is not right for me, even though we are no good in bed. I keep expecting to drill through to some deep dark passionate heart, beneath the layers of permafrost. Holding Eva's scarred wrist, I kiss its innerside and think about asking her about her adolescence, asking her why she has razor scars on her wrists. But I know

71

she will demur, dissemble, talk about something else. I have to find some other way. Squeezing Eva's fingers, I look into her milk-and-emerald eyes and say: 'There's something I've got to tell you . . .'

Resting her head on my faithless arm, Eva sighs and says: '*Ja*? What is it?'

'Well. It's about . . .'

On my tape the last song is segueing into the next song. My favourite on the tape. Ah well. Taking the cue, I start singing along. The rain is lashing the windscreen like thrown fistfuls of gravel; the cars and buses on either side of me are kicking up angled sprays of rain; we are all speeding out of London, out into the wet and dreary countryside. As we do so I sing the lyrics, making Eva laugh and kiss me, as I warble.

'Space travel's in my blood, there ain't nothing I can do about it.'

Long journeys wear me out, but I know I can't live without it, oh no . . .

And as the rain comes down, and Eva continues to kiss the side of my neck, I start going into autopilot, provoked by this song into remembering another journey, another girl, another car ride, another planet.

For two years of university life, Simon and I were best friends. We used each other, as best friends are meant to do. He was my intellectual counterweight, my ballast, my getaway from the drunken, stoned excesses of my normal life. When I wanted to talk about death or God or architecture, when I wanted to connect with that student life of the mind – the life I had deliberately eschewed – he was the one I went to. In turn, I introduced him to girls whom he failed to get off with; I showed him how to roll a spliff, which he failed to learn; I taught him to add up the numbers on a bus ticket, to see if they made lucky twenty-one.

Then it all changed. Halfway through our third year at UC – just as I was beginning to question my entirely hedonistic existence, just as I was beginning to wonder, for a minute or two, whether I would ever fall in love – Simon fell in love. The first time I really needed his philosophical wankiness, he left me waiting. By this time Simon had moved to a new flat in Regent's Park Road, while I was in a squalid, lagery flatshare in Montagu Square. One afternoon I went round to see him and he told me. I was stunned. All he could talk about was this sexy French girl he'd fallen for: Nathalie. When I wanted to talk about my need for a relationship that lasted beyond the first wordless breakfast, he told me he and Nathalie were going to the opera; when I wanted to chat about the way I had a better relation-ship with minicab drivers, than with any particular woman, he informed me that Nathalie was a trained singer; and when I wanted to discuss the enervating effect of all my drinking and dope-smoking and happy highliving on an otherwise sensitive spirit, he told me that what Nathalie liked best was for them to make love in the back of his Citroën DS.

It was more than flesh and blood could bear. My only choice was to escape to the Union and get drunk, which was precisely where I was one afternoon when a friend of mine and Simon's – one Josh Diamond – came in, sat down, and invited me to stay on his family's island in Scotland.

'Uncle Guy . . .'

Alice is saying something. I ignore her, stepping on the accelerator.

'Uncle Guy, watch me!'

Checking the speedo, I see that the needle is creep-ing past ninety. It would be good to do a hundred, I think; I always feel agreeably irresponsible and laddish

73

when I do a hundred.

'Uncle Guy! Pleeeeze!'

This time my niece's voice sounds less happy. Strangely distant. Again, I opt to ignore it. We are on the M4, heading for Swindon, and making good progress. Turning up the volume on the tape-player I sing along to the epic doggerel of one of my favourite pop songs:

> *You touch me with your spirit*
> *You touch me with your heart*
> *You touch me in the darkness, I feel it start*

In the last half-hour the sun has come out: glancing across the front seat I see my girlfriend has been lulled into sleep by the windscreened warmth. Slow moments elapse; more lyrics are insinuating themselves:

> *Hot dog, jumping frog, Albuquerque*
> *Hot dog, jumping frog, Albuquerque*

Then I hear Alice's voice again. This time it sounds oddly muffled: loud and quiet, then loud again: like a radio signal at its horizon.

Gently I tap my girlfriend's knee. She stirs:

'Mmmnn . . .?' Her eyes are low-lidded. 'I was asleep. What is it?'

Keeping an eye on the Mercedes in front, I jerk my head rearwards:

'Check Alice out, can't you? She keeps asking me to look at her.'

Irritably, Eva leans and looks behind. Her reaction freezes me.

'Alice!' she shouts. 'Alice!!'

'What?!'

'No! Alice! NO!!!'

Without an explanation, Eva jumps and twists and climbs out of her seat. Chafing against my seatbelt I

74

crane to the mirror. And I see. Alice is hanging halfway out of the window. My niece has opened the window and climbed up the door, and she is about to topple onto the rushing road below. Blindly blinking, and clutching the wheel I check my speedo and see we are doing eighty in the fast lane. Eighty miles per hour. 80 mph!

'Don't slow down!' says Eva.

'What??!'

*'Don't slow down!'*

'Why not, Eva?!'

'Just don't fucking do anything!' she is yelling. 'Don't slow down or swerve. She'll fall. Alice come back inside!!'

Behind Eva's yells I can hear Alice. I can hear the little girl's voice. She is crying and calling my name:

'Uncle Guyyyyyyyy! Uncle GUYYYYYYYYYYYYYY!!!'

'Jesus!'

'Stay in lane —'

Alice's voice is snatched away by the slipstream.

'Eva! What's going on?'

'Uncle GUYYYYYYYYYYYYYYYYY!!!'

As Eva goes for the girl I look to the mirror again. Alice's foot is snagged on the rear seat belt.

'Christ!'

'Eva —'

'Uncle GUYYYYYYYYYYYYYYYYYYY!!'

'Wait!'

One jolt and Alice will go flying onto the bumpy, thundering road. As I grapple with the wheel I envisage Alice's skull being squashed and popped, under the tyre of a speeding juggernaut. Feeling sick I clock the mirror —

'Get her now —?'

'No!'

'What does she —'

75

'— GuYYY —'

'Don't go slow!!'

In the corner of my eye I see a car level pegging; the driver is signalling to me and pointing frantically at my rear window.

'Fucking hell!' I say. 'Does he think I don't know!'

'Hold it!'

'Just grab her ankle!'

'Nearly —'

'Christ —'

'Ja —!!'

'Jesus!'

In the last moments I have taken my eyes off the road for half a second; too late I see that the car in front of us is braking. Careering towards the car's bumper, I yank the wheel down and swerve us into the middle lane. Horns are blaring; headlights flashing. Accelerating away, I try to swerve us into the slow lane, but as soon as I do this I have to tug the wheel again to avoid a lorry. I am losing control of the car. We are yawing left and right and going way too fast. Too fast! Squeals fill my ears – Alice is screaming. Gulping air I check the side mirror, take a gamble and yank the steering wheel hard left, and then left again, slicing us left and left and fast onto the gravel of the hard shoulder where I stiffen and slam the anchors on and bring us to a convulsively juddering stop. We have stopped. *We have stopped.* After a minute of deep breathing I unlatch my seatbelt and turn around.

The drama is over. The window has now been shut and Alice is being comforted: my girlfriend is rocking back and forth in an attempt to quieten the sobbing child, who is hiding in her lap.

Opening the car door I step outside into the warm, buffeted air; I can hardly hear the whoosh of the motorway traffic for the thump of my beating heart. I have to relax, if I am to drive again: gazing at the cars, I let my mind drift. Until I am just watching the cars. The cars. The cars.

There were two carloads of us. There was Josh and Dave and me and Simon and another friend of mine from UCL – Peter Curtis. And there were three girls: Georgina, Amy and Nathalie. I could see Nathalie was pretty and chic, and exotically coquettish; I also hated her as much as she hated me. We took against each other the first time we met, while waiting for Josh to get his car started in Gordon Square.

Our antipathy was easily explained: she hated me for being Simon's best friend, I hated her for taking my best friend away; she hated me for resenting their happiness, I resented their happiness. Our animosity was so instant and electric I made sure she and I travelled to Skye in separate cars. I was in the boys' car.

We were planning to be gone for four days. Josh had therefore packed six grams of coke, eight tabs of E, an ounce of Thai sticks and some hash. These drugs worried me. Although I was more than *au fait* with marijuana, and had snorted the odd line of amphetamine sulphate, I was not keen on the idea of sharing a vehicle with Class A narcotics. Up to that point in my youth I had considered myself a cut above the hard drugs abusers, even though I was a committed boozer and spliff-toker. In the way an armed robber in prison looks down on a sex offender, my thinking was – hey, I might be bad, but I'm not as bad as them.

All that began to change when I got to know Josh, properly: on that long, rainy car ride to Scotland. Listening to Josh Diamond talk about drugs, as we sped North through the mizzly hills of Derbyshire, I found myself being seduced by the glamour. Like a rarefied socialite, he seemed to be on excitingly first name terms with everybody, with every drug: he called them skag, or blow, or hooter, or whizz, or Eccies, as if he knew them personally. Like they were people who he hung out with in trendy Notting Hill drinking clubs. Which he did.

Nevertheless, I did my best to fight the allure, the magnetic drag. As I swang the wheel and overtook a speeding coach I tried to get a grip. Three years of double standards must mean something, I decided: surely I was not going to give in so easily. There was no way I was going to do LSD, for instance. That was the drug that made people jump out of windows. Nor was I going to do cocaine: that was the drug that obliged you to have aluminium inserts in your nose. Clutching the gearstick I shook my head and explained my misgivings.

'OK, OK . . . Loosen up dude . . .' Josh was sighing in that effortlessly cool, superbly Trust Funded, ex-Westminster schoolboy way. 'If you don't want to do any Chan, that's OK. No hass . . . Now, if you'll excuse me, I've got to give this my best shot —'

Stiffly, I drove on, trying not to look across the seats as my passenger hoovered up a huge line of white powder. It was impossible: staring into Josh's gaunt, sallow, ravaged, pockmarked, prematurely ageing young face, it seemed so appealing.

'Er . . . Josh —' I said.

'Yeah —'

'You got any of that . . . stuff left?'

Grinning, he reached for the breast pocket of his denim jacket.

'*Pas de problème . . .*'

Swiftly the mirror was extracted, two lines were chopped, and another nose did the sniff, to the consternation of the van-driver alongside us. From then on it blurred. At one point we were lost on the M1: it was

78

foggy and dark. I was drumming manically on the steering wheel, singing along to the stereo; then, all of a sudden, we were on a single-tracked road in the Borders.

'Jesus, how the fuck did we get here?' This was Peter, rubbing mist from the window with a jacket cuff and staring across the darkened moors. Moments later we were speeding through the bluewashed, dawnlit terraces of Glasgow, where I turned and saw Josh swigging whisky and sniffing coke and driving the car: at the same time. Two hours after that it was morning and a whole night had passed and the boys in the back were asleep, and Josh and me had swapped roles, again: he was back in the passenger seat, scraping the last of our second gram out of its wrap, only looking up to gaze, curiously, at the sunlit Highlands, at the windswept mountains and the green-gold heather and the limpid blue of the lochs.

'Look at this place. Trees. Sky. Mountains.' He sighed and dropped his nose and sniffed the coke. 'Should build a few car parks.'

Passing through Fort William we bought some pies for breakfast; then we took the ferry to Skye, feeling the sun and the wind as it bit at our cheeks. Finally we drove down the Hebridean coast to a little inlet where we parked, and where the other car – containing the girls, and Simon – pulled up alongside. Here Josh pointed over the wavelets to a small outcrop of rock.

'That's it,' he said. 'My island. My family's island.'

Rubbing my unshaven chin I gazed across the hundred and fifty yards of causeway and seawater that divided the mainland from the miniscule islet, on which stood a tumbledown cottage, and a toytown lighthouse.

'Josh,' I began, 'when you said we were going to stay on your dad's island, I kind of imagined . . .'

'Yes?'

'Well, I kind of imagined . . . an island.'

Despite the smallness, it was big enough for us. For a weekend it was all the world. We smoked coke on the beach and did hash in the lighthouse; we found antlers in a rockpool and dead sheep in a cave. In the mornings we played Scottish rock music on our little stereo and in the afternoons we played pat-a-cake with the cow-eyed seals that lazed on the shore like festival hippies. And at night, in the sweet, sacred night, we gathered round the hearth and drank and sang, and listened to flamenco; and afterwards ran outside to dance with the girls, beneath the hills of Knoydart, beside the Sound of Sleat. Standing there on that pebbly beach, inhaling the delicious night air, my head swimming with all the new things I had consumed, I saw Nathalie staring at me. Angrily. Resentfully. Oddly. Although I didn't know it, the weekend in Skye had seen two seeds sown in my soul; two bulbs that would burst into flower. Soon enough.

We are here. Stourhead. The earlier rain must have driven away the busloads of rhododendron-fanciers, because the National Trust car park is empty, even though it is now a lovely, sunny, late-summer afternoon. Helping Eva out of the car, and then Alice, the three of us step across the gravel towards a knot of ruddy-faced, puffa-jacketed middle-aged ladies, who are standing by the wooden ticket offices. At the scrunch of our footfall the women turn and gaze and as one they smile. It is obvious what they are thinking: what a lovely young family.

Collecting the tickets I guide my womenfolk through the turnstile. Once inside we are confronted with the portico of a large and elegant, early Georgian country house.

'Uncle Guy, who live there?'

'A rich man.'

'Can we go and see him, then? The man inside, can we? Can we? Uncle Guy?'

'Well . . .'

'That's a black poplar,' says Eva, pointing out a big, tall, irregularly branched tree.

I turn, surprised. 'You know that?'

Nodding, Eva explains the significance of this tree, this black poplar: 'They are very rare. There are only a few of them left, dotted around the country, I think. And because they are now so far apart, they cannot fertilise each other . . .'

Together we look at the tree. Her face has an expression of distant sadness – even sadder than her normal demeanour – as she goes on: 'So you see what that means?'

'No.'

'It means . . . that they are probably doomed to extinction. Because there are now so few of them . . . they are sort of dying of loneliness.'

As Eva finishes her disquisition, I start to feel peculiar. My girlfriend's strange story has perturbed me: not just for its content, but for its existence. I had not expected Eva to be so botanically knowledgeable. And now that I know of her facility, I am hugely envious. I have always despaired of understanding nature; of naming and knowing its constituents. I can spot a few distinctive trees: a birch or a beech, an oak or a horse chestnut, but that is it. For the rest, when I go for a walk in the country I feel like a philistine in the National Gallery; I do not understand the architecture and am envious of those who do. Now here's my German girlfriend annotating the English landscape like she was brought up in the backwoods of Berkshire.

'That's a hornbeam. And that's a maple. These seem

81

to be sequoia, and larch ... These are the famous rhododendrons, and tea roses, that's a peach tree, that one's from China —'

My face says it all: I'm staring at the girl, dumbfounded. If I was in a fanciful mood I would say she had swallowed the concordance to Creation; as it is, I am sticky with admiration. While we pass by the house and step down some steps towards the famous gardens proper, I ask her where she learnt all this lore.

'My father was a lover of English gardens. They are very popular in Germany. You know this is perhaps the most famous garden in the world?'

Content to be her pupil, I nod.

'This is the horticultural equivalent of ... the Sistine ceiling. Or Chartres Cathedral. Or Bach, even. This garden is a classical object, I think. The very best of its kind —'

As Eva asseverates we round a pathway between some big holly bushes and step out on to a kind of natural belvedere, a lawned viewing ledge, and as I go to speak my breath is whipped away by the disquieting sight that greets us. Before my eyes is the most beautiful view I have ever seen. A serene silver lake lies in the groove of a thickly wooded valley whose rainwashed hills ascend to a sky of emblematic blue. Dotted between the glades and copses are several classical temples and pavilions, their silent white beauty reflected in the lake water. Birds are singing in the beeches; a warm breeze is tousling the elms. In front of me Alice has sat herself down on the damp grass; her normal talkativeness has been confounded by the majesty of the aspect.

Eventually, my niece says, in a very small voice: 'Guy – does he live here?'

'Who?'

'Him?'

'Who?'

'Is it where God lives?'

Before I can answer, the child gets herself into a state; the thrust of her question has evidently got her thinking about heaven, and about dying – and probably about her recent near-death experience in the car – and suddenly she is standing up and shouting, putting her hands over her eyes. This sends me: I don't know what to do; expertly, Eva intervenes. Picking Alice up, my girlfriend croons some consoling absurdities in the child's ear.

Now we progress down the path towards the lakeside. All the way down I listen to Eva's breathless and enraptured commentary, said half to me, half to Alice. Eva is describing all the plants and the trees and birds and insects; she is naming them: the dainty tulip trees, the Macedonian pine, the cedar and catelpa, the dawn redwoods with their beautiful crimson barks, the sitka spruce and the cypress, the beech trunks surrounded by golden leaves – like sackfulls of krugerrands – and as I attend on this poetic litany, it melds with the sky and the clouds, and the hexagons of sunlight spangling Alice's happy young face.

Hand in hand, we sit on the damp, mossy grass that inclines to the lakeside. Once seated, Eva says, her eyes as wide as they go: 'I love you.'

In response, I smile, absently. I am thinking what a clever colour green is. How it was a good choice to make Nature predominantly green. One can only imagine the effect if it had been tartan, or orange, or black.

# 10. Manufacturers Hanover

'Sixty Eighty! Sixty Eighty!'
   'Seven —'
   'TWO!'
   '*Fuck it!*'
   I am standing at my desk with a phone in each hand and I am grinning and laughing as I sell millions of pounds for Deutschmarks. The adrenalin is buzzing. The hormones are fizzing. Leaning from my desk and my flashing Telerate screens, I see that I am not the only one seized by bloodlust: today the vast, grey-carpeted Osaka Bank dealing rooms are a battlefield; they are a frenzied cockpit of dealers and bond-traders and analysts and researchers all screaming at each other and themselves and the walls and their intercoms.
   Turning to a white-shirted Andy Mackay, who is clutching a phone in one hand and a dribbling Lucozade can in the other (he is unaware that in his excitement he has upended the can), I go to interrupt my friend. But he is bellowing so loudly at his broker, at the other end of his intercom – 'Duncan you wombat, I said sixty shagging EIGHTY!' – I can see there is no point in trying to butt in. Switching back to my own screens and my own intercoms, I juggle some numbers and make some frantic deals. Then I gulp some cold coffee and sweep a ream of Tuffs Reports off my desk,

and start attacking the pound again: 'Fifty Sixty!'

'Seventy —'

'Paid —'

'Fiver! FIVER!!'

Today is Wednesday the 16th of September, 1992. In years to come this will be a famous day: the day the European Monetary System – the Exchange Rate Mechanism – began to collapse. It's happening as I stare at my screens: the hyenas are patrolling Threadneedle Street; the vultures are circling Bank Station; the sharks are swimming up the Thames, en route to Tower Bridge. In other words: the guys at the Bank of England are finding it impossible to keep sterling above its legally permitted ERM floor of DM 2.7780. *Big* surprise.

As I shout into my intercoms, trying to get John Hellings from Godsalls to sell me some Marks for pounds at seven eighty four – 'How much? Jesus!' – Mackay swivels to face me, and I see he is trying to communicate. Given that I have a phone pressed to one ear and another religiously attuned to the shrieking intercoms, I can't hear him: by way of reply I make a circle with my thumb and forefinger. Then another phone starts jumping off my desk, and a girl rushes up with some figures, and a friend starts yelling at me from the Swissie desk, and my Bloomberg computer starts scrolling more information about the financial madness that is engulfing Europe.

'Fifty Seventy —'

'Forty Fifty!'

'Forty Sixty —'

'OK John – that's six-tee. Six-tee!'

Rubbing my chin, I try to get a grip. To get a handle. The pound is now hovering at or below its permitted floor in the ERM widebands and I can't see how the Treasury can keep this up. It is absurd. They must be pumping billions of dollars and Deutschmarks into this futile effort to maintain sterling near parity. They must be spunking the national reserve. It is insanity. It's a fiscal equivalent of the Somme. Wave after wave of our country's finest is getting mown down by the remorseless logic of the global Forex market. The upside to this is that I am one of the machine gunners. I am one of the bad guys. And I love the fact. My lips are spittly with zeal, I am giddy with joy – I am, in fact, reminded of Oliver Cromwell, laughing with glee at the Battle of Preston, as I straighten and smile and shout at my colleague Alex Henderson.

As I observe, things change: Sandy Henderson drops the paper Spanish flag he was waving and thumps the pane of his screen with the side of his fist. Something is up. A different buzz is descanting across the general tumult. Scanning the scene I see that everyone is staring at the various TVs suspended over our heads. The TVs are switched to Sky News, and as we all watch the TVs flash a picture of the Prime Minister. Dangling his handphone Andy spits: 'Major! You toilet!'

His views are broadly echoed. This sight of the PM has got everybody riled: everybody is jeering and swearing and hissing and nudging their friends. Pretty soon it becomes obvious why Sky News is showing a picture of John Major. The Treasury and Number 10 and the Bank of England are trying to fight back, they are trying to stop the exodus from sterling. The base interest rate is being raised from 10 to 12 per cent. From ten to twelve per cent! Christ! This is a huge jump. A practically suicidal leap. Yelling some new commands into my speakerphone I continue my dealing with renewed zest.

Such an interest rate hike is otiosely counterproductive and everybody knows it. Far from stabilising the pound, this futile gesture simply confirms the

86

Treasury's desperation. The British economy is in Deep Recession. Recent retail sales figures may have hinted at recovery, but today there was also news that unemployment figures have reached a five-year high. What the entire country is crying out for is these absurdly punitive interest rates of 10 per cent to be hacked back to 8 per cent, or lower. But that can't happen, not as long as the PM and the Chancellor are in power. They've staked their reputations on defeating inflation through the rigours of ERM membership, and so we are not allowed to lower rates until our financial brethren in Frankfurt do the same. And of course the Germans won't, because their economy needs the Mark to be viewed as inviolable so as to combat the destabilising effects of Reunification. This, in turn, means the markets now see a huge discrepancy between present UK monetary policy and the interest rate drops demanded by those recessionary economic indicators.

'Jesus on E's! Arsehole!'

I am happy. I am part of a team; I am enjoying the *esprit de corps*. As I stand here and dump the pound like a dirty nappy I know I am aping the actions of ten thousand other dealers in Midland Montagu and Salomon Brothers and Nomura Corp and Manny Hanny, in Lazard Freres and Credit Agricole and Bank of America and BZW – not to mention Frankfurt and Paris and Sydney and Singapore and Bangkok and Seattle – and I relish the fact. The sense of atavistic camaraderie is seductive: the way we are tearing at the soft and vulnerable underparts of the European Monetary System reminds me of a pack of African hunting dogs bringing down a wounded wildebeest.

'Forty-seven —'

'Yours!'

'Randy bastard!'

'Jimmy – you mincer —'

Time for a breather. I have been on the go since 7.30 this morning and I need to clear my mind, to think about something else; if only for a minute. Picking up my packet of Turkish cigarettes I walk across to the wide picture windows and peer down. Below me is London Wall; standing here I decide this is what I shall think about. Architecture. The Architecture of London Wall. Even today, on such a balmy September morning, the architecture of the benighted district below me looks scary and bleak. Not quite the funky, groovy, multilevel futuropolis the postwar planners intended. Not quite the Corbusieran dream of a kinetic city. All I can see from my bird's eye vantage is an area that looks like it belongs in East Berlin. All I can see is a place where it takes half an hour to walk three hundred yards to the dry cleaners. All I can see is a whacking great motorway that callously obliterates the medieval street-plan. So why did they build like this? Why were they allowed to build like this? Why did they think people would enjoy living and driving and walking around towns built like this? Why why why —

'What's up?'

It is Mackay. He has joined me at the windows for a quick cigarette. As he drags on his Marlboro I notice that he is yawning: he is smoking and laughing and yawning, simultaneously. As you do when you are on amphetamines. Flicking ash onto the grey carpet, Andy grins at me and says, apropos of the day's business: 'Just like the lira, isn't it?'

I concur. Two days ago the Spot markets over-whelmed the Bank of Italy and forced them to devalue the lira, to decouple the Italian currency from the Mark. Now the same thing is happening to sterling. Exhaling smoke, Andy says: 'There's no way the Bank can hold out. They'll have to drop out before close.'

'You reckon?'

'Pony on it —'

Disagreeing, I reach out a hand. Slapping my palm to confirm the wager, Andy replies, apropos of zero: 'What happened with you and the medic, anyway?'

'Sorry?'

'You know. That doctor who you got pregnant. What happened?'

'Oh. Right. I offered to marry her.'

'You did what?'

Andy's incredulity is written on his face; any higher and his eyebrows would be invisible beneath his fringe. Vaguely, I admit: 'I don't know what came over me. I just decided I wanted the child . . . and it seemed the best way of persuading her.'

My friend is thinking; I can hear someone shouting his name from his dealing bay, but all his attention is focused on me:

'Christ, I knew you were a bit off the boil, Simpson, but this takes the biscuit. What did she say?'

'She rang me up last night —' Another shout tempts me to return to my Reuters screen, but I resist: 'She rang me up and she told me she didn't believe me. I think she's going to go ahead with the abortion any-way.'

'And you're throwing a party, right?'

'No.' I avoid Andy's eyes. 'I dunno . . . I guess it was a symbol of something or other.'

Loosening his silk Hermès tie, Andy says: 'A symbol of you losing it, I reckon.'

The conversation is scuppered by yet another shout; this time imperative. Throwing me a kindly, sym-pathetic, I'm-afraid-you-are-off-your-rocker expression, Andy drops his cigarette butt in a trashpan and returns to his yowling speakerphones. I do the same. We are going back to our task: crushing the Bank of England, as we crushed the Bank of Italy. Leaning predatorily

89

over my desk I chase a broker down and shout and snap and do some more deals, then I make some scribbled calculations, then I keep yelling. And yelling. And dealing. It's wonderful. I actually can't lose. No matter what absurdly long position I take, no matter how much sterling I oblige myself to sell – the Bank of England keeps buying. And dishing up Marks in return. It's an all-you-can-eat buffet. The palaver is wondrously stupid. For all the Old Lady's reserves-wasting, rate-rising efforts, this financial Battle of Passchendaele is bound to end in abject defeat for the Treasury, the Bank and for Number 10. It's just like Mrs Thatcher said: you cannot buck the market.

'Thirty fifty?'

'Nine quid?'

'Gimme eight!'

'Mine!'

What is incredible to me is that after a decade of Thatcherism the people that took over from her didn't grasp that salient truth: that you can't buck the market. I mean, where were these guys hanging while Maggie was in power? What exactly were badger Lamont and the eunuch John Major actually doing during Mrs Thatcher's tenure? Were they, perhaps, sitting in her Cabinet, advising her to enter the ERM at an unsustainable rate of 2.95?

Now there is another buzz around the room, over and above the general madness. Glancing at my watch, I see it is 2.17pm. Glancing back at my Telerate screen, I gulp. I cannot quite get on top of this news. Even though the pound's decline has accelerated following the interest rate hike the Treasury imposed just before lunch, the Treasury has now gone and done it again. They've raised interest rates again – this time to 15 per cent. *Fifteen whole per cent!* It is disastrous! It is moronic! It is great! Making a whooping sound I crush my plastic cup and I toss it backwards over my shoulder and I wink at Andy as he grins the hugest grin, as he unbuttons the collar of his starched white shirt, and says to me: 'OK mate – this is it. Fill your boots!'

Over the next three hours Andy and I together sell approximately 100 million pounds – in return for hugely underpriced DMs. It is a feeding frenzy. A fiesta. A bonfire of the vanities. A crucifixion of the Conservative government. It is also over. We know it is over when the news goes round that the Swedish government – whose DM-linked currency has also been under the cosh – has raised the country's short-term interest rates to 500 per cent. This surreal news comes like a scene of knockabout farce at the end of a tragedy: the stuff the playwright puts in so as to prevent us going home depressed.

The second signal that this particular drama is drawing to its conclusion comes at about 6.30pm., when Norman Lamont appears on TV, standing on the front steps of the Treasury. Staring at the suspended TV screens, the whole Osaka Bank Dealing Room goes momentously quiet. Lamont is adjusting his tie and approaching a row of microphones. Although everyone has a strong idea what the Chancellor is about to say, the atmosphere is tense. Here in the Bank of Osaka, you could hear a Punt drop.

Now the Chancellor speaks: 'Today we have all witnessed an extraordinary series of events. As president of the finance ministers I have, as a consequence of these events, called a meeting of the monetary committee in Brussels to consider the situation. In particular how stability can be restored to the foreign exchange markets. But first I will be reporting to the Cabinet and discussing the situation with my colleagues, and I may have further statements to make in

91

due course. In the meantime I *can* inform you that the government has concluded that Britain's best interests are served . . . by suspending our membership of the Exchange Rate Mechanism, forthwith.'

Uproar. Total uproar. As Lamont turns from the cameras I turn from the TV and survey the arena. I have never seen Osaka Bank so full of revelry and merriment. Some dealers are singing the national anthem and kissing their secretaries; others are hunched over their screens and shouting at their intercoms; still others are ordering champagne, and telephoning their girlfriends, and cancelling nights-in with their wives. Suffused by smiles, Andy turns to me, and mouths something. Distracted by the continuing mêlée, I slap him on the back. As I do so it occurs to me that I have been truly happy today. Not because I have played some significant part in geopolitics, not because I have helped to weaken an important pillar of Euro-Federalism, but because I have shoved my hand up the Bank of England's skirt. I have fucked the Old Lady over the sofa. And that satisfies the man in me; it makes me happy; it uses my testosterone. Yes. If I am honest with myself – and I am trying to be honest with myself, as I watch a line of traders doing a conga around the dealing rooms – what I like best is Winning. Imposing my will. Conquering. It's a male thing. It gives the same masculine satisfaction as smashing another man's head in. Or screwing your best friend's girlfriend. Or pissing your name in a snowdrift.

Or blasting a four-lane motorway right through the centre of the City of London.

# 11. Minories

The oak-panelled room is filling with cigarette smoke. Balancing my fuming cigarette on the rim of a metal ashtray I look at my old friend, and say: 'So. What's the sitch?'

Crossing the carpet, Neville Griessman says nothing. Over his shoulder, outside the sash windows, I can see the yellow-leaved plane trees of Inner Temple, their twigs tapping importunately against the pane. Neville turns: 'There's not a lot you can do, legally. If she is determined to have the abortion then your options are really rather limited.'

'To what, exactly?'

'You could cart her off to Saudi and force her to have the baby, under Islamic law. Failing that . . .'

'I have no rights whatsoever?'

'None at all. As far as the law is concerned, certainly as it is applied, the baby – the foetus, I should say – is no more than an appendix to the mother's body, until at least the twenty-eighth week. Thereafter, it's a grey area.'

Absorbing this, I say: 'In other words . . . abortion law is a bit one-sided?'

Running his fingers through his thinning red hair, Neville sits himself behind the rampart of his mahogany desk.

'It does seem somewhat invidious. The whole thrust of Conservative legislation vis-à-vis the family has been, ostensibly, to make people assume responsibility for the children they conceive. Hence the Child Support Agency. Yet women are, in practice, allowed to use abortion as a kind of *ex eventum* contraception. They are still allowed to sleep around and be cavalier and they can still abort if the outcome doesn't suit them, or suit their careers, or suit their flat tummies. Which is rather iniquitous.'

Churching his fingertips together, Neville pouts, and continues: 'As it happens, I've been dealing with a lot of divorce and custody cases, recently. And I have to say there's little doubt that the effect of feminism on British jurisprudence has been almost completely pernicious. The man's role has been reduced to that of putative miscreant. He is only consulted and involved when the time comes to pay . . . But don't blame me. Blame the Tories, or yourself. I'm sure you voted for them.' Before I can object, he carries on: 'If Mrs Thatcher had really been serious about family values she would have tightened the abortion laws, making it as difficult for women to escape their maternal duties, as it will, in future, be for men to run away from *their* responsibilities.'

All through Neville's speech I have been examining, with interest, his balding pate and thickening stomach. Neville Griessman and I were exact contemporaries at university. We attended the same tutorials, and yet here he is: a sad, fat, virtually middle-aged slaphead. Thank you, God.

'So,' my friend sighs, 'who is this poor woman, anyway?'

'She's a doctor.'

'Nice girl?'

'Mm . . . Good legs. Bit lippy.'

94

'And you love her, yes?'

I bridle: 'God, no —'

'But you said you wanted to marry her?'

'It was the only way I could get any leverage. And, I guess the idea kind of appealed, for a sec.'

Wrapping his hand around the inner lapel of his pin-stripe jacket like a particularly pompous headmaster, Neville wags a forefinger at me. 'Marriage is a serious business, young man —'

'No, really?' I make a sarcastic face. 'I only made the offer because I genuinely thought it might change my life. Give us both a bit of ballast, you know.'

Silence fills the room. My cigarette has gone out. Fingers rested against chin, Neville says: 'How are the other chaps, anyway?'

I shrug: 'Josh is a total stoner.'

'*Plus ça change.*'

'Alex is making some serious dosh. Simon's got a kid.'

'So I understand. He married your sister, correct?'

'That's right.'

'They happy?'

'No. But coping.'

'I see . . .' Turning around in his swivel seat Neville gazes through the window at the courtyards and gardens of the Temple. It is mid-afternoon, the sun is being obscured by a front of dirty grey clouds.

Suddenly Neville stiffens and growls and says: 'Jesus! Look at those funbags! YES!'

Crowding to the window I follow Neville's gaze. Ascending the steps that lead to some neighbouring chambers, a few doors down King's Bench Walk, is a young woman barrister. She is wearing a black jacket and skirt and carrying a brown cardboard wigbox, but her large and jouncing breasts are still eminently noticeable beneath her white blouse. Neville splutters:

'God, is she stacked! She can't be any more than twenty-two. Christ! The mouse's ear, Guy, the mouse's ear!'

He is slapping me on the back and shouting. And I can't help laughing. My old friend might be a sad, ugly, carrot-topped Jewish lech but I like his company. As we lean out of the window to take in the overview of the oblivious young woman, we are both, for a moment, undergraduates again: ululating with lust at the Summer Ball.

Once the girl has disappeared inside her chambers we retreat to our previous positions and our previous conversation; with a practised air Neville takes a bottle of Macallan from a bottom drawer and pours us both a topaz-coloured tumblerful. Then he mentions Eva.

'I heard you were consorting with jailbait.'

'She's not jailbait. She's nineteen.'

'Nineteen, nineteen . . .' Glass in hand, Neville gazes mournfully at the ceiling. 'The sexiest word in the English language. Have you told her about Belinda?'

'Nope.'

'Sensible man. There's little point until you sort it out in your own head first. If I were you I'd go to church.'

'Come again?'

'I find it immensely helpful.'

'You're Jewish, Nev.'

He smiles: 'Everyone in the world is Jewish, Guy. It's just that most people won't admit it. They're in denial. I've always suspected that you were a bit semitic, for instance.'

'Come off it —'

'You see, you're denying it.'

Reluctantly laughing, I listen to Neville's own guffaws subside. Finally he says: 'Look. Forget this doctor, for me, OK?'

'OK,' I say, downing my Scotch. 'I had decided to,

96

anyway. This was just a bit of curiosity. I just wanted to know all the legal facts . . .'

Neville nods. 'The legal facts are – that'll be six hundred quid.'

Chuckling again, I place the whisky tumbler on the desk, return my chair to its corner, make my goodbyes, and then take the stone stairway down into the collegiate precincts of the Temple. Outside the afternoon is ending with a cloudy chill; buttoning my suit jacket I head off towards Fleet Street. Halfway to my destination I come across the Temple Church.

Going inside I take a pew and gaze at the Purbeck marble colonettes and the waterleaf capitals and the grotesque heads that adorn the spandrels of the circular nave. It avails me not. Try as I might to elicit some religious feeling in myself I cannot do it. Maybe, I think, maybe I should pray . . . Closing my eyes tight, I focus on the image of a Saviour, on a Christ who suffered for our sins: on the image of his sweating brow, his bleeding scalp, his cruelly speared torso – but it doesn't assist. I am still faithless. Affixing my gaze on the supine statues of dead Crusaders, at the distant centre of the nave, I am filled with a strange desire. I wish I could go to war. I yearn to do that: to shoulder my father's old rifle and kiss my distraught old mother and walk grimly but determinedly out the door of life. The thought fills my sails: as I sit here, gazing haplessly at the triforium and the ambulatory, at the statues of Norman knights clutching their pomelled swords between their mailed marble hands I feel a keening need. All I get to do, in my pond-skating existence, is show how much I can drink, how much money I can make, how fast I can drive, how many dippy girls I can pick up. Whereas what I desire is to temper the Toledo steel of my soul in the cataract of cruel experience; to prove my martial virtues; show how nobly I can die.

97

Rising abruptly from my pew I step outside and walk under an arch and shortcut down an alley to Fleet Street. Here I dodge through the snarled-up traffic, ducking between taxis and buses and swearing courier bikers; then I saunter up Chancery Lane, heading past the Victorian Gothic of the Public Records Office. Eventually I reach the Tube, where I catch the Central Line to Bank.

Ten minutes later, when I emerge from Bank Station, I am knocked off course, again. Confronting me is the strange, foreshortened view of St Mary Woolnoth, but it is not this that is unsettling me. It is the crowds of scurrying people: all the twinsets and Burberrys, all the commuters that are streaming into the Tube and buying copies of the *Evening Standard* and lighting much-needed cigarettes and swaying dangerously into the street to hail taxi-cabs. While I stand here under the aedicules and niches of Hawksmoor's masterpiece, surrounded by this mêlée, I find my mind is filled with an image. Of a huge forest. Of a great forest of black poplar trees that fills the pavements of Cornhill, that shades the buildings of Bengal Court – that marches from Biliter Square, to Fenchurch Street, to Bevis Marks, and Minories.

Maybe I shouldn't have had mussels for lunch; maybe I shouldn't have gone into merchant banking. Gazing at the fumes that fug from a chugging taxi-cab, I swivel on a heel and make my way home.

# 12. Chiswick Pine

'So you're flying to Bangkok next week?'
   'Yeah.'
   'And this is a reward? Your holiday?'
   'For destroying the ERM.' I chuckle. 'Job well done, if you ask me.'
   His lips stained by cheap claret, Simon returns: 'But . . . I don't quite understand. When is Belinda having the abortion then?'
   Jesus. I had hoped to avoid this subject; I had hoped to get through Sunday lunch at the Reeves's without having to talk about this.
   Grudgingly, I reply: 'She's getting it done on Friday. It just seemed right. I don't love her. She doesn't love me. OK? Can't you stop banging your bloody tambourine?'
   Shifting Alice to his wife, Simon stammers: 'I'm not trying to change your mind. You must believe that.'
   'Sure . . .'
   'I merely wanted to know why you waited so long. It has been quite a while, hasn't it?'
   Stumped for a truthful but uninteresting answer, I stare around. The early autumn sun is flooding through the window, illuminating the full meanness and tininess of the Reeves's ground floor flat. Ignoring this, I say: 'I don't fucking know.' A glare. 'Can't we talk

99

about something trivial?'

Simon swallows his spoonful of apple crumble, and says: 'Such as?

'How about God.'

He nods: 'If you want. What aspect?'

'Got any stunning new proofs?'

'Well ... yes. I have ...' Stroking his chin, Simon adopts his special it's-so-obvious-if-only-you-could-see tone of voice, the one he usually reserves for discussions of Brutalist architecture. 'I have had some thoughts. But there's very little point in me explaining them to you. If you don't have faith, you wouldn't understand. That's the paradox.' He smiles. 'Rather exquisite, really ...'

Resisting the temptation to grind Simon's wine glass into his face, I demand that my friend stop patronising me. To his credit, he does: dropping the pomposity, he starts to explain the ins and outs of his latest theory. I find his approach unpersuasive, but interesting. Traditionally, a Simon Reeves lecture on The Necessity of Faith commonly revolves around the unspeakable beauty of the Universe, the playful loveliness of Creation, the inexplicable grandeur of the Heavens, and other such hippyish tosh. This time Simon has a new angle: his latest theory is that God exists because Evil exists. I say: come again, and Simon obliges. He mentions Belsen and Auschwitz and Treblinka. To this I slurringly respond that yeah, sure, the Holocaust was a pretty nasty turn of events, but it doesn't exactly prove God exists. *Does it*?

Undeterred, Simon claims that if we accept that Evil, i.e. the Holocaust, exists, then we must accept that Good exists, and that, if Good exists, then so does God: the fount of all Goodness. Now I turn to Sarah and say, 'Can I have some more apple crumble?' – then I point out that my friend is applying an arbitrary moral construct: I point out how, in presuming the Holocaust proves the existence of Evil, he is merely approaching the argument with an *a priori* belief in Evil.

Raising a forefinger, Simon moves the conversation on to the Moors murderers. His next claim is that even the blindest, stupidest moral relativist – by this he means me – must admit that there is something in *that* particular case which is intrinsically bad, that is irredeemably horrible, that is conclusively and definitively Wicked.

Perfect. Quite recently I have been reading about this Sixties murder case, so I am well armed. Toying with my wine glass I inquire whether Simon has heard about Moors Murderer Myra Hindley's famous statement at her trial. Simon shakes his head; in a flat voice I reveal how Myra Hindley explained to police that one of the reasons she and partner Ian Brady tortured and buggered and slaughtered the children on those bleak, cold, windswept northern moors was to prove that there could be no God. Poutingly, Simon looks through me. He is gazing at me, saying nothing. Blindly I knock back the rest of my wine and when I open my eyes I see that Simon's gaze has achieved a certain frostiness. I am not sure what this chilliness means. Maybe this means that, somewhere, deep down, he still resents me: maybe this means that even though he can dazzle me with his theological and epistemological footwork, he hates the fact that I can stick one past him from thirty yards when it comes to girls.

If this is true, it is very sad: Simon and I *aren't* talking about morals or God, we are merely dancing around the handbag of History. He and I are simply chain-ganged together by that surreal series of events, that started six-and-a-half years ago, and ended with him saving my life.

*

The catalyst of this chain reaction was Nathalie and me becoming friends. It happened a few months after the Scottish trip had proved to my satisfaction what a shallow and uninteresting tease the girl was. I was round Simon and Nathalie's Regent's Park flat, one April Sunday morning, having my normal stiff and sullen conversation with Simon's true love – when something changed. We were drinking coffee and eating excellent croissants, and suddenly Nathalie started pushing back her curls of black hair, and laughing, coarsely and robustly, at some sex-story I was relating. My intention had been to scandalise and annoy the girl; to my surprise she was lapping it up.

The rest of the day Simon and I had planned to spend alone together; instead we decided to gamble on the new warmth and risk a day as a threesome – walking up Primrose Hill, having lunch in Camden Town, boozing it up in the pub, getting each other to talk about ourselves. By the end of it I knew the gamble had been justified: my previous conception of Nathalie was entirely wrong. She wasn't shallow, merely endearingly hedonistic; neither was she a tease – rather, refreshingly feminine. Nathalie Saure was, in fact, sexy and articulate. And wild. Over her sixth drink she explained why: how an indulgent upbringing with rich and loving parents had left her with a curiosity for horizons, and the confidence to explore them. If she could put it in a phrase, she said, she wanted to spend every day as if she was going to die that evening, and as if she had been born that morning. Necking my beer in the gin-palace pub on Primrose Hill Road, I could only agree. The girl was enunciating my own 22-year-old sentiments exactly. It was uncanny. From that moment on I resolved that she and I should be friends: firm friends. The happy by-product of this would be that it would enable Simon and I to renew our own friendship, which had fallen into abeyance since Nathalie's appearance on the scene.

A *menage à trois* ensued. A true, and equilateral, triangle. Thereafter, we did everything as a trio: whether it was a trip to Camden Market, or a gig at the Marquee, or a foray into the North Essex countryside – if there was something to be done that season, Simon and Nats and I did it together.

Then, as spring turned into summer, things changed, once again. Simon had always maintained he was going to get a First: as his final year loomed, he started achieving it. From late June onwards he began spending more time in the library, and less time with me and Nathalie. This meant she and I were perforce left together, to our own devices. The first couple of times this happened we were mildly embarrassed – hitherto we had always been diluted by a third. Then one morning I went round to Simon and Nathalie's flat, carrying my guitar: I was on my way back from the repairer's. As soon as Nathalie saw the case slung over my shoulder, she got excited. Leading me into the empty living room we started making music. I played guitar, she sang; an hour later our faces were flushed and happy.

Thereafter my visits to Regent's Park Road, to see if Simon was in, became explicit visits to see her and to see if *she* was in. I liked hearing her sing; she liked hearing her sing. Over the following weeks, we tried our hand at everything: Van Morrison, the Incredible String Band, Debussy, Peter Paul & Mary. We tried it all. We tried hard. We became pretty skilled: sitting in the sunlit living room at Regent's Park Road, I would pluck a plangent chord, she would hit a dulcet top note, the two of us would prolong the harmony . . .

Afterwards, at the conclusion of these laughing duets, we talked. Every time we put down our music sheets and went to share a wine bottle or two, Nathalie had us chat about her ideas and fantasies and dreams and frustrations. They were nearly always sexual.

One conversation had especial significance. It was a mild summer evening; Simon was working late in the library; we were sitting on the balcony of the Regent's Park flat. From this balcony you could see across the back-gardens of Camden to the sward of the Park. From the Park, that evening, came scents of just mown grass, from the streets came summery laughter, from under Nat's dress came the aroma of coconut sun-oil.

'So,' she said, sipping her wine, 'Guy.' Sometimes she pronounced my name ghee like the Indian butter, just to annoy me. 'Tell me, Ghee. Do you like doing it from the behind?'

'What?'

'Do you like . . . to do it from the behind —'

'From behind . . .'

'Yes. I know. *The* behind.' Putting down her wine glass, she smiled and arrayed her bare feet on the balcony rail: 'But do you like it?'

'Yes, definitely. One of my faves.'

'And what else? *Sado-masochisme? Frottage?*'

'What's that?'

'It means . . .' She looked at me with a sly curiosity. 'It means rubbing yourself against women in the Metro.'

'There's a word for that?'

'*En français.* But what else do you like?'

'Oh, everything. You know. Outdoors. Spanking.'

'Spanking? You like to be the dominator, then?'

'Yep.'

A silence. She grinned: 'Would you like to spank me?'

This span me out. For a moment, I was dumb. The chances were this statement was a joke, one of Nathalie's incendiary quips. Yet it was still provoking.

Along with the wine, a bad thought entered my head. Sitting there on the balcony, all I could think of was Nathalie and me – naked, together. It was monstrous: as we spoke, Simon was less than two miles away, designing velodromes, and here I was discussing the merits of spanking his girlfriend, *with his girlfriend.* Momentarily, the bile of guilt filled my throat. Then it didn't. Instead I was overwhelmed with resentment. I loved and respected and admired Simon immensely, but he was still a wanky faggot. A gonk. What was he doing with this adorable slut? This mischievous plaything? This angel in lingerie? She was mine; she was his; she was meant to be mine. The conviction sent me: I knew that if Nathalie and I ever got around to having sex it would be true, final passion: she and I were designed to share a bed. Not her and Simon. While I sat there, and looked across the North London backyards, smelling the early evening barbecues, the very idea of Simon and her doing it seemed reprehensible and ludicrous. Did he use his bicycle clips in bed? Did he truss her up with his woollen ties? Did he hoarsely whisper in her hot Parisian ear about strainer arches and choirscreens and the interesting Saxon crypt at Repton?

Letting my eyes rest on Nathalie, as she curled her toes and wrinkled her nose and laughed that sexy, drunken laugh – it became clear. Clear as the clearest Carolingian rock crystal. Effortlessly I concluded that if anything was going to happen, if anything was going to result between Nathalie and me, it would all be Simon's fault, anyway. The way I saw it, if it hadn't been for dear, kind, honest, loyal, trusting, quite possibly impotent Simon, we would never have met in the first place.

Our family lunch is over. Sarah and Simon have set off

in Simon's battered Citroën, with the intention of buying some furniture at Chiswick Pine, and seeing some foreign film at the Chiswick Plaza. Consequently I am alone with my niece.

Setting Alice on my lap I read her a story about Spot the Dog and his birthday present. This story goes down well. Alice is a rhapsodically selfish little girl – she is completely obsessed with birthdays and presents – nevertheless she does it in such a nice way, I actually don't mind. After ten minutes of listening to me she is snuggled up close, with her thumb in her mouth, and her clear blue eyes focused on the page. Meanwhile, as I drone on – 'Look, there's Spot's present. What's in the present? Can you guess . . .?' – I find my own mind hazing over. I am remembering what happened later. That year.

That fateful year.

One of those Simonless days – the Saturday after the balcony chat – something happened. I had been retuning my guitar in the living room, waiting for Nathalie to finish her *toilette*. Then I forgot myself and decided to use the lavatory. Walking into Simon and Nathalie's bathroom, I caught the lady of the flat stepping fresh and wet out of the shower. For a second, neither of us did anything: she didn't grab a towel; I didn't move. She was staring right at me, scrutinizing my reaction; I was staring back – at her nubile body, at her young but heavy breasts, at the black Afro curls of her pubic hair. Her naked body was the most beautiful thing I had ever seen in my life. I was rooted. I would have stayed there all summer, if a gurgle from the boiler hadn't brought me to my senses: mumbling an apology I bolted out the door – and the flat.

Back in Montagu Square, the image obsessed me, guiltily. I tried to get it out of my system by masturbating. But it was useless. Every night I still had dreams about her: whether I masturbated twice, or three times, or forty-six, I still woke up with a memory of a dream about Nathalie, a dream about a naked, smiling, shower-wet Nathalie quizzing me wickedly about *le spankeeng*.

Such an intolerable situation could not go on. Things came to a head, one morning, when I picked up the phone, and heard her voice: 'Wake up! It is me.'

'Who?'

'Nathalie!'

Coughing, I queried: 'Christ . . . What time is it?'

'Eleven o'clock . . . 'urry up!'

'Why?'

'I want you to come and meet me.'

'Where?'

'The Wallace . . . I will see you there in half an hour? Bye!'

She had gone before I could argue. Sleepily I tumbled into some clothes and out into the summer air, and shuffled across Baker Street to Manchester Square. Seconds later I saw her, skipping round the corner of Spanish Place; she was wearing a very short dress that showed her thighs, and a top that set off her slim-but-dimply shoulders. And her dark hair was wet, just like her shining eyes.

'You look 'ungover, Guy.'

'Thanks. So do you. What are we doing here?'

'Nothing . . . I just thought . . .'

'Where is Simon?'

A Parisian shrug. I persisted: 'Why did you want to meet here?'

'Because . . .' I could see her estimating me. 'OK. I will tell you. There is a painting I must show to you.'

Once inside, she dragged me down some corridors, past a famous Rembrandt, before calling a halt in front

107

of a big, sombre canvas. The picture was of a naked man and a woman; they seemed to be gliding through space. The caption said Francesca da Rimini; I vaguely knew what this was about: Dante, or something.

'Why this one?'

'Because,' she said. 'Only because . . . You see the woman?'

The woman in the painting was holding onto her airborne lover, as they flew through the blackness. There was a look of wistful longing in the woman's low-horizoned eyes. Standing beneath the painting, Nathalie toyed with a twist of black hair. She was finding it hard to explain: 'So. You see. I saw this painting for the first time, last week. And I thought . . . that is how . . .'

'What?'

'That is how I feel. Sometimes.'

Returning my gaze to the painting, I nodded, calmly, although my heart was thumping. In an attempt to lighten things, I said: 'So you mean, you feel like you're whizzing through space with no kit on?'

'Please . . .'

Nathalie wasn't amused; her eyes were brimming with tears. Mock-casually, I tilted her chin with a finger.

'C'mon,' I murmured, 'What's the prob?'

'Oh,' she said. Her voice was weird, wrong: 'I am just . . . very confused.'

'Confused. Why?'

'Because . . . I wish I did not think what I do. But I cannot help it. I just . . . do.'

Our lips were three inches apart. Hers were trembling. I still had her chin cupped in my hand.

Stooping to her face, I went to peck her, comfortingly, on the cheek. Her skin was a smear of warmth, salty with tears – but I didn't have a chance to wipe it; placing a forefinger against my chin, Nathalie guided my lips to her lips.

It has been a pleasant afternoon: Alice and I have made a big Lego castle and watched a Disney video; we have eaten choccies and biccies and drunk pints of Ribena; now I am explaining to the girl why she is not in the photographs of her parents' wedding.

Pointing to the big silver-framed photo I am holding up, Alice wonders: 'Where am I, Uncle Guy?'

'Um. You didn't exist. This is before you existed. Not long before, actually.'

Shaking her head, she says: 'Am I in heaven? Is that where I am?'

'No. You just weren't . . . born.'

'Not born?'

'No . . .'

Now she raises her piercing blue eyes: 'Uncle Guy, who made me not born?'

'No one.'

'Where are you?'

'I'm not in the picture. Look, that's your Gran, in a particularly stupid hat. And that's your Grandad, looking like he's had thirty-six pints . . .'

Alice laughs: 'Izza joke!' She is clapping her hands. 'I want to get married. I am going to marry James and have a long dress, like Cinderbrella . . .!'

'Of course you will.'

'Will you marry me when I'm old?'

'No —'

'Why not?'

'It's not . . . the done thing. Look – there's the moon!'

As if to save me from my cross-examination, the moon has risen over the streets of Chiswick: it is clearly visible through the living room window. Picking up my niece I carry her to the window and point at the clean white disc in the early evening sky.

'Look,' I say. 'Can you see it?'

Knuckling an eyesocket Alice nods, and then turns to me and asks: 'Uncle Guy. Is the moon going to marry the sun? Is the moon the Mrs of the sun?'

'In a way,' I say, adjusting the awkward weight of the child in my arms, feeling the warmth of her thigh on my wrist. 'In a way. The moon and the sun are like your mum and dad, and all the stars are their children, all the beautiful stars . . .'

Absorbing this bollocks, Alice gazes seriously out of the window at the heavens, and then slowly shuts her eyes and snuggles closer. She is falling asleep in my arms. Gently I pad my way down the hall, past the kitchenette and the bathroom, as far as Alice's tiny room, but when I go to lower the child on to the bed, she stirs and tightens her grip round my neck. She might be dog tired but she's not letting go of her uncle. I have no choice. Lowering myself onto the bed, with Alice clinging to me like a baby monkey, I lie us both down, side by side. From this angle I can watch as Alice slips away. Indulgently I brush the hair away from her eyes, and touch the back of my hand to her frowning forehead.

And then I just lie there. Sensing. I can sense everything that makes the child. The Ribena on her breath, the Vosene in her hair, the Zig Zag bath-foam on her skin. I can sense the Apple Crackles, and the TCP, and the Noodle Doodles; I can sense the Coco Pops and the Numberelli and the Frazzles and Dairylea: I can sense the bananas and Nik Naks and Toffypops and peaches and Tip Tops and Scallywags and Alphabites and Pot Shots and Ricicles and Ketchips and Donkey Kong Shreddies.

# 13. Number 59, Portland Place

Walking up Portland Place, I try to focus on what Belinda is saying; politely I attend to her nervy, febrile, pre-abortion chatter. But it is no good. All I can think of is Zapruder: the film he made of John F. Kennedy's assassination. I can remember how my mother behaved when she watched the film – how she would cover her eyes and say, with real conviction: *no, please, no – don't let it happen.* It was as if she believed that the atrocity would somehow be averted, that for once the President's cranium would not explode, would not burst into a bloody flower. At the time I did not understand my mother's dread: she knew what was going to happen, there was nothing she could do about it – so why all the sweat? Now I understand. In a small way it is the same sickly feeling I experience whenever I walk up Portland Place.

Every time I walk up this street I think, no, surely, it can't be as bad as I remember. It is. As Belinda and I halt in front of the Chinese Embassy, waiting to cross the road towards Harley Street, my attention is inexorably drawn to the frontage of Number 59, and I am forced to wince. To flinch. I can't believe the way this charming building has been knee-capped, has been tarred and feathered, has been brutally tattooed. I can't credit the way the pediment and pilastering of this house have been neatly sliced in two, in order to make way for a very inferior piece of Thirties Residential Speculation. Rooted on the street corner, staring at the mutilated pediment of Number 59, Portland Place, I find I am reminded of a war-wounded amputee, forced to beg in the street; or of a half aborted foetus—

Turning to Belinda: 'How are you feeling? OK?'

'Oh, great,' she retorts, now aware that I have not been listening to a word. 'Really. I *love* having abortions. I wish I could have them more often. It's *such* a nice break from dull routine . . .'

Noticing my expression, Belinda relents. 'I'm sorry. I'm just on edge.' She squeezes my hand. 'It's jolly nice of you to come, actually.'

Self-consciously, I demur: 'No problem —'

'A lot of men would have just sent a few flowers and washed their hands, after that.' She smiles, showing white teeth. 'You aren't so bad, sometimes, are you?'

'Guess not,' I reply. I am wondering whether to feel patronised, or insulted. Deciding on neither, I lead Belinda across Wimpole Street, guiding us past a Lutyens townhouse, until we come to a junction and turn left; thereafter we stroll north to Number 16: the Well Woman Clinic.

Standing outside, I press Belinda's palm and kiss her on the cheek and say: '*Courage, ma brave.*' And then I feel stupid for saying that. Trouble is, I have no idea what to say; I do not know the etiquette. I am beginning to wish I had just sent a few flowers and washed my hands.

'I'll come back in about . . .'

'Two hours,' says Belinda. 'It's just a vacuum aspiration. Shouldn't be more than a couple of hours. See you later —'

Swivelling on a low, sensible heel, she turns and steps inside the foyer of the building; for a moment I

112

stand there watching the glass doors close and flash; then I turn and head off. Vaguely I wander the streets of the area: strolling past the medical shops of New Cavendish Street, and the Italian delicatessen of Thayer Street, and the fine bay windows on Hinde Street.

Eventually I turn left onto Marylebone High Street, and halt. From this viewpoint the villageyness of the district is apparent: the bakers and the butchers, even the parochial spire in the distance . . . But I do not give a toss, today. Today there is only one thing to do: get drunk. That is what expectant fathers are meant to do; perhaps this experience isn't so different. Nipping into The Cross Keys I squeeze between the Trinity students and the dusty-jeaned builders, look at the fanciable bar girl, and say:

'Triple Glenlivet. Neat.'

Three triple malt whiskies and four pints of mild later, I fall out into the Indian summer sunshine, the strange October warmth, and I stumble away towards the Well Woman Clinic.

The Well Woman Clinic turns out to be a sleek, shiny establishment. It is evident Belinda is getting value for my money: the place has a generous air. As soon as I am through the doors, I am offered a coffee and a glossy mag. Suppressing a burp, I sit on the pastel sofas and flick through the copy of *Cosmo*, while waiting for my de-foetused ex-girlfriend to emerge. The magazine bores me; dropping it on a pile of other mags I go to pick up some promotional literature. This latter is more absorbing. It describes the various methods used to abort, herein. Such as vacuum aspiration. Clearly I picture what this means: sitting here I imagine Belinda as she is now: lying with her heels in the stirrups, smiling bravely at the ceiling, as the nurse inserts the steel nozzle. For a moment, all is quiet. Then someone flicks a switch, and the motor starts throbbing, and the

113

machine starts shaking and with a sudden thwock, shluuuurrrp, ka-CHOF, the stuff that is our unformed baby is felched out of Belinda's uterus, sucked along a plastic hosepipe, forced through a metal grille and squirted into a Pyrex glass canister.

Maybe I shouldn't be dwelling on such unsavoury matters. Can't help it. As I sit here I let the leaflet droop and my mind wanders again: to the name of the Well Woman Clinic. It occurs to me now that this is a little bit of a euphemism. Perhaps they should call it Cuntbusters. Or Motherdon'tcare. Savouring the whisky on my breath I sit back, trying to stop the room spinning, as I wonder what would happen if there were complications. God, I hope not. I truly hope not. I can imagine how it would happen: I can see the nurse turning to the consultant as she tells him that only half the foetus has been extracted. Sagely the consultant nods, checks the dials, and strokes his senatorial jawline. Then the same physician instructs the nurse to pick up the forceps. Her face red and puffy, the nurse obeys: gripping the handles of the forceps she begins squeezing and mashing, using the forceps to pulp the half-formed flesh-and-bone inside Belinda's uterus. Eventually the nurse is spooning what's left of my child out of my ex-girlfriend's womb, like a tanner scraping fat from a cowhide —

I'm going to be sick. Pitching to my right I lean over the armrest of the apricot-coloured sofa, and position my mouth over the brass pot of a potplant. I am going to be sick. I am going to be sick. I am going to be . . . No I'm not. The moment has passed. Gratefully dabbing my head with a tissue, I right myself, exhale and smile cheerily at the receptionist. My embarrassment is mercifully interrupted by the appearance of a moon-faced Belinda. She is stumbling towards me. Grabbing her arm I escort her to the sofa. I probably need to sit down as much as she does.

'Uhh . . . How was it?'

She rolls her eyes. 'Bit horrid, actually. Bit . . . grim.'

'Really?'

'Yes. They say I'll be OK, in an hour or two.'

I am still drunk. 'What do you want to do now? Do you fancy a coffee?'

'Coffee?' She shrugs. 'Suppose . . .'

Helping Belinda and myself outside I manage to guide us down Devonshire Place and across Marylebone High Street as far as Maison Sagné, the Viennese tea house. There we take the last table and I order two *cafés au lait*. Looking up from her lap, Belinda eyes me, sniffs the air, and wearily says: 'You've been drinking.'

'Just a couple. Do you fancy a croissant?'

'Sorry?'

'I'm starved.' Burping again, I lean to a waitress and order two croissants. When they arrive, I feel more uncomfortable. I love my Maison Sagné croissants with lashings of sour cherry jam; somehow such luxurious indulgence doesn't seem right. Morosely I nibble the croissant dry while Belinda watches her coffee get cold. Desperate for something to say, I manage: 'Hope it didn't hurt . . . I mean —'

This makes it worse. What is there to say? 'Sorry you had our unborn child ripped out of your womb – still, ne'er mind, eh?'

It is pointless and sad and embarrassing and I almost leap for joy when Belinda finally opens her mouth and says: 'Guy, I'm tired. Could you lend me the cab fare?'

'Course.'

Gratefully I get my wallet out and shove a twenty in her hand; then I take her into the street and shove her in a cab; then I shove off myself towards the sunny Octoberyness of Regent's Park and the Zoo and the

115

Nash Terraces – God's own housing estate.

An hour has passed. My post-abortion wanderings have taken me past the madcap skyline of Hanover Terrace, and close to the limos parked outside the Central Mosque; they have escorted me via the toytown pavilions of Hanover Gate to the 3-D puzzle of the Snowdon Aviary, where I have paused, for a second, to listen to the squawks and chatter of the parakeets, to the high-pitched one-liners of the mynah birds. Ignoring the traffic lights I saunter south to the beginning of the eastern Terraces. This is one of my favourite views in London: the enfilade of Cumberland Terrace. Seen from this oblique angle the reckless length of John Nash's masterpiece goes on and on: a gay parade of stucco columns, of confectioner's Corinthian. Beneath the portico and pediment of Cumberland, it strikes me – for the thousandth time – how strangely clean the area's pavements are: how smartly blacked are the cast-iron Crown Estates lamp-posts.

Beyond the lawns and paths I come to a wilder section of the Park. I am slightly tired. Leaning a hand against a tree trunk I watch some girls watching some boys play football. One of the girls, who is seated with her legs tucked asymmetrically underneath her, has hair as black as black purple. It is so glossy and clean and shiny I want to sink my face into it and breathe.

Belinda. Belinda Belinda Belinda Belinda Belinda.

The private police are cruising Avenue Road, the American lecturers are quitting the Business School. Considering things, it occurs to me that this park, the Regent's Park, has been everything to me: it has been the arena of my youth, the venue of my love, the Colosseum of my brawls with destiny. I have tripped and fucked and drunk and laughed and kissed and

116

chased and got lost in this park; I have ambled across it at dawn when you can hear the anteaters coughing in the Zoo; I have stood amidst its cherry trees and gazed at the unrevolving restaurant of Telecom Tower, I have paused by its chestnut sellers to tenderly button-up the duffle of my true love; I have rowed across the oily lake en route to absolutely nowhere; I have bought hot dogs and tried to rollerblade and had amiable frisbee sessions with ex-girlfriends; I have trailbiked and sunbathed and tried to fly kites; I have romped with springers and thrown bagels at mallards. I have done all of this and more.

And yet.

Setting my forearms on a railing, I look down at the tarmac that inclines to the Regent's Park lake and I see green-and-white splodges of Canada goose-droppings, tiny tumbleweeds of silver sweetwrappers and the scuffed toes of my black leather boots. I have no choice. I have to think about it. About Belinda. About my recently unborn unbaby. I could get very sad about this. Very, very sad. Even now I feel like I am driving through a cold wet night and the windows of my car are misting faster than I can wipe them. Everything is misting. Everything is grief-stricken: the willows, the benches, the streetlights flickering into pink on the Marylebone Road. Stiffening, I spit, and turn, and look. From here I can properly see the bogus beauty of the Nash Terraces, those jerrybuilt, plasterboard palaces.

Hailing a cab on Albany Street, I open the door and slump in the back, watching all the other dour, sooty, late Georgian houses, repeating themselves.

# 14. Marine Ices

'So it's legal speed, then, yeah?'

'Yep. It's legal. Ish.'

Andy and I are in the vibrant, *Blade Runner*-ish bustle of Patpong, the Bangkok red light district. I am trying to explain to him the precise effect of Captagon, a locally-available speed: 'The effect is . . . somewhat like coke. Except it's cheaper. And easier to find.'

He nods, impressed. I relish the fact that the normally supercool Mackay is impressed by all this, by the tumult of the Bangkok pleasure zone: by the dazzling neon signs, the crowds of Jap tourists and the myriad shouts of 'fucky fucky?'; by the smells of spices and fishballs and perfume and rubbish and diesel and sewage; by the curses of the *tuk-tuk* drivers and the smiles of the beautiful transvestites and the leers of the Siamese wideboys hawking fake Cartier watches and 555 cigarettes and boxes of so-called Lacoste, on every street corner.

'So, where do we get this . . . Capt stuff, anyway?'

'Any of these chemists. Watch it!'

Dragging my lost-looking friend out of the way of a skidding moped – on the back of which is sidesaddled a couple of slashskirted Laotian whores – I help us both across the street, into the bright, white Happy Bird Pharmacy. Once inside, I confidently ask the Chinese pharmacist for Captagon. All I get in return is an awkward shrug and a nervous no. This is repeated at three more chemists; slowly it dawns: 'The police must have cracked down, I guess. They must have banned it, since last time . . .'

Into yet another Chemist we traipse, anyway. At the mention of the brand name we get the expected gesticulations: I'm-sorry-sir-but-this-is-impossible. Exasperated, I flash a twenty dollar note. This elicits a more promising response. With an anxious 'Oh-kay. Pee'ah. Yoo wai'?' – the man disappears into a back room.

'Peter?' says Andrew, squinting at me. 'Why does he think you're called Peter?'

'It's how they say Mister. Hey – I think he's got some!'

I am right. The pharmacist has returned from his antechamber, bearing two dusty packets of Captagon. He gives me the packets. I give him the twenty bucks.

The exchange made, Andrew and I step out of the cooly air-conditioned chemist into the humid mayhem of Patpong's nocturnal streetlife.

'So . . . what now?'

I smile. 'Now we wash these pills down with a few drinks.'

Having a few drinks, however, is not so easy. As soon as we start walking the streets in search of a vodka and tonic, we are accosted by a million young Thai men in suits: each of them trying to drag us back into their go-go bar.

'Hey meester! Meester! You wan' good time?'

'Girly show?'

'Come see girl!'

'Lazor brade! We do lazor brade!'

One of the men even shoves a menu in my hand. At the top it says *Good sexy show. Girly show. Bannanas. Smokking cigarete. Ping Pong.* Handing the menu back

I go to escape, but the man is especially insistent.

'Wha you wan, man?'

'Sorry?'

'We hav many gir. You come see.'

Intrigued, Andy leans nearer: 'You reckon you've got everything – in your sex show?'

'Yes. We hav!'

'How about a woman sucking off a woman?'

'No problem. We have sucky sucky.'

Mackay sniggers. 'OK. What about an old man with his mum?'

'Yes! Same same. We hav ol' man.'

'Really.' Andy says. 'Then . . . I don't suppose you've got . . . The Duke of Edinburgh getting shagged up the bum by a horse, have you?'

The man smiles: 'Oh yes Pee-ah we hav Duke Edinburr. We hav Duke Edinburr with horse! No problem!'

An hour-and-a-half has elapsed. We are ensconced in the Pink Pussycat go-go bar. Reaching into the breast pocket of his dark blue Valentino shirt Andy takes out a fistful of Baht to pay for the dozen or so drinks we have consumed. The drinks are quite cheap, considering the floorshow on offer: fifteen semi-naked teenage girls dancing on a dais behind the horseshoe-shaped bar.

Collecting his new Simla beer and handing me my next vodka and tonic, Andrew shouts, above the thumping sound of the Rolling Stones: 'What was that message you had at the hotel?'

I shrug: 'It was nothing. It was from home. They want me to ring home.'

'So. Did you?'

'Nah,' I say, flippantly sucking my vodka through a straw and gazing up at the gyrating girls, one of whom

120

is wiggling her bikinied little arse *just* for me. 'I can't be arsed. It'll only be someone wanting me to buy something. Some cheapo CD player. Jesus – look at her!'

Following my gaze, Andrew turns and takes in the full beauty of the new dancer who has just appeared on the dais. 'Strewth,' he says. 'She looks like that girl at Marine Ices. Remember?'

'You mean the one you were really in love with? Your true love?'

'That's right.'

'What was her name again?'

'Er . . .'

Turning from my friend's amphetamined laughter, I look at the girl again. The sight of her makes me happy. Clad in white knickers and black stilettos and a scanty red tee-shirt, this whore can be no more than seventeen – nevertheless she is so well-developed her hard and large breasts are making the front of her tee-shirt hang down flat, about four inches in front of her stomach.

As Miss Marine Ices starts headbanging wildly to 'Brown Sugar', Andrew leans his speedy beery breath to my ear and says: 'These chicks are giving me religion.'

'Me too.' For a moment I feel a twinge of guilt – thinking about Eva; then I don't. 'Do you wanna buy one?'

'How much are they?'

'A lot. But you can usually beat them down.'

'Really?'

'Sure. It's extra, though.'

He laughs. I continue:

'We could always go to a massage parlour.'

'Whassat?'

'I was told about it . . . last time.' I shrug, semi-knowledgeably. 'When I was here with Josh. Apparently you get these two girls and they rub you

121

and . . . stuff.'

He grins: 'Two?'

'Two.'

That clinches it. With a burp and a hiccup and a quick 'Try anything twice' Andy and I quit the bar and load ourselves into a taxi; minutes later we are pushing open the plate glass door of the Tiger Eye Massage Parlour. Herein, we are positioned by the manager in front of a big window, behind which are sitting at least thirty nubile, nearly-naked girls. Each of the girls has a numbered card pinned to her bikini-bottom. Under the watchful eye of the proprietor I explain to a wild-eyed Andrew that he has to choose two of the girls by number. This he does, as do I. Whereupon we are led through separate doors, by our chosen playmates.

Inside, the two teenage girls order me, politely, to strip. Once I am naked, the prettier one, who gigglingly tells me her name is Ni, hands me a dressing-gown. Obediently I put this on; they remain bikinied. So far this is quite painful: I am keen to get my hands on the girls' bodies, which are so excruciatingly near, but I can't. Instead we are going into another room.

In this next room is a huge bath full of water. Under orders I doff the towelling gown and step gingerly into the perfumed water. It is deliciously hot and full of girls: they have stripped off their costumes and climbed in alongside. After lathering my chest, they comb knots out of my wet hair, and knead the tension out of my stiff back. My shoulders feel broad and manly under their nimble hands. All through this, Ni giggles; her friend is more serious. Both of them have lovely, big, in-your-face breasts, the pink nipples of which look like dollops of cranberry jam on golden sponge. Staring at these nipples gets my penis swelling: the girls notice this and one of them reaches out, and starts washing my erection. She rolls it like dough between her palms

122

and then she goes 'Hoh!' as it stiffens further – as if she is surprised and slightly shocked by how big my penis is. A very professional touch. But then it hits me: what have I paid for? I want to *fuck*; I want to get my hands on their supple young bodies. That's what I want, yet they will not permit it. When I reach out they just laugh and sidestep, and say 'no Peetah no!' Then they assist me from the jacuzzi into another white room; in the centre of which is a huge bed. The girls are still wet and soapy from the bath; after towelling me down they lie me down on the bed and climb in alongside, sandwiching me between their bodies; then they start slathering their wet naked breasts up and down my tingling skin. Ohh ... Staring at the ceiling, I nearly choke on my saliva: shocked by the deliciousness of the sensation; it does not last long enough. Soon the girls cease their slithering, and they divide their attentions: one of them begins kissing my thigh and kissing my upper thigh and moving my thigh out of the way so she can lick my perineum with an expert tongue. I have never had this done to me before. For a second I am embarrassed – for her and for me – but soon I relax, let myself slip away, and as the girl licks and licks, exquisite little darts of pleasure start needling through.

Meanwhile the other girl has saddled herself across my stomach and as her long hair softly flays my neck and face she starts kissing my chest and stomach, and I can feel the muscles in my stomach tense as she does this. It feels funny. So funny I actually start laughing. As if everything is funny, as if the world is a joke I've only now understood. This gets the girls laughing, too. We are all smiling, now, all smiling and laughing – until the girl who is straddling me gets a different idea and reaches for the root of my cock and commences to suck me. She is swallowing my penis, whole, using her white throat, shaping her lips into a ruby red vowel.

123

Simultaneously the other girl has gone down to lick my balls, again; expert slow licks that moisten me, that make me tingle. As she does this I look at her, desperately.

Enough. Cuffing the same girl by the calf I drag her nearer and kiss the heel of her little foot; nuzzling her instep I lick around her toes. After this I kiss the sweet hinge of her ankle, and again, and in between kisses I start mouthing my way up the length of her legs, to her thighs; then I part her embracing thighs and her thick lashes flutter as I stoop to her sex and tongue her, lavishly, boozily, beerily. Now I can taste her, properly: the cuisine that makes her, the Siamese spices, the coconut milk and red chilli oil and the tart lemon grass, and as I eat her all up, as I bite her and kiss her I have to wipe my mouth dry on the skin of her soft inner thigh and then I draw back for a second and gaze at her cunt, at that complicated headwound – as it twinkles and glistens, yawning and drooling, like a retard. Between my legs I can sense my penis nodding, heavily, throbbingly close to climax.

Not now. Not yet. To stop myself coming too soon I stiffen my arms and retreat and I start kissing the second girl: slapping; nuzzling; groping; grazing. After a while, a few minutes of this, I turn and move and find a different place, longing to be lost in the Delta; to be adrift, marooned, anchorless . . .

Lazily grabbing one of the girls, like a Roman choosing fruit at the end of a banquet, I take her fifty kilograms of warmth in my arms and casually flip her over so that she is face down. Into the bedclothes she says something, slurrily, something submissive. Between licks of my nape, her friend laughs. Slipping a pillow under the girl's waist so that her arse is better positioned I shift myself over. Tightly gripping the handlebars of each buttock I slide my hard aching penis home, at long last. The sensation is so sweet, so terribly, unexpectedly sweet, I find that I shut my eyes and cry out, quite suddenly: 'I love you.'

Back at our hotel I fall straight into bed, with the scent of the Delta still on me.

Before going to sleep, however, I remember I have to shut the curtains. Dawn is already rising over the Chao Phraya river and I do not wish to be woken by the hot tropical sun on my dehydrated face, five hours hence . . .

On my way back to bed I notice a hotel envelope: inside the envelope is a telegram from my father. Wearily turning on the bedside light I unfold the paper and read:

'Your niece has drowned. Please come home. Dad.'

# 15. The London Ark

Stepping outside Terminal 4, into a misty morning, I breathe deeply. The air is cold; sharp. It has an edge. I ascertain that it is autumn. When I left London ten days ago it was warmish, an Indian summertime. Now the air is full of cold and wind and mist, and memories of ex-girlfriends. Stepping into this October morning gives me the same headrush as walking through a department store's cosmetics bazaar, where I can smell the different scents, all the Chanels, Guerlains and Diors that remind me, respectively, of Nathalie, or Nathalie, or Nat —

Lugging my cases off the trolley and into a black cab I bark at the driver: 'Islington. King's Cross. Fast as you can.'

And sitting in the back seat I watch Heathrow disappear behind. Half an hour of tunnels and motorways later, we turn into Hammersmith. Here I crane my neck to look at the weird new top-heavy office block that sits alongside the motorway: Ralph Erskine's London Ark. Gazing at this oddly shaped building helps to take my mind off Alice: instead I can ask myself key architectural questions, such as: why does the Ark give the feeling of being a dim gentle giant? Why does the decaying copper carapace of its roof look like a badly made toupee? How come Alice drowned?

126

While the taxi accelerates over the flyover I yearn across the skyline of West London and think of other things, determinedly. This whole Hammersmith area is haunted by an architectural might-have-been: Richard Rogers' inspirational Hammersmith Broadway Project. That rhapsody on a theme of shopping malls would surely have been better than the present architectural centrepiece. The one that sits here now. This great, boring, pink-and-grey post-modern monolith – Centre West, by EPR Associates – is entirely crap; its newness insults rather than improves the surrounding decrepitude: like a yuppie waving cash at the winos. Of course, other areas of London – *Alice, little Alice* – are also spooked in this way. By buildings that could have been, like Rogers' Hammersmith, or were, like London Bridge. As we head up Knightsbridge I strive to think of other places that are haunted: such as the North Bank of the Thames between Charing Cross and Somerset House, where once was Robert Adam's elegant and noble strandside terrace, The Adelphi. Somedays, when I find myself in this area – promenading on the Victoria Embankment or stumbling drunk down Villiers Street or sipping Pimms on the sunlit terrace of the Royal Festival Hall opposite – I perceive the nondescript buildings that obesely squat where The Adelphi paraded, and I find myself wistfully imagining, through the mists of time and pollution, that maybe I can glimpse a segment, just a hint . . .

But now I am thinking of lives that can be haunted by what once was, and what might have been. Will my family now always be haunted by what *might*: a grown-up niece, and what *was*: a lovely and vivacious two-year-old, *now dead*?

We are waiting at the lights. Now we are veering past Albany Street and the turning for Camden and this area makes me relax. Here I can justifiably reminisce. So I shall. Once more I take the silk kerchief of memory and press its scent-soaked lawn unto to my nose, like a Regency fop in Bermondsey slums, thus to expunge the malodours of my present situation, of *Alice*, my *Alice*, little *Al* —

The night Nathalie and I first made love was one of the hottest of an exceptionally hot summer. We were in Camden, lodged in a sweaty, crowded, noisy rock-and-roll pub near the Lock. For several days since our kiss in the Wallace Collection we had been trying to avert the inevitable; that night it became too tough. The sultriness of the air made everything seem dangerously heady; wondrously tropical. Every word we spoke vibrated with eroticism.

'Fancy another pint?'

'Yes. And some pork scratchings?'

'I think I'll have peanuts.'

She was wearing a tiny skirt; scarcely decent. Her legs were bare; her nose was tilted; her eyes were melting, already. Looking at her beauty I felt the noose of lust around my throat grow tighter. I couldn't help myself: sitting there I even adored the way her instep was white against the red leather of her sandals. She made me think of the *Ballet Russe*, of a mad flamenco.

'Where's Simon?'

She eyed me, significantly.

'Away.'

'Really?'

'*Vrai*. He won't be back . . . until tomorrow.'

'Fancy a long one?'

'Vodka. Ice. Cranberry juice . . .'

Too warm, too warm. The summer had already been supernaturally good, now it felt like it was about to explode. Dizzily I wiped the sweat from my eyebrows, watching a shirtless man shout at another guy, across a pool table. It was noisy in this pub: some young women at the bar were singing and laughing and fanning themselves with beer-mats. Water was trickling down Nathalie's frosted vodka-glass; lifting the cold glass she pressed it to her cheek, then she looked at me. Her face was as sombre as I had ever seen it.

'Guy. What are we doing?'

'Sorry?'

'What are we doing? How can we do this? How can we do this to Simon?'

'I don't know.'

'It is terrible.'

'I know.'

Setting the glass on the table, Nathalie exhaled, hugely. Then she raised her eyes again, and gazed through me. And then, as if on cue, we both said: 'Let's go —'

Grabbing her hand I led her outside. Skipping up Parkway, we tried not to look at each other, or say anything, as we keyturned ourselves into her cool, wicker-chaired flat. The place was empty, Simonless: the floor was black and white with shadows from the streetlights outside. Taking one of the wicker chairs, I watched as Nathalie poured us both a refrigerated glass of white wine. Even at this late stage we were trying to prevent it . . .

Sometime later we moved onto the sofa. Seated, I looked at her looking at me. That close I could smell the wine on her breath and see the languish in her eyes. And then, then it was the moment; oh, the moment.

'Just here.'

We have arrived. My house. Leaping athletically out of the taxi I drag my cases after. My cases strew themselves wantonly across the pavement, but I do not care.

Paying the man I unlatch my door and rush in. I am swallowing dryly. I have to do it. I have been postponing this moment for too long. So.

Going into the hall I pick up the phone and dial my sister's and Simon's, in Chiswick. Four rings: a switch: the answerphone. 'We're in Winchester. Double three, double eight, four nine. Please leave a message.' Sweating, I try to gauge from my sister's tone of voice what she is thinking. Her recorded voice sounds neutral – with, perhaps, an appoggiatura of weakness, right at the end. But despite or because of the fact that the voice is so neutrally clear, it is for me, thick with sadness: like she's been drinking all day on her own. Indeed, I would almost have preferred that my sister had screamed 'God why are you ringing us don't you know our daughter has drowned you ... sob ... sob...' Anything other than this dismal terseness. This chilling normality. 'We're in Winchester ... Please leave a message.'

But why are they in Winchester? Have they buried Alice already? Is she being buried in the country? Why?

Another call: Winchester 338849.

It is answered by my father.

'Hello?' His voice is weary.

'Hello ... it's Guy.'

'Guy. You got the message?'

'Yes, at the weekend —'

'But —' my father coughs; I can hear a voice in the background; my sister's? 'But you didn't ring —'

'Uh, no ...' I am stammering. 'I just ... got the next flight out, Dad. When did it happen?'

'She's not dead.'

'What?' She's not dead? 'Sorry —?'

My father stalls me: 'Alice is in a coma. She fell in the pool. I think you better come down.' Click ...

I know that click. That's different. It's different from

130

my father's normal phone-replacing manner, which is normally a quietly dignified *click* or an urbanely world-weary *click*. Never that sad and faintly admonitory *click* . . .

But a coma? She's in a coma?

Unannounced, my flatmate appears. I ask him if my car has been fixed: he says yes. I grab my car keys, without explanation. Then I get in the car and start off down the London roads to Winchester. My mind is in a blur; I slap some music in the stereo, a mixture tape. For a second it clicks and whines and then switches into play. The first song is insipid and inappropriate. I find another tape: this time it is 'Girlfriend in a Coma'. I fast forward again: to some Seventies jazz rock. A bit of Gospel. A snatch of quite jocular Handel.

No good, no good, no good. For some reason every-thing I play, today, is Elgar's Cello Concerto. For some reason, while I have been away, my glove compart-ment has been cleared out and swept clean and filled with tapes of sad, awful, tragic, miserable, elegiac Edward Elgar, played by Jacqueline du Pré.

Turning the stereo off, I urge the car down Chiswick High Road. I want to go faster. The traffic won't let me. Come on come on *come on*, I say, slamming my hands impatiently against the steering wheel. Come the fuck *on*. It's no good. I have to calm down, to think of something else, or nothing, before I emotionally hae-morrhage all over the newly hoovered interior of my Spyder. Remember something happier. I try to remem-ber something happier. Like falling in love with Nathalie.

The summer was halfway gone by the time I started to realise I was falling for Nathalie. Right from the outset I knew she was special – she was funny, quickwitted, and seriously irresponsible – but it still took me a while

131

to see quite how exceptional she could be. She wasn't just wild, she was ravenous. Extreme. Out of control. Her dresses were either Romeo Gigli, or second-hand rags with holes in the right places; likewise, her lingerie was either Yves Saint Laurent, or she simply went without. All or nothing: all or nothing. Nathalie was the only girl I had known who wanted to drink and dance and go out as much as me; sometimes more than me. Her fancy didn't just run away with her, it kidnapped her: if we were going to have sex *al fresco* it had to be sex on champagne in the park in the middle of the day while listening to Mozart.

It was the day we made love in Regent's Park that I realised that I was losing it properly. After making the assignation on the phone I had a shower and caught the bus and alighted at Great Portland Street. It was yet another hot sunny day: my feelings were a mixture of giddy unhappiness and rhapsodic anxiety. I was abuzz. Rubbernecking over the hedge by Ulster Terrace I squinted and visored, and caught sight of her and I felt my heart syncopate. Running across the grass I grabbed her by the shoulders and kissed her, hard. She was laughing, I was beaming. Without either of us saying *yes* or *no* or *how about if*, she led me by the hand into a nearby copse and there she lifted up her arms like a diver, wanting me to peel her cotton dress away . . .

Under the dappling arches of the lime-trees we did it. There and then. At first it was our normal rampant filthy sex; then it got different: groaning and sighing Nathalie started to bliss out, to freak. Flinging an arm across her sunsplashed face she tried to keep quiet: but she couldn't help it – stuffing her knuckles against her small white teeth she spat out the words: '*Je te déteste – je te déteste – je – te – déteste—*' And so it happened. As I stroked my penis and leaned on my arms, as I looked into the dark shiny eyes of my best friend's girlfriend I felt myself get dizzy, get vertigo: I felt like I was looking down into the depths of the Thames, at night. Like a suicide. It was mad. Taking Nathalie's knuckles out of her mouth I put them in my own mouth and sucked the salt off her lovely fingers, and as I did it I closed my own eyes and felt a shudder of happiness, and then I knew this was Not Just Fucking. Not Just Fucking. For the very first time in my life I Wasn't Just Fucking.

It was terrible, too frightening. Rolling off Nathalie, suddenly, I reached for my jeans and started pulling them on. I could hear the taxis on Albany Street; I could smell the roses from Queen Mary's Garden. Leaning over, Nathalie touched my steel-tensed shoulder with a hand.

'Are you . . . OK? What's wrong?'

I couldn't do it. I couldn't tell her. I couldn't tell her that there was suddenly a void in my heart. A great empty echoing place that had never been there before – that was shaped like her. Turning, I looked at Nathalie's puzzled, sad, sunburnt, pretty face, and kissed it.

And so I am smiling, too. I am smiling, sadly, at the memory of this: as I take the Stockbridge Road out of Winchester. As if to contradict my indulgent nostalgia, the sign for my precise destination, King's Somborne, pulls me up, short. I am almost there, and the reality of what is about to unfold mobs around; like a load of angry locals thumping on the side of a prison van.

Tyre-scrunching my father's gravel drive I notice my car is merely one of several. The whole tribe has gathered: even my mum's car is there and she hasn't seen my father in years. Through the back door I find a group of people drinking tea around my dad's kitchen table. I scarcely recognise them: neighbours

133

and friends of my father's. They stare at me as if they scarcely recognise me, too. After I have explained that I am the Son of the House, they tell me that everybody else, everybody important, is at the hospital, at Winchester General. With Alice. It's visiting hours.

Then someone mentions that Simon has returned early and that I will locate him in the living room.

In the living room, the expensively Turkish-rugged living room, I find Simon staring at the wall, smoking. He is listening to Elgar's Cello Concerto; the Jacqueline du Pré version. Going to the stereo, I switch it off. Simon doesn't blink. He just sits there in his stupid blazer, smoking. And staring at the wall.

'Simon,' I say, quietly. 'Si —'

He turns. His eyes are bloodshot.

'*Simon?*'

His nails are bitten. His chin is unshaven. I notice he gets a red beard. I also notice I have never noticed this before: because he has never let himself get this unshaven before.

'Simon —'

Finally, he speaks: 'Hello, Guy . . . How was Thailand?'

Flatly, I return: 'Fine. What the fuck happened?'

Again he vacillates.

'I've got to know. Dad said she fell in the pool. How did she fall in the pool?'

'We were in the kitchen . . .'

'*Sorry?*'

'When it happened.'

'Right.'

Disjointedly he unfolds the scenario. Coughing and sighing, he tells me how he was snoozing in a chair; how Sarah was talking to our father; how they were consulting maps. With a grimace, Simon explains how it was an uncommonly hot day, which is why they had the pool uncovered, which is why he was sleepy because he'd been working half the night.

Ignoring my puzzled expression and half-mouthed query, Simon tells the rest – how someone asked where Alice was, how they all looked up and gazed at each other, how they rushed out into the road, how they realised she wasn't in the road and so they rushed as one, back round the house and down the garden lane, to the uncovered swimming pool, where they leant over.

A vacant pause. A long, meaningless pause. Simon completes the picture: 'She was just lying there, Guy. With her eyes open. She must have been there – God knows. God knows how long. Just . . . lying there. At the bottom of the pool —'

I nod. All I can think is how cold it is; it feels cold in the room. It is so cold I have to get up and go into the kitchen. Here is no better: the kitchen is chillier, even though it's full of people. Self-consciously I approach the sink and turn the tap to fill the kettle; I don't want to drink tea or coffee but I am embarrassed by all these strangers, and perplexed by my own lack of reaction to Simon's story. As I sort this I look out of the window at the covered pool; the pool looks guilty. Almost sullen. Across the lawn slants of autumn sunshine are outlining shadows of trees: long, Cinemascopic shadows, like you get at the end of a film.

Setting the half-filled kettle on the counter I feel for the car keys in my pocket, exit through the back door, run round the house and jump in my car. After that I drive at about ninety into Winchester, search for the hospital, park, go in the hospital, ask for Alice Reeves – a two-year-old girl, nearly drowned? – and I am directed along three corridors, past a flowerstall and through a dozen floppy see-through perspex doors until I find myself in one of the paediatric wards. Here

135

I spot my mother by the coffee machine, and my dad conversing with a doctor, and finally the tragic loneliness of my sister in a room at the end of the corridor.

Tightening my fingernails into my palms, as I used to do when I was a child to stop myself from laughing in class, I step along the corridor past children in calipers and children in pyjamas and children in wigs, until I am in the little room and I am shoving through the knot of doctors. I can hear people saying *daughter* and *mother* and *uncle* and *pulmonary surfactant* but all I want to do is see my niece.

I can see her.

She is in a bed with tubes stuck up her nose; with tubes coming out of her neck and her mouth. The bed is small but Alice looks even smaller. Too small to be in hospital, to be connected to machines, to be treated like a dying person. Going close I lean over the bed and it's there that I see what I did not want to see.

Alice's eyes are open. Her hair looks glossy, her cheeks are red, her face is facing the side like she is sweetly asleep. But she isn't: her eyes are open; they are pitched to the corners; they are full of an infinite sadness; they are dead.

# 16. The Yorkshire Grey

'This is Peter. He is holding a dog. What is Peter holding? It's a dog. The dog is called Jason. Can you see? Can you see Jason? He has a blue collar on. Can you see Jason's blue collar? Can you?'

No . . .

'Now Jason is licking Peter. There's Jason, licking Peter with his tongue. Lick, lick, lick. Jason's tongue is very wet. Lick, lick, lick. Can you see Jason's tongue? Now Peter is laughing. Jason's tongue is tickling him. Do you like being tickled? Do you?'

OK —

'Now Peter and Jason . . . Now Peter and Jase . . .'

That's it, that's all I am doing. Placing the book, face down, on the bed, I stretch, and rub air into my face. I have been sitting in this claustrophobic hospital room for about three hours, trying to stimulate my comatose niece by reading from her favourite picture-book. And I am tired. I am tired of trying to be pitiful and compassionate and unrevolted.

Since arriving here in Winchester, a few days ago, I have spent my afternoons in vigil, over Alice, and I am beginning to feel something close to anger. The whole charade is so cruel and drawn-out: when I look at the stiff, dribbling, lifeless patient, with her catheters and cranial bolts, with her Electroencephalograms and

137

Bilateral Pressure Monitors, it is impossible to be optimistic. The signs of medical mistreatment are too distressing: the flecks of blood where the tube has abraded her soft mouth, the bruises where her physiotherapy has been overenthusiastic. How I wish Alice wasn't like this. I especially wish her eyes weren't like *that*. It's those sad blue eyes that do it, that send me: the way they are pitched to the left as if she's all the time averting her face, like a lover rejected, and saying, sans words: why the fuck are you bothering? Vexed, again, I am about to ask some fiercely pertinent questions of the day nurse, who is rinsing bits of tracheotomy tube in the stainless steel sink-unit opposite, when I hear a voice down the corridor. It is my sister, returning from her sandwich-break.

Picking up the picture book, I wearily persist: 'Peter and Jason are going for a walk. They are going for a walk by the sea. Look, can you see the sea? It is full of boats. Can you see the boats? Peter would like to have a boat. He likes boats. Now Jason is —'

'Hi.'

It's my sister.

'Hi,' I say. My sister sits down at the end of Alice's bed. She looks terrible. My sister's face is so etched with guilt and remorse and despair and – worst of all – *hope*, I cannot bear to look at it. Instead I bury myself in the picture book, pretending to be interested in Jason and Peter. Sensing my wilful distance, my sister chats with the nurse: 'I think she's looking better today, don't you?'

The nurse nods, vehemently: 'Oh yes. She'll be . . . her breathing's much better. Definitely . . .'

A pause.

'What about you, Guy?'

I pretend not to have heard.

My sister repeats: 'Guy – don't you think she's looking better?'

138

'Uh . . .'

'You only see her every so often . . . so it's easier for you to see all the improvements. Don't you agree she's looking better?'

'Well, yes. Of course.' I am desperate. 'She looks much more . . . relaxed.' Relaxed is obviously the wrong word. My sister's pale, ageing, pretty face twitches. She looks down to the carpet and, to distract herself, starts taking more toys and teddy bears from an orange plastic Sainsbury's bag. I am grateful for this respite. It gives me the chance to interpret my sister's body language. My interpretation is worrying. Looking at Sarah's fraying jeans, and her muddy trainers, and her why-bother make up, I can only wonder: What did she do? How come my sister deserves this? Why the special treatment? I can't begin to conceive what Sarah must think. What she must be thinking, right now.

My anguished empathy is interrupted. My sister is asking me another question, her voice vibrating with emotion.

'But . . . don't you think she's more alert? Wouldn't you say?'

Shut up, shut up, shut up.

'Yyyess,' I intone. 'Yes, she does look a bit more . . . alert. Sort of more . . . with it. You know? Her expressions seem more . . . aware.' That saves it. Slowly my sister's anxious frown softens, and relaxes, twists into a half-smile; then she gets up and switches on the TV. It is time for *Neighbours*. This particular soap opera was my precocious little niece's favourite viewing, primarily because of its catchy signature tune, and seeing as the Intensive Stimulation Programme we have adopted, as a family, is based on the use of recognised stimuli, it has been mooted that the theme tune to *Neighbours* might assist.

It is certainly embarrassing: horribly, shockingly grisly. The lunchtime News concludes and the announcer cues the programme, whereupon my sister and the nurse start singing a duet. Nodding and wagging their heads like children's TV presenters, making the various mobiles suspended above Alice's bed start rocking and revolving, they commence a thin and reedy singalong:

*Neighbours, Everybody needs good Neigh-bours,*
*With a little understanding,*
*They can make the perfect daaay.*

Getting up, I place Alice's book on my chair, and exit.

Once in the corridor I decide on a coffee. Approaching the drinks machine I chance upon a gaggle of physicians: a fraternity of white coats, visibly hierarchical. They are the same doctors that did the rounds this morning, the same doctors who discussed in suspiciously confident voices the levels of Alice's liquid tranquilliser, her emerald-green Diazepam cordial.

I intrude on the oldest, the top man: 'Doctor Mortimer?'

'Yes? What is it?'

His abruptness unsettles me: 'Uh – I'm sorry to interrupt, doctor . . . but – I'm Alice Reeves' uncle and . . .'

'I know. How can I help you?'

'Well . . . I was just wondering what you thought. About her . . . chances.'

'Chances?' The doctor eyes me. 'I see. It is serious, of course. With a case like this, we have to be very careful what hope we offer . . .' He seems unsure how to treat me: 'Tell me again: how long was she under water?'

'We're not, er, certain . . . We still don't know exactly when it was she fell in, and . . .'

'I understand.'

'But – we think it must have been at least seven, or eight minutes?'

The doctor frowns, caressing his jaw.

'That is a long time. She's quite a lucky girl to be alive at all. Having said that . . . I have known similar cases of pre-natal, or indeed post-natal anoxia – where there's been truly remarkable improvement. The brain is very unformed at her age, so that gives us grounds for optimism.'

This is flannel. I recognise it all too well. Abandoning caution, I tackle the man head-on. 'OK, doctor – I know all that. What I really want to know is what you really think? Will she get better, properly? Will she one day be the way she was?'

'Well . . .'

'*Yes?*'

He shakes his head: 'If you want my own opinion, the prognosis is not particularly good. Miracles do occur – but that's precisely what they are: miracles.'

At last. This is what I want. This straight-talking stuff is just what I need to hear after four weeks of waffly, well-meaning, my-uncle-once-fell-in-a-boating-lake bollocks. I go on: 'So, the brain damage is . . . irreversible. Right? She will at least be severely brain-damaged. Right?'

Nodding, the doctor affirms: 'I'm afraid that is quite likely. Given that she's already been in a coma for four weeks, it's probable she will suffer some kind of brain damage. Possibly rather severe. And that is to presume she will come out of the coma.'

I hadn't considered this. Slightly thrown, I say: 'You mean, she might not come out of the coma . . . *ever?*'

Checking his expensive-looking, metal-strapped watch, the doctor sighs, tersely. 'Brain traumas are notoriously unpredictable. One simply cannot predict.

141

If there is any improvement it's more likely to be a slow resurfacing. Nonetheless —'

'What?'

He reassumes his doctorly air; that infuriating air of vague positivity. 'We mustn't give up hope. Must we? There's always room for hope, especially with such a young patient.'

And that's it, that's my lot: as I try to frame a reply the doctor turns to his adoring colleagues and disappears down the corridor, away from me and my troublesome niece.

Life is a long swim up river. A long swim up river that ends in the sea. And yet, still. Still. Even though we all know that, sooner or later, we shall all be swept away, sometimes it still feels good to struggle, to fight, to strain against the coldly surging torrent, to feel the sensuous ache in one's muscles.

Trouble is I just don't feel like struggling tonight. I feel like turning turtle. I don't give. It all seems stupid and pointless, and sad. I am sitting in the darkened kitchen of my father's house, Blue Cedars, and I am watching the moon slide across the semi-cloudy sky, and the November rain lash helplessly against the French windows. And I am agitated. I have a whisky in my hand; I sip it, I am pensive. The house seems empty: my sister and my father and my stepmother are all asleep. Tomorrow I will go back to London; but what am I going to do now? I am going to do nothing. I am going to smoke a few Turkish cigarettes and look at the vague shape of the cedar trees – beyond the insulting cover of the swimming pool – and I am gong to try and empty my mind. But I cannot think nothing. I have to think something. I have to read something.

Going into the dining room I reconnoitre the bookshelves. There I find a lot of slim poetry volumes and oily car manuals: the dining room bookcase is the fourth division bookcase – here is the place to find books that haven't been read in years and that won't be read in years but that are still too useful or too poignant to be relegated to the garage. Scanning the spines I see a whole foot is taken up by my *Narnia* books, and my sister's *Malory Towers*. Left of these are remnants of later adolescence: a dog-eared *Catch 22*, my sister's old Brontës, some French/English dictionaries. None of these interest me, right now. For whatever reason they are not quite right.

Just as I am about to give up, I see something more interesting. On the extreme bottom shelf is a selection of my university textbooks. A few of them notably mint. One catches my eye by its colour: Le Corbusier's *Vers un Architecture Libre*. It is bright yellow, memorably so. I first glimpsed this shocking canary-in-a-coalmine yellowness in the gloom of the Yorkshire Grey: a goodish pub near the Tottenham Court Road, where the Bartlett School decided to hold the bulk of our Freshers' Induction Weekend.

Opening the cover, I see my name, scribbled across the frontispiece: *Alisdair Guy Simpson. Fitzrovia.*

The sight of this intrigues me. Was I really that naff? *Alisdair* Guy Simpson? Of *Fitzrovia*?

Flicking into the book and lighting another Turkish, I try to imagine the youth I must have been then. Keen, uncynical, gauche. As I do I am distracted by some late-adolescent marginalia in the book. Scrawled down the side of each and every page is a litany of remarks: *stupid French cunt, mad Marxist bastard, what is he saying the wanker?* It obviously didn't take long for my Induction Weekend enthusiasm to subside.

Wandering on through the pages I sip the Laphroiag, and smoke more Turkish, and think some stuff: until 2am, when I rub my tired eyes. Then, at the last, I spy

143

a final margin-note. Next to Corbusier's dictum: *a house is a machine for living in,* I have addended the note: *yeah, just like a gas chamber is a machine for dying in.*

In my present frame of mind, this strikes. It provokes a few thoughts: What was I thinking when I wrote that? Was I being deep, or flip, or wanky? I must have hated Le Corb so much – I maintained he could and would have admired gas chambers for their noble functionalism, for their teleological streamlining. And in that, it occurs to me now, maybe I was completely wrong. Perhaps Le Corb was, after all, OK. Perhaps he was rather fine. It is possible. As I sit here, malt whisky in hand, I dwell over a grainy black and white picture of the *Unité d'Habitation* – Corbusier's seminal apartment block in Marseilles – and it occurs to me that this building is actually very impressive. The *Unité* might have been the model and inspiration for many of the barrier blocks that blight the cities of England, yet there *is* something frankly grand about its massivity, its ugliness, its ruthlessly brutal, almost sociopathic arrogance —

Ruthlessly brutal? Sociopathic arrogance?

It's late: *too* late. Grinding my cigarette out and necking the last of the whisky, I slap the book shut and retire.


But I do not sleep easily. When I am woken by my beeping alarm at eight, the rain is flooding through the window, not the sun. Turning off the alarm with a phlegmy curse, I wonder why I feel so groggy. Then I remember: bad dreams. Weird bad dreams. I cannot remember what or how or why they were bad; I just know they were.

Yawning into my suit and shirt I slouch downstairs. Here I grab a milkless Nescafé and some butterless toast and then, wordless, I drive my sister into hospital;

I am on my way home to London – I have work to do, after all – but last night I promised to look in on Alice, one more time, however briefly.

Nearing the hospital entrance, I start to wish I hadn't promised. As my sister and I park, and disembark, an unsettling feeling kicks in. A nasty feeling. While we are trudging down the corridor to the Children's Ward, passing the kitchens and the lifts and the visitors' rooms, this creeping dread intensifies – until it becomes almost unbearable. I am feeling nauseous. Faint. Giddy. This sickly horror abates when we enter Alice's little chamber – to be replaced by a different emotion. A startling *déjà vu*. Looking at my niece – lying there in bed, intubated, spasticated, invigilated – I am reminded of an image. A disturbing image, a remembered photograph, a recollected picture of somebody with a – somebody with tubes in their face – a picture of a —

With a kiss for my sister, I make my excuses, and go.

# 17. Bananas

Women are stupid. Simple. Slow. Like dogs. I have always known this – yet it still surprises me. It still surprises me what swans, what horses, what mad animals they are. Particularly my girlfriend.

It is Saturday morning. We are at my home in Islington and we have been making non-orgasmic love for over an hour – and still my daffy girlfriend is so daft she hasn't realised that it is now her duty to pretend, to finesse, to do us both a favour and fake. Fake. F-A-K-E. For a fleeting second I wonder whether it would be worth turning homosexual: it must be so much easier, a quick strum and you're done. Guaranteed.

As I lick at my sweetheart's snatch I get another strange feeling. I am having the unexpected sensation that I am a nineteenth-century whaler, standing on the icy deck, staring out to sea. The Arctic storms are swelling, the bitter wind is howling, the salt water is sputtering from the brow of my leather sou'wester – and then it happens. Suddenly, without warning: the boat rocks, the waves heave, and from far above a sailor's cry goes out: Thar! She Blows!

My mistake. It was just a sneeze. Eva is just sneezing. Dutifully I recommence my efforts. Shifting Eva's thighs apart, I nuzzle the salt-lick of her genitals again. I am trying to be patient but I can feel the impatience rise inside me: like a bulimic's last dinner. Just a sneeze? Just a sneeze? Here I am being a carnal Stakhanovite – and she *sneezes?* Disengaging myself from Eva's matrix I wipe my mouth, and change my mind: moving up Eva's body I stretch to lock my elbows and penetrate her with my penis. As I do this I gaze away. Out of my bedroom window I can see the grey November skies, louring over the drizzly streets of Islington.

This depressing sight reminds me of Alice. Not good. Refocusing on my task, I start to do it longer, and slower, and better, pressing the shaft of my penis hard against her clitoris. This technique sometimes does the job – especially if, simultaneously, I kiss Eva's earlobes. Manfully I complete these manoeuvres: then, as a finishing flourish, I duck and bite the hard unripe peach of her shoulder. As soon as I have done this, Eva seems to get the message. Eva is making an attempt. She is rolling her hips and gurgling. She is pretending to come. At last. This is it . . . she's come. Good. Now I can have some breakfast.

Rolling off my girlfriend I reach out a cold arm and pull a cigarette from the bedside packet, ignite it and blow the blue smoke straight upwards.

Next to me I can sense Eva squirming. She doesn't know quite what to say; whether to admonish me for my obvious disinterest or enquire as to why I didn't want to climax or get weepy because she still loves me and it is all going flat. So instead she traces the bridge of my nose with her fingernail. Quite why she does this, I don't know. Perhaps she saw someone do it in a movie and thought it looked cool. I wish she'd stop it. It annoys me. Just completely annoys me. So much so I get a sudden urge to go downstairs and find a crowbar and use it to stove Eva's skull in.

Perhaps some of the gloss has gone off this relation-

147

ship. It could be. It can't be right that I want to murder the poor girl. I have to do it: say a sweet but sad *adieu*.

Duly resolved I turn over and look into the melancholy eyes of my nineteen-year-old Swiss/British girlfriend, and I say: 'Fancy a coffee?'

Later, after coffees and a belated breakfast of some lox and cream cheese bagels bought early this morning in Brick Lane, after a night on the razz, we drive down to Foyle's. A couple of days ago I promised Eva that I would help her in her quest to buy more books for her Art History Course. Thus we are now driving down to Foyle's. As we go along, as I shift a gear to get us round Russell Square, Eva squeezes my thigh. Two months ago I would have liked Eva doing this, I would have found it agreeably saucy. Now it pisses me off that she's interfering with my driving. But I don't say this: I am, despite my cruel cynicism, still rather fond of Eva. I don't want to hurt her. Well, not much. Even as I look across the car, as Eva winds down the window and fills her blonde hair with the breeze, as she coughs and yawns and flattens her long rosy fingers in front of her mouth, I am aware that my girlfriend's very presence fills me with gloom: she is a living reproach to my straitened emotional circumstances.

Turning into Great Russell Street I have a minor panic attack. Maybe I will never fall in love again. Maybe that was my lot. Maybe that was it. Just that.

Then again, if I *have* used the teabag of love for the one and only time, what's wrong with that, anyway? Why should I want to fall in love again? It's torrid and painful. As history has tutored me. And he that does not learn from history is condemned to repeat it. To repeat it.

Oh God, let me repeat it.

*

Crawling through Soho I seek out somewhere to park. As usual it is impossible: the place is chocka. Affably I suggest we try the little sidestreet that runs from Charing Cross to the Pillars of Hercules; Eva shrugs. Over the last ten minutes of our drive – probably because I'm being a bit more solicitous of her feelings – young Eva Speisser has chameleoned from her normal sad and slightly nervous demeanour, into her occasional, ultra-confident *alter ego*. The I-am-blonde-and-pretty-and-I-am-also-under-twenty-years-old persona. The same persona that has women staring at her in the street with pathological jealousy.

It never ceases to amaze me how women glare at each other publicly: if looks could kill, half the women in London would be in Holloway. It happens here and now as I park the car in Sutton Row: while Eva is unravelling her endless legs from the front seat of my sports car, an ageing and over-tanned harridan on the other side of the road slips Eva a glance that says, *girl, if I had a knife, I'd chop your tits off.*

Feeding the meter with pound coins I order Eva to meet me back here in an hour. Then, after watching her disappear into Foyle's, I turn from the predictable dys-functionality of the Centre Point fountains and head into Soho, down Sutton Row. Here I pause, before stepping into the Pillars for a bottle of Budvar: I have just recognised the building opposite. Rather, I have recognised it because it is unrecognisable. What used to be a nightclub called . . . Bananas . . . I think . . . is now a record shop. Weird. This is always happening to me in London. I am always only noticing buildings when they change role, or fascia, or name. I suppose it's like only hearing the clock when it stops. Or only realising you are in love when your girlfriend dumps you.

But anyway. Stepping inside the pub I clear my mind

and seat myself at the bar and nod to the bar girl, and when she has poured the bottle of Budvar into a glass I lift the hoppy freshness of the beer to my face. Inhaling its scent I am reminded of what happened on October the 17th, years ago.

It was a chilly autumn day. Simon was in College; I wasn't. Instead I was on a bus on Prince Albert Road, on my way to his flat. My intention was to go round and fuck our girlfriend: to have a quick knee-trembler against the freezer.

When I crossed the threshold these plans evaporated. I found Nathalie making some delicious-smelling, cardamom-spiked coffee, and I decided to set aside thoughts of sex and have a coffee instead. And a biscuit. And a bit of a chat. Such uncharacteristic behaviour was becoming increasingly common. Loathe as I was to admit it, even to myself, I had reached the stage with Nathalie where I just liked being with her. The sex was great; her company was even better.

Before we knew it we were sitting on the balcony, singing and joking and talking about music, until we got hungry: chivalrously I offered to nip down the road to Camden to buy a few bottles of beer and some picnicky food. It took ten minutes.

Observing Nathalie unpack the blue Tescos bags and pour us both a half pint of Budvar, I felt a need to ask.

'You are going to tell him, aren't you?'

Munching a slice of Bayonne ham, Nathalie shrugged.

I implored: 'You have to, Nats. We can't go on. The guilt's giving me migraines.'

'Mmmm . . . *oui* . . .'

She was making sandwiches, laying watercress on Normandy butter on bisected baguettes. Her movements were confident; somehow chic. It struck me, as

I watched her prepare lunch, how she did everything with a self-possessed grace: even when we were alone, when she was walking nude around the bedroom, she did it like she was on the catwalk, like her nudity was *haute couture*.

'I do not know, Guy. Put some music on?'

'What do you want?'

'Poulenc,' she said, decisively, wetlipped by the beer. 'The piano concerto, it is on the table.'

Slipping the CD into play, I returned.

'Does he guess, anything at all?'

'No.'

'Poor bloody bastard.'

'He's your *friend*.'

'He's your *lover*.'

Her eyes evaded mine. She was listening dreamily to the concerto: one of her favourites. I persisted.

'Are you still sleeping with him?'

'. . . I told you. No. He . . . doesn't . . .' She handed me a plate, with a sandwich. 'He doesn't try anything, OK?'

Biting into the baguette I shrugged, and spoke: 'I'm sorry, Nats. I just get jealous. I can't work it out. I mean – what did you see in him in the first place? He's a wonderful guy, and all that, but . . .'

'I saw exactly what you saw. He is intelligent. Kind. And good. And when I first came to London I was . . . lonely.'

'I see . . .' Placing my baguette back down, I wondered: through the kitchen windows I could see leaves being detached from the trees of Regent's Park Road. 'Christ, it's terrible, Nathalie. He's just a decent bloke, and I'm just a cunt. A total and utter cunt.'

Her hand reached out: 'You are,' she said. 'You are a bastard. You are an arrogant, aggressive, selfish, violent bastard.'

151

'Whereas you are vain. And spoilt. And frankly a bit of a lush.'

She shrugged: 'So then ... There is no hope for us ...?' Without waiting for an answer, she sighed, urgently: 'Fuck me, Guy. Now. Against the *réfrigéra-teurrrr* ...'

Twenty minutes later there was food everywhere.

'*C'est impossible,*' she said. 'Look at the mess!'

Picking up a rag and a brush, the two of us got to work: filling an entire binbag with empty bottles and foodwrappers. The bag I briskly jettisoned outside; relishing the clean apple smell of the cold autumn air as I dumped the thing in the dustbin.

Afterwards I went back, into the bedroom, where Nathalie was smoothing the duvet: although we hadn't been near it. Glancing at my watch, I said: 'I've got to go.'

Nathalie looked up, a French chambermaid in a Whitehall farce for a second.

'*Oui?*'

'It's four, he'll be back soon.'

'Nn.' Her posture was strange, slightly spastic. I saw something sparkly fall from her face. A teardrop.

Disturbed, I went over; instantly she twisted and sighed, and slumped into my arms. 'Oh, Guyyyy ...' she said. 'I love you.'

Her embrace was stifling; pushing her away, I said. 'I know, honey, I know. But I have to go.'

'Yes, yes ...' She said this as if she accepted things. She didn't. Instead of letting me go she sank to her knees and wrapped her arms round my thighs: like the mother of Achilles, pleading with Zeus. Embarrassed, I tried to lift her up, but she just shook her head and started fiddling with my fly buttons: reaching inside my jocks she extracted my semi-erect penis which she began to suck, soft and hard.

God, it was sweet. Too sweet. It felt so pleasant I shut my eyes and laid a hand on her bobbing head, like a bishop blessing a novitiate priest, and I let her go to it.

At which point Simon walked in.

He just walked in. No front door noise, no cough in the hall, no footsteps in the corridor. He just walked in. And saw. Saw his true love giving head to his friend.

At the click of the door Nathalie turned, the end of my cock bulging out her cheek like a gobstopper.

Blinking furiously, my first thought was: no way, it's not true, Simon isn't here, he doesn't exist, it's a dream.

When I opened my eyes, Simon was still there.

Taking me out of her mouth, Nathalie wiped her lips with the back of her hand, and croakily said: '*Simon . . .?*'

Now Eva and I are back in the car, driving North. We are going to Hampstead Heath for a walk. But first we must go via King's Cross Station so Eva can go to the photobooth and get her picture taken; she has to renew her Travelcard. Parking the car on York Way I sit and switch off the engine, and watch the pimps and whores chatting at the corner of Pentonville Road. There is, I recall, an old English folklorism which says it is good luck to pass a prostitute in the street: that makes the residents of King's Cross the luckiest people in the world. Dismissing this pleasing absurdity I lean across the gearbox and open the door for Eva to get out, then I lift and sniff my fingers, simultaneously observing the pretty bottom of my girlfriend as it disappears into the station. My fingers smell of sex, or smoked salmon, or both. I need a shower . . .

The minutes pass. I read a newspaper. It bores me. Glancing up my eyes are drawn across the street to a

153

tall, dark-haired, heartstoppingly beautiful girl marching round the corner from the Tube. The girl is carrying a big leather portfolio: she is obviously a model. Behind her comes another beauty, a long-legged teenager. Then two more: two lofty blondes. There are a lot of Photography Studios in this warehousey area of Pentonville, so I often spot the odd model. Today, more unusually, there's a dozen of them: parading up York Way, swaying past the carpet shop, sashaying right into Caledonia Street. They look great. They look like a train of Newmarket racehorses, with their superb buttocks and their fragile necks and their glorious, expensive thighs. They look beautiful, and stupid, and miraculous. Like swans, or gazelles, or Borzois.

# 18. Covent Garden

Today I wake up, yawn, scratch, cough – and despair. Last night I had another argument with Eva. For the life of me I can't remember what it was about. All I know is that it was nasty. Really nasty . . .

In an attempt not to think about this, I abandon my normal morning ritual: of slouching downstairs and glugging black coffee and snapping bad-temperedly at my flatmates; instead I lean over to the bookcase. My intention is to rid my mind of gloom by playing a Mozart tape: a selection of his Vespers. Unfortunately, I can't find the *joie de vivre*-ish cassette where it should be. What I locate instead are some old love letters I once sent to Nathalie.

Picking these out, I muse: for a while. I had forgotten I had these; I had forgotten how she, in a spasm of guilt, sent them back. Flicking through the pages, it surprises me how much they surprise me. I haven't read these letters in years but their highly strung lyricism still has the power to move: especially the beginning of the last letter. This page, the most crumpled of the lot, relates to the highpoint of our affair, when we were truly dizzy with love. When I am not comparing my Nathalie's breasts to *white Italian peaches*, I am calling her vulva *a billionaire's plaything* and her sexuality *a Spanish stallion's cabriolet* and her orgasmic tremors

155

*the very Alzheimer's of desire ——*

True sadness. Clutching these crumpled old letters and staring out of the window at the rainy, windy, 29-year-old world, I feel truly sad: I cannot believe that I was once twenty-two, that I was once in love, and that I once wrote love letters like this. The imagery might be slightly overwrought, the poeticism may be slightly received, but that still leaves the sincerity. Was this really me? Can it be? Was I once so truthful about my feelings, and were my feelings once so true?

Traipsing downstairs I draw some coffee, scan the *Times*, and snap bad-temperedly at my flatmates; then I grab my coat and step into the raw winter morning. Outside, the sky is the colour of stained concrete. This matches the dismal leaflessness of the trees. Meanwhile, by Beresford Pite's library a black girl is sullenly watching her muzzled dog take a crap in the gutter. This girl is wearing a huge, fake-fur-lined anorak: the hood is so big in comparison to the girl's head it makes her look microcephalic.

I have decided to buy some Christmas presents; I am going to walk into town. On the way it starts to rain. Quickening my pace I take the corner at King's Cross, turning right onto the Euston Road. Pacing down this dilapidated avenue, dodging the puddles and the derelicts, I try not to think about my relationship with Eva; I can't help it. Am I even having a relationship with Eva? What is a relationship, anyway? And if I am having a relationship, what's the point? One of the reasons I can't get on top of this girl, of Eva, is because of her abiding melancholia: her sadness perplexes me. Because it is paradoxical and bizarre. Sad girls are commonly great between the sheets: their lack of self esteem seems to make them uninhibited. *Do anything to me*. Whereas Eva is the opposite. Carnally speaking,

Eva seems irredeemable; unhelpable; I have done my best but she is still scared, still scared of being out of her depth, still pathetically frightened of swimming out too far.

I should have guessed Eva was terminally unsexual the first time I saw her take off her knickers. Girls have two ways of dropping their knickers: some do it with an almost imperceptible wiggle, a Girl-from-Ipanema hipswing that they are barely aware of. It is as if their hips are doing it automatically, the way a heart beats. Other girls take their knickers off like they are about to go for a dump: even when they know you are lying in bed, smoking, and watching. For this is the dichotomy of woman: some have sex in the bone, carnal RNA; others think of sex as defecation, despite their best intentions.

And yet Eva is also hauntingly beautiful.

Shivering these thoughts from my head, I nip across the road and nearly knock over a policeman. I am at the top of Kingsway, at the edge of a bustling Covent Garden. It is time to start. I am determined to get my Christmas shopping done in one go: to spend the afternoon buying all the gifts I need – for my mum and my dad and my sister and Simon and Eva and my step-parents – and for . . . and for Alice? Now it hits me, as I check out a saucy punkette loitering by Holborn Tube. What am I going to do about Alice? What on earth am I going to buy Alice? What is the protocol? Should I buy her something that says to her: I know you are going to get better and be clever, that is why I have bought you a book? Or should I buy her something she will appreciate in her present state? Like a rubber blanket, or a year's supply of Kleenex?

Dejected, I pause. I cannot buy my niece a blanket; but nor can I buy her a picturebook. Because. When I unribbon the wrapping and offer the gift, what am I going to do then? Carefully place the opened picturebook across the child's unmoving, comatose face? Or crack the spine and tuck it under her chin, and watch her dribble all over the text?

Effortfully I immerse myself in the hubbub of the city: in the people and shoppers and taxis and drizzle and Salvation Army choirs. So successful am I in my self-distraction, as I pass the Sugar Loaf Pub I am nearly knocked over by three drunken, stilettoey secretaries, who have just rolled out of the tavern wearing tinsel on their heads, singing a pop song.

Dusting myself off, and stepping around this inebriate sorority, I progress: past an ad agency and a curry house and a ticket booth, all of which are brimming with aggression and good cheer. Everybody is soused, it seems. From Jenevers on Drury Lane I hear a shout of 'Suck his dick you old boiler!' This ribald cry obliges me to look through the windows of the Jenevers bar, into the tumult of another office party. The cause of the shouts is a Strippagram: some topless middle-aged woman is removing some poor guy's baggy white underwear in the middle of the pub. The victim is so out of it his eyes are almost shut and his friends are having to support him – nevertheless I notice he has still managed a semi-erection. Strangely disturbing. Just before I move away the semi-naked stripper takes an aerosol out of her bag and starts squirting the man's bollocks with shaving foam. *I have presents to buy.*

But where? And how? And what? I want to start at the end of Neal Street, beyond the First National Bank of Chicago, but I can't. I have been stalled. My attention has been diverted to an arse that belongs to a girl in red velvet flares, who is bending to sweep up the curls and clippings in a hairdresser's. This arse is amazing: it is cute: it says *spank me.* As does the girl's face: when

158

she turns and straightens I see she is hideously ugly. Ashamed I drop my gaze and pretend to be interested in the items displayed in the window: in the metal tubs of Dax and NuNile and Brylcreem that sit on the shelf next to the C'est La Force Shampoo, and the KNY Silker Gel, and the bottles of Polybaume Untangling Balm. There is a lyricism in this. Enough to distract. As I move on I break into a smile. A steamy, rainy, Decembery dusk is falling and the whole of Covent Garden – of Neal's Yard and Long Acre and Shorts Gardens and Earlham Street and Slingsby Place – is lighting up in a dazzle of neon and halogen, of streetlamps and fairy-lights. While I wander down Neal Street and look in the tinselly shop windows and listen to the novelty radio songs and revel in the shouts and the whistles and the jokes and the carols, and the got-the-time? catcalls of the hippie chicks heading for Wagamama, I exult. In the profligacy of life, the Christmasiness of it: I adore it all: the Jacet clocks and nankeen hats and Voodoo chokers and Classix Jackets; the silver handcuffs and La Rocka bombers and Spinbak Boomerangs and Orange Caterpillars; the singing bowls and zodiacal buttons and Hard Yakka Footwear and Yard-o-Led pencils and Lylokai cypresses and Marakissi biscuits . . .

Even now, as I squeeze myself through a mob of identically-dressed Japanese girls, only to find my way blocked by a van out of which two men are unloading huge Stilton cheeses – I am moved. By the sentiment-ality of the image. The men look like roadies unload-ing amps at the end of a Heavy Metal festival: and their *sod you, I'm working* attitude seduces. While I wait here in the drizzle, as these great cheeses are stacked in rindy, leprous, yellowy-grey columns, the smell and the dark and the lights and the steam overwhelm.

Onwards. Past Shelton Street and Cucumber Alley, and the Thomas Neale Shopping Mall, I come to Terry

Farrel's Comyn Ching triangle and the Seven Dials monument. Here I nip into an upmarket toy shop and spend £300 on an exquisite stuffed toy, a large and beautiful leopard. For Alice. My hope is that the lavish expense of the gift will disguise its helpless unsuitability.

After leaving instructions for delivery, I exit the shop and opt for a breather. Leaning against the monument I smoke a flippant Turkish and gaze at the barrow of flowers at the end of Earlham Street. This barrow is lit-up by the dazzling new Westminster Council street-lamps; a lurid klieglighting that makes the flowers glow, makes them fluoresce, makes them throb with over-exposed colour. They are lovely: these African violets, these snowdrops, these tall Bells of Ireland, these pine wreaths and tulips and Casablanca lilies, these blood-red Jaguar roses . . .

Turning down Monmouth Street, I feel big cold water-drops sliding down my face. This is most peculiar. This is intensely weird. I know that men should only weep in a war, just as women should only swear in bed, but I cannot help it. It is true. For the first time in ages, for the first time in *years*, I am crying.

# 19. Simpson's-in-the-City

'Do you boys want to go up? I think we can squeeze you into a corner —' The blue-aproned headwaitress of Simpsons-in-the-City is talking to three men in their early fifties, one of whom I recognise as the Vice Chairman of Unilever. The three industrialists do not appear to mind the woman's overt condescension; they even seem to warm to it. This is either because they like the idea of being one of the lads, or because her nannyish tone reminds them of childhood, or because they are so hungry they simply don't care. This last is the likeliest: we have been waiting in the chilly eighteenth-century courtyard of this ancient restaurant for what seems like hours. Worried my lunch partner might be getting restive, I advise: 'Don't worry. We'll get a seat pretty soon.'

Simon shrugs: 'I don't particularly mind.'

'No . . .'

'It's nice to get out of the office, anyway.'

Despite this upbeat remark, his face is downcast. Worryingly so. My intention in asking Simon to meet me here, for lunch, was to cheer him up – to somehow take his mind off Alice. But Simon is as morose as I can remember him at any time since the accident.

Doggedly, I try again. 'So . . . how's everything? I mean – at work?'

He shrugs: 'Oh, not bad . . .'

'Everything's OK – then?'

'Yes. OK.'

'Seen any good films?'

'No. I haven't.'

'Really. Uh. How about books?' My anxiety shows in my tone. 'Read any decent books?'

Taking another gulp from his pint, Simon wipes his mouth with the side of a wrist: 'I'm reading Dante.'

'Dante, that's interesting —'

'Backwards.'

'What do you mean?'

'I mean backwards. From the end to the front. I started with Paradiso, then I read Purgatorio, now I'm finishing Inferno.' Necking more beer, he glances at the sad December sun. While he does this, I check his attire: he is wearing a pale pink cardigan, a Regimental tie, a blue striped City shirt. As I finish my appraisal, Simon expands: 'Something struck me, actually . . . In the book. You know that final Canto – when Dante sees all the souls, entombed in ice? When he sees the condemned people staring up at him from the ice, with their mouths locked into screams?'

At last: we have a conversation. Gloomy, but a conversation. Enthusiastically I nod: 'Yes – yeah – I know that bit.'

'Well,' he says. 'When I read it, yesterday evening. You know what it reminded me of?'

'Uh, no.'

'It reminded me of Alice. Of the way her soul is entombed in her body, the way she is locked in the ice of her crippled body as she screams at a pitiless, Godless sky.'

The captains of industry are starting to shoot looks. Discomfited, I say: 'How is she? I saw her last month, but . . . you were there last week, right?'

162

'I was.' Simon stares at the ground, darkly: as if he has just spat blood onto the pavement. 'I was. How is she? Hnnn. Can she be anything?'

'Sorry?'

He flaps a hand: 'If the statement has any sense, she's all right.'

'What?'

'She's the same as ever. Her eyes are open, she moves her hand. A fraction. That's about the extent of it.'

'Right. Yes. But —' I am keen to counter Simon's pessimism, but it is difficult. What can I say? What do I know?

Nevertheless I must speak; if only to disperse the silence that threatens to last through lunch: 'Don't get me wrong, Si, but . . . I reckon you are . . . overdoing it a bit. I mean . . . It isn't *that* bad.'

'Yes, it is.'

I struggle: 'No . . . come on. It's not. Remember the doctors said you mustn't give up hope for at least six months. And then there's all the tests she can have – the whatsit, the second Cat scan. I mean . . . before then . . . you know nothing, really . . .'

Simon anchors me: 'What you are in fact saying is that you can't tell me what you truly think. That she is as good as dead. That's the case, correct?'

I want to argue: I am unable.

Simon continues: 'Have you noticed her hands? Did you notice her hands, when you went down?'

'Sorry?'

'The way the tips of her thumbs are protruding through her fingers? Did you see them?'

I shrug, dumbly.

He goes on: 'And what about her feet? Have you noticed the way they have become scissored, sort of crossed over?'

163

'I presumed it was some reaction to being in bed, or the physiotherapy . . .'

Simon shakes his head: 'I looked it up in a textbook. It's called adduction. What it indicates is that her mind has gone. The adduction of the hands and feet is a symptom of palsy.'

'Palsy?'

'Cerebral palsy.' He says the words with a disgusted moue. 'Her brain is very nearly shot. She'll keep on growing, of course, as long as we keep feeding her, but at best – at the very best – she will be severely palsied. Bilaterally haemaplegic. Or tetraplegic. Or whatever the word is. She's going to be . . . a blob. A human vegetable.'

'Don't,' I say. That's all. 'Don't. You shouldn't be so . . . like that. It's unfair. On Sarah.'

'Is it?'

His eyes are piercing, demanding the truth. In this they differ from his wife's, which always demand lies. Presently I am not sure which is the harder to cope with. While I am wrestling with the dilemma, Simon finishes his pint, and asks: 'Go on. Tell me. If you don't agree. Tell me what you really think. Do you really think she's going to get better?'

Now. This is it. What to do?

Brightly, I lie: 'Yes, I do.'

'Truly?'

'Yes.'

For all Simon's aggressive pessimism, my reply has fanned a small flame of hope. I can see it in his glancing eyes, his quivering lip. In which case all of his gloom and despair must be fake: the poor, sad, hopeful bastard.

'But . . .' Simon is saying, slurrily. He has sunk three pints already. 'But why? What grounds do you have for . . . for thinking she's going to get better?'

164

'Because she's a fighter. She's come this far.'

'And? What else?'

'Well. There's that evidence of brain stem activity. And the fact that she is so young. And the fact that she's seeing some really top neurosurgeons . . .' I look up: 'OK? So. I might not be as hopeful as Sarah, but I still —'

Snorting, he interrupts: 'You are not wrong there. No one could be as hopeful as Sarah. We're not in her league.'

'Her what?'

His cardigan looks too pink in the winter sun: 'You didn't know about all this evangelical business? She didn't tell you? Didn't she tell you that she'd found Jesus and it turns out he's a folk singer?' My friend is chuckling, tragically. 'It's a bloody nightmare. Every day when I come home the house is full of beardy priests promising that Alice will wake up tomorrow and say "I'm hungry, Mummy". I loathe it, Guy, I totally loathe and despise it . . .'

Before I can think of a reply, the Simpson's waitress interrupts, telling us there are seats free.

Obediently – and, for my part, relieved – we climb the stairs into the loud, clattery dining rooms. Herein we are seated at some high-backed chairs next to two boozed-up brokers I vaguely know from Citibank. As I take my place I order a brace of kümmels; if I have to sit through another hour of Simon's rhapsodic nega-tivism, I am at the very least going to do it drunk. Across from me, across the wooden table, Simon has started auditing the menu, incredulously: 'Chops, chops, and . . . chops. Is that all they do?'

'It's a chop house.'

'Sure.' He tuts, not unkindly. 'But what on earth is this? Stewed cheese. What on earth is stewed cheese?'

'A kind of rarebit,' I say. I had trusted the happily

165

bibulous ambience of Simpson's-in-the-City would infect Simon. It hasn't, yet. Quickly I aver: 'The chops come highly recommended.'

'Really,' he says, and at last there is a hint of a smile, as he lifts his glass of kümmel. 'Good God.' He smarts, slamming down the tumbler. 'What's that?'

'Kümmel' I say, 'It's a traditional City drink. Made of caraway seeds. Happy now?'

'Yes.'

'Good . . .' I grin. 'So drink, drink, and be drunk, you miserable git.' As soon as I've said this, I wince: this remark is the sort of thing I normally come out with, but these are not normal times. This is not a normal lunch. Is Simon robust enough to still appreciate my humour? A pause. Then his teeth twinkle, even if his eyes don't. 'Sweet,' he says. Ten minutes later we are diving into platefuls of thick, sear-grilled chops served with creamy mashed potatoes and stacks of lavishly buttered parsnips; I have drunk three pints of 6X and three huge kümmels; I am now happy, despite everything. In this spirit of corporeal contentment I opt for some small talk. I say, through a mouthful of mashed potato and beer: 'What are you doing for Christmas?'

And immediately I have said this, I regret saying it. Again.

'Christmas . . .' Simon muses. 'Christmas . . . I can't honestly say I'm looking forward to it.' His eyes appear misty. This could be the kümmel; I hope so. 'Presumably, you are coming down, to your father's?'

'Uh-huh.' I reply. 'Sarah told me . . . Alice will be there – that Alice will be . . . out of hospital. Just for the day, like?'

'That's right.' Simon nods, tentatively. 'Just for the day. There'll be a nurse of course . . .' The mist thickens. He drinks some more kümmel. The horrible silence looms over us again, like the shadow of Nosferatu.

'Tell me,' he says, 'you did this stuff. What does Philosophy have to say about The Problem of Evil?'

'You what?'

'*Evil.*' Simon repeats, napkinning his lips. 'The Problem Thereof. The Philosophical Approach.' He hiccups. 'What is it?'

'Oh, right,' I say. 'Sure. 'Course. The Problem of Evil. Mmm . . .' I am belching. He doesn't respond. I repeat: 'I must admit I don't remember that . . . quite so well.'

Placing his cutlery at five o'clock, Simon stares at me over his empty plate.

'Come on. You must have learned something when you were beavering away.'

'You mean when I wasn't beavering away —'

He smiles. 'Precisely. When you weren't sleeping around, or doing drugs, you did do a bit of Philosophy. Didn't you? So . . . wasn't it . . . Hume? Didn't Hume say something about Evil?'

'Yes . . .' I murmur. 'He did . . . I think . . .' Simon nods, impatiently. I go on: 'As far as I can remember, if you're talking about human evils, that all . . . depends on faith . . . Because if you believe in the Bible they can be explained as part of our Fallen —'

Holding up a hand, like a traffic policeman, Simon stops me: 'I'm referring more to horrendous natural evils. Earthquakes and . . . diseases . . . and so forth.'

Another pause. I suddenly feel cold: as if I have been sunbathing and a cloud has passed across. 'OK . . .' I demur. 'Well . . . With all that . . . bad stuff . . . The problem is much more difficult. So . . .' Before Simon can reply, I answer myself: 'So, some philosophers have posited a God that has limited powers. That can only intervene in the laws of physics in certain ways. In which case maybe God hasn't got much choice . . .'

'Yes.' Across the now cleared table, Simon is draining his kümmel: 'I understand the metaphysics. What

167

I've forgotten are the religio-philosophical justifications for horrendous evils. Were there any, in classical philosophy? Or is this too tricky?'

This is an affront. Mildly insulted, I snap: 'If you really want to know – Hume reckoned that Evil as a problem was probably insoluble, in religious terms. He thought leprosy and plague and run-over children – and . . .' Nervously, I hurry on. 'He thought these things were simply irreconcilable with a benign, omnipotent Deity. So he got rid of the least likely hypothesis, he got rid of God.' Simon nods; I continue: 'Others, however, felt able to justify natural Evil, all the same. They thought that Evil is a kind of moral spur, that if there was no famine, there would be no agriculture. Without sorrow, there'd be no pity. And without war, no Wilfred Owen. Right?'

My explanation is, I feel, not bad for a semi-drunken Foreign Exchange dealer, eight years out of college – but it does not seem to satisfy my friend. When I say – 'Of course that still leaves the problem of facing Evil. Of seeing it. Of coming to terms with its in-your-face unspeakability' – he disdainfully replies: 'You mean the instantiation.'

'The what?'

'It's called instantiation.' A sigh. 'It's what finally dissuaded Dostoevsky from believing: the horror of Evil, the awful horror of seeing an actual single instance . . . of it . . .' As Simon speaks his face starts to cloud, and he grabs the next kümmel out of the waitress' hand. He doesn't even let it reach the table. He is obviously thinking of Alice; he is obviously determined to get drunk. Utilising the silence, I look out of the window. The sun has gone in; a light drizzle seems to be falling. Which is only right: it is winter, after all; and without winter, there would be no snowball fights.

Like a chemist dissolving powders in a beaker, Simon

is meditatively swirling the liquer in his tumbler. After the fifth swirl, he drains the drink, grimaces, and looks at me: 'Actually, I believe you have a point. It's a bit Jesuitical, but it's a point . . .'

My friend is complimenting my arguments: a rarity. Smiling anyway, I start writing a cheque for the bill, not giving Simon a chance to prolong the discussion. Then I slip myself into my cashmere coat and skip down the stairs, out of the door, into the rain-spotted courtyard. Moments later he joins me. 'Bloody evil weather,' Simon says, but as he says this, he chuckles. Evidently he is not quite the same morose bastard of before. This is because he is very drunk. And I fear for him when he sobers; I truly fear for him.

'Got to get back to the office,' I say.

'Walk with you?'

'Course . . .'

Past the Jamaica Tavern and beyond the George & Vulture, and out into the drizzle and bustle of Bishopsgate, we stride as one. I am nearly cheerful, again. I am feeling better because, as we near the door of St Michael's Cornhill, I can hear a choir, rehearsing a Bach chorale. The sound is quite beautiful. It chimes with the taxi-signs glowing in the lunchtime twilight, it chimes with the Corinthian rhythm of Soane's Bank of England peristyle, it chimes with the rain that is raining on all the couriers and the ship-brokers and the market-makers, and all the German bankers in their brand new Barbours. It is good and it is great: I have to resist an urge to play in the puddles. I am truly up. Genuinely happy. And I know this feeling. I have experienced it before: sometimes when I am drunk and in the City of London I get the strange sensation that it is a kind of paradise. When I am in this euphoric mood I see the City of London as it could be, as it nearly is: a perfect city; a grand, historic place populated solely by suavely affluent young people doing glamorous, overpaid jobs in the midst of beautiful modern architecture.

The difference with today's pre-lapsarian rhapsody is that I have just had lunch with Simon, with the serpent in the grass.

Heading towards the courts of Lothbury and the new barrel vaulted Barclays HQ, we pass a gaggle of sexy, Essex-ish office girls standing beneath their portico, smoking Silk Cuts. Once we have cleared this landmark we cross Threadneedle Street, duck under the arch by Throgmortons, and make our way into the elegant ovoid of Finsbury Circus. Here the rain abates, and we pause. Standing in the middle of the Circus Simon and I have an architectural debate: or what was intended to be an architectural debate. The problem is that when I start by saying how I like Lutyens' Britannic House, Simon just agrees; and when I provocatively praise the self-evidently inferior post-modern structures on Lutyens' left, Simon – the arch modernist – just nods. Like he doesn't care. Like he doesn't care about anything.

Shaking hands, we disperse.

# 20. The Docklands Light Railway

After Simon had shut the door and walked out of the flat, I sat down and weighed my head in my hands. Across the room Nathalie knelt on the floor, sobbing. We didn't dare look at one another, for fear that we might confirm in each other's gaze our own, keening guilt. We didn't care to share a glance: not when I got up, not when I walked past, not when I downstaired out the door into a twilit Regent's Park Road.

Striding away from the flat I began to formulate my plan of action. This was – to get fucked. Specifically, I was going to get totalled on dope, or crack, or LSD, at Josh Diamond's new squat. With this in mind I started South, crossing Parkway at the blue-glass Design House; I was en route to Albany Street. I knew that the previous month Josh had moved from our flat in Montagu Square to a squat, somewhere here, at the bottom of Albany. I also knew there was more than a chance there would be enough drugs, wherever Josh was, to stop me thinking about Simon, to prevent me thinking about Nathalie, to stop me re-seeing the way Simon had looked, as he stood in the doorway ... Wrapping my coat against the evening chill, I made for the end of Albany Street, past the Queen's Head & Artichoke pub. It dawned on me, as I did so, that I was slightly lost. On my left was the only church in London

171

with eight dildos on top, otherwise known as John
Soane's Holy Trinity Church; directly in front of me was
the best wind tunnel in Western Europe, otherwise
known as the forecourt to Thames TV. But where was
Colosseum Terrace?

There.

Traipsing back towards the right place, towards the
run-down and grimy Terrace, I felt the slipstream of the
passing buses tug at my overcoat as I reached for the
bell button.

Moments passed. I pressed again. Finally a dishev-
elled Josh came to the door; yawning: 'What's up
Guido?'

'Nothing much.' I paused, and said: 'Uh . . . Josh . . .
You haven't got any . . . drugs, have you?'

'Maybe . . . How hard, man?'

I shrugged, sheepishly: 'Rocks?'

Beckoning me to follow, Josh ambled away down a
corridor, weaving past a pushbike and a surf board. At
first glance, the entire squat appeared to be as cold as
it was dirty and squalid: not exactly an improvement on
Monty; but so what? It had base so it was heaven.
Stepping inside Josh's particular sector of the hovel, at
the rear of the ungentrified Georgian house, I sat down
and cleared my throat and did freebased cocaine for
the very first time. Sitting on the end of an unmade bed
I took a knife-tip of white powder, tipped it onto a
sheet of foil, torched it with a lighter-flame and smoked
it; afterwards flopping back onto the crispy duvet, to
estimate my reaction.

My next thought was: I wanted Simon to kill himself;
to top himself; to save me from my guilty misery. The
only thing that seemed logical, as I lay there and stared
with exultant aggression at the nicotine-stained ceiling,
was the obvious fact that if Simon did the decent thing
and killed himself I wouldn't have to face the prospect

of facing him. And apologising. Nor would I have to suffer him try – and fail – to beat me up.

Simon didn't try to beat me up. He couldn't have done so, if he had wished: the following week I lodged in Josh's squat. For seven days I hibernated there – drinking and smoking and listening to dance music – until my conscience had been put to the sword.

Then I decided it was time to eat: getting myself in gear, I sloped off down the road to the supermarket on Great Portland Street, where I fussed over the cheeses and the fruits and the health-conscious yoghurts, the green beans and broccoli and spinach and lettuce, before returning to the squat with three samosas and a Galaxy bar.

'Hey —!' said Josh, as I opened the door, ushering a whirl of autumn leaves and litter into the hallway.

'Hey what?'

My friend puckered his brow, and looked at me, blankly.

'Can't remember,' he admitted, simultaneously bending down to take a huge inhalation of smoke from a milk-bottle-cum-coke-pipe. Silence followed; smoke came out of Josh's ears; he sighed and closed his eyes, and smiled like Saint Theresa. Then he looked at me again: 'Oh, yeah . . . I remember. You had a call from Nathalie. She wants you to ring back . . . asap.' I shrugged. Josh eyed me, hazily: 'She sounded pretty hatstand, man . . . You aren't knocking her off, are you?'

'Nooohh,' I said, swiftly changing the subject: 'Fancy a samosa?'

'What kind?'

'Meat.'

'No veg in it then?'

'I would say it's pretty likely this samosa has no nutritional value whatsoever.'

173

Josh grinned: 'Sounds wicked. Bung it over.'

Two days later, after a series of furtive and emotionally incontinent phone calls, I found myself standing in the plush new London City Airport in the Docklands, looking for Nathalie. Dressed in a selection of Josh's colourful rave gear and a tatty baseball cap, I looked a little out of place amongst the double-breasted business types bustling around. This conspicuousness did not go unnoticed. Once Nathalie had spotted me, from her position in the check-in queue, she tutted.

'You look good.' She was fingering the hooded, cider-stained sweatshirt. 'Dior? Lacroix?'

'OK,' I sniffed. 'I was in a . . . hurry. How is he, anyway?'

She made a sad face: 'Tsch . . .'

'What?'

'I think,' she said, 'you do not have to ask that?'

I affirmed: 'No. But he is OK, yeah?'

'*Non.*' She tilted her head. 'He is . . . very sad. Very very sad . . .' The queue in front of Nathalie was growing shorter. Kicking her suitcase forward, Nathalie exhaled, emotionally: 'He says he never wants to see you again.'

'Never?'

'Ever. But he also . . . he says he will try and forget what . . . happened. If you do not see him for a few years.'

'That's OK,' I bridled, unjustifiably. 'That's fine. I'm not exactly keen to take tea with him.'

'Yes, yes . . .' She averted her gaze. '*Naturellement* . . .'

From this proximity I could see Nat's eyes were wet: visibly teary. I also noticed that her red lips were glistening, and for a self-centred second I speculated on the chances of some sex. Then it occurred to me. Looking down at Nathalie's luggage an unhappy notion

174

thickened my throat.

'Why did you invite me here?'

'Because I am going away. And I needed to speak with you.'

'Sure. But . . . You must be . . . going away for a long time, right? I mean, all this luggage?'

She smiled: 'I am going away for a very long time.'

'How long?'

'. . . I am not coming back.'

This silenced me. And her: she went to explain something, but before she could do so, a tear escaped and rolled down her cheek, to the corner of her lip-sticky mouth.

'Oh, Guy —' she said. 'Guy —' And as I reached out to thumb the rosy trickle from her chin, she opened her arms and embraced me.

'I did not want to tell you because I thought . . . I hoped . . . you would try and persuade me not to go. But I have to go. I have to . . .'

Unromantically, our embrace was interrupted by a terse little cough from the woman at the check-in. It was Nathalie's turn. Helping Nats load her cases onto the conveyor belt, I struggled to think of something to say. But I couldn't, I couldn't think of anything: I was tongue-tied by grief. A flash flood of emotions was rising inside me, threatening to carry me away.

'Nathalie,' I tried, 'Nathalie —'

'*Viens.*'

Swallowing hard, I followed Nathalie out of the warm Departure Lounge, on to the cold, windy, autumnally sunlit runway. A propeller plane was coughing into life. Next to it a score of businessmen were queuing to ascend the gangway.

Finally I spoke, shouting over the noise of the propellers: 'It's a bit like *Casablanca*, isn't it? The last scene?'

'Maybe.' She said, fingering a strand of dark hair from her mouth. 'But maybe you are thinking of Woody Allen.'

'Yessssss . . .'

Behind Nathalie I could see the shimmering, wind-whipped waters of East India Dock, and the toy town monorail of the new Docklands Light Railway; beyond that I could see the fray-ended stump of the unfinished Canary Wharf Tower. It seemed apposite: the unfinished nature of the Docklands townscape matched my crushed and unresolved feelings. I knew now that I was totally in love with Nathalie Saure – that I was totally, utterly, inexpressibly in love with someone else – and that someone else was leaving.

It was ironic. I had an ironic desire to smash the air steward in the face as he came up and tapped Nathalie on the shoulder.

'We are about to take off, Miss.'

'Yes.' Nathalie nodded, then swivelled to peck me on the cheek. '*Adieu.*'

Before I knew it she was picking up her bag and walking to the plane. Rooted, I watched her climb the metal stairs: standing there I observed her chic shoes and her nice little mini skirt, and the way her black hair was blowing this way and that in the chill Docklands wind. Then, as the doors were brought shut and the plane taxied away, I felt my head froth with questions.

So that was it? That was the big number of my life, the showstopper? That was the best song in the show? That was the tune that I'll be whistling at the end, when I walk out of the theatre?

Encore, encore, encore.

# 21. Goldhawk Road

I am walking from Liverpool Road to Upper Street. It is hot. The pavements are dusty and empty. Crossing one traffic-free junction I take a left and a right, strolling past a rusty old Bentley with green leather seats. Now I find myself in a pretty little square that I don't recognise. Backhanding the sweat I survey the houses. They appear to be Georgian: very early Georgian, almost Queen Anne. I have no idea what square this is – Gibson? Nelson? Something else?

Finding the corner I duck through an alley; squeezing past a young woman with a pram. The next square, just beyond, is even older: the houses are made of stone, and wood: a kind of grey weatherboarding. Again I fail to recognise the place; nor do I recognise the architectural style. I try to picture my route on the A to Z, but it doesn't help. Somehow I have overshot Upper Street and crossed into Clerkenwell, or Hoxton, or another district I don't know too well. Agitated, I swivel, and retrace. But the faster I walk the more unsettling and surreal things become. I am pacing now, jogging down roads and through sidestreets, and every new turning brings me into a stranger square than the last: a row of Tudor houses, a section of oak paling and brick, tiny little emerald green gardens full of wild roses. Running round the back of a building I come to

177

a yard littered with oyster shells and wine bottles; in a panic I press on through a hedge and over a rise and find myself in a wide green meadow.

It is deathly quiet. The sun is still hot and high. Sitting down on a mossy tump I rub air into my face and try to calm myself. In the distance, on the crest of a hill, I can see a team of brown deer, quietly grazing. Watching these deer a feeling of vast sadness overtakes me; a sadness so immense and unarguable when I wake up my eyes are pools of tears.

That dream was six hours ago; I am still disturbed by its oddness. When I close my eyes I can still taste it. It would be easier if this bizarre dream had not been preceded by nightmares, but it was. I have been having nightmares for days now: dreams of babies with no bodies, of babies with liverspotted hands, of dogs with babies' heads. It's as if there has been some Chernobyl in my unconscious. All I can give birth to, dreamwise, is deformity. Eyeless embryos. Mutilated corpses. They make me feel achey and nauseous.

The dreams make me feel hungover, even when I haven't been drinking. This is ironic: this morning must be the first Christmas Day since I was a teenager when I haven't woken up with a throbber of a headache. Nor was it a conscious choice to stay sober. I am only without a hangover because last night my sister insisted the family join her in Winchester Cathedral for Midnight Mass.

Happily, despite my complaints and apprehensions, Midnight Mass wasn't so bad. Carols are the nicest kind of hymns and my irreligious heart is yet susceptible to the Disney-esque imagery of the Nativity. The bad side of religion is exemplified by the situation in which I find myself *now*: standing in a very different church to Winchester Cathedral – a chilly, ugly, big, echoey

178

Victorian church on the outskirts of the city.

I am here because, over breakfast this morning, I was volunteered by my father to drive my sister to her third religious service in twenty-four hours. Presumably, my enforced altruism was meant to reward me with a puff of spiritual pride. Instead I feel bored and embarrassed. Pious devotion is discomfiting gener- ally – this happy-clappy stuff is the worst. As far as I can see, the people in this Evangelical warehouse are not just worshipping God, they are getting fresh with Him. Showing God their tits. Some are even falling to the ground and moaning – like Jesus has just located their G-Spots . . .

Christ, Christ, Christ; I have to ask myself: why can't they do this at home? Why do they feel the need to do it in a crowd, in a public building? Does it operate on the same principle as surburban orgies, or soccer hooli- gans, or those otherwise sensible London Irish who end up singing Republican songs in Kilburn pubs – that en masse their rationality and probity and inhibition disappear?

Nevertheless.

As I sit here in my sister's adopted church three things strike me. The first is that, actually, these happy- clappyites are not quite as ugly as some congregations I have seen: they are not so heartstoppingly bumfaced as the average busload of Anglicans, for instance. There are even a few acceptable young women, one of whom – a high-breasted brunette – keeps turning round and giving me the eye.

The second item is that their Evangelical singing is, surprisingly, rather fine. For all the swaying and salut- ing and extra-liturgical arsing about, the singing poss- esses a dash, an undeniable brio. There is even a descant, made more beautiful by the fact that it comes not from the choir but from an ordinary worshipper

179

somewhere in the middle of the congregation. The descant is raw, but pure; it is the sound of young Mozart; it is the untutored soprano of the human soul; it belongs to the girl with the tits, three rows in front.

The third point, as I listen to this lovely girl using her lovely voice, is that If It Helps My Sister, What's So Terribly Wrong With It? Do we object to medicine because the drug company's methodology was suspect? Do we ever demand to see relevant back issues of *The Lancet*, before grudgingly accepting our prescription? We do not. We take the pill on trust. Its effectiveness is often and simply because we believe in it, just as we do with Religion. There is therefore no difference between the everyday placebos of medicine, and the cornflour and saccharin of Christian Faith. I can have no logical objections.

But. But but but . . . As we leave the church on a silent high, I am immediately re-depressed: it is winter. The rain has stopped, the anticyclones haven't. Oppressively aware that even as I pull open my car door, banks of black cloud are ganging up somewhere over Salisbury Plain. I seat myself in the Spyder alongside my sister, and accelerate away. The ensuing drive doesn't alleviate my gloom. While driving the silent car, motoring us through the Georgian centre of Winchester out into the rainy, gusty farmland on the other side, I begin to feel paradoxical: I want this melancholy car journey to end; but I also want it to go on for ever. Because if it goes on for ever I won't ever have to go home to Blue Cedars: to that place where everybody is sitting around the Christmas lunch table trying not to think about, or wonder over, or worry about, or look at – little Alice.

Remarkably, Christmas lunch is worse than anticipated. As soon as we have sat down to the brown bread and smoked salmon, Simon and Sarah start up. This is the worst argument yet.

He says: 'Pass the pepper, Sarah —'

And she says: 'Here —'

But as she hands it over she spills her glass of wine. Instinctively Simon reacts, using his paper hat to mop up the winestain. Watching him, his wife advises: 'Don't use that, silly – use the napkin —'

'If I use the napkin then I won't have one, will I?'

'But that's what napkins are for. Not paper-hats.'

I know what's coming.

'Good God,' says Simon. 'Thank you so much. Perhaps if you weren't so bloody clumsy —'

'Me? Clumsy? For God's sake Simon you haven't been able to sit down without spilling something all morning —'

'Rubbish!'

'It's true. Every place we go you seem to end up *breaking* things.'

This last remark had a nasty undertone. At the other end of the table I wonder about intervening, suggesting that we pull some crackers. But I presently realise that there's no point. This is just the way things are, and always will be: from here on in, *every* phrase will have a nasty undertone.

So what are we to do? Exchanging glances with my father and my uncle, I shrug, implying – let them, maybe it's for the best.

It isn't. Simon is retorting: 'Shut up, Sarah. If you hadn't been at church for the ninetieth time this Christmas lunch wouldn't have been late.'

'Ohh – and I suppose you were helping out, were you?'

'Yes.'

'You mean you weren't sleeping?'

'What does that mean?'

My sister half-stands: 'You know what it means. You know damn well what it means —'

'That I shouldn't have been asleep when Alice fell in the pool? And what about you? You're her mother. What were you doing? Making lasagne? *Watching the telly?* Why weren't you bloody looking after her!'

They exchange glances. Then, with a stifled cry, my sister pushes back her chair and flings her paper hat onto the floor and runs from the dining room, leaving behind her an unfinished lunch and an unpulled cracker – and a room completely quiet except for the tiny suck-suck-suck sound of Alice breathing, laboriously, through her tracheotomy tube.

My niece is propped up in her specially-adapted version of a highchair, at the end of the dining table. Beyond her, by the windows, sits Sally, the NHS nurse, who at this moment is diligently reading a shiny-covered paperback and trying to pretend she hasn't noticed our grotesque familial spat. The nurse's presence has made everybody self-conscious all Christmas. It is as if we are examinees being invigilated; as if we are prison-visitors, shrinking from the eye of a warden. Sally's presence hasn't even saved Alice from suffering: in a vain attempt to include her daughter in festive family life, my sister has stuck a Christmas paper hat on Alice's head. A Christmas paper hat! The pathos of this is unbearable. It makes Alice look as if she were the object of an ill-judged joke, like a corpse adorned with a stetson by Rag Week undergraduates . . .

Conversation slowly resumes – Simon has done his duty and apologetically pursued his wife out the door, and I turn back to my lunch; thence to my niece. This is the first opportunity I have had to get a good look at Alice, outside hospital, and I find it hard. I find it hard to look at her; once I am looking at her, I find it impossible to stop. Her strange zombieness simultaneously repels and transfixes. Sipping my wine I recall what Doctor Mortimer told me – how he said Alice might not ever wake up, in the traditional sense. I can see what he meant, now. Alice has definitely emerged from her coma, she is definitely conscious in some ways – but she is utterly, utterly different. Just utterly changed, and degraded.

While everyone else indulges in a desultory conversation about the future of the Royal family, I gulp my drink and confront the still from a horror film that is my niece. I see that beneath the brim of the festive paper hat Alice's sad blue eyes are pitched to the left, staring sidelong at the dining table; those eyes are alive, but they are also growing less blue; they are fading, dimming. Dropping my gaze, ashamed of my curiosity, I sneak a look at Alice's hands, at her little thumbs. I can see that these are stuck between her third and fourth fingers. Likewise her chubby legs – they are twisted and crossed, they are adducted, just as Simon said.

Indeed, as I munch on a homemade mince pie, I gaze at my niece and I realise with a sickening lurch that these deformities are not the end of it. The poor child is still growing. Her nails need cutting, her hair needs trimming, she is getting fatter. My niece, who was once so pretty, is actually growing obese. Presumably this is a result of the crippled child's vast intake of drugs; whatever the cause, it is detestable. Bleakly, I wonder: How much more must she bear? How much longer must we mutilate her body with Diazepam and paper hats?

My drunken depression is interrupted. A noise from the other room tells me that everybody has gone through to watch TV, apart from Sally and me. We are alone.

Getting up, I lean and palm my niece's cheek, and kiss her damp little forehead. Then I step back, and reflect; next to Alice's highchair stands an emerald green bottle of linctus. Her Diazepam cordial. Picking up the sticky bottle I examine the label. The nurse, who has been watching me, pipes up: 'It's to relax her, and to help her sleep. And it helps with any general pains.'

Nodding, slightly irritatedly, like a shopper interrupted by an over zealous assistant, I replace the bottle; then look at Sally.

'Is it strong?' I say.

She chuckles: 'Ooh yes. Very. Half a bottle of that and you'd be out for a week.'

'Really?'

'Definitely.' The nurse looks almost proud. 'It's really effective.'

Picking up the bottle she unscrews the metal top. 'You know, now you mention it, I think she's due a spoonful . . .'

Not wishing to witness the feed, I retreat to the other side of the room to finish my wine. Perhaps this drink will have the same effect: to relax, and help me sleep, and take away the general pains . . .

Later, driving back to town, I feel the anxiety and tension subside: I have done my bit: I have made my excuses: I have fled. It feels agreeably selfish and pleasantly lonesome. The motorways are empty and wet. I can see grey veils of rain, sweeping across the sliproads. Leaning over the gearbox I rifle through my glove compartment, until I find an old tape, a selection of Nathalie's favourite songs. Duruflé, Debussy, Richard Strauss. The nostalgic sadness of this music is just right: it chimes with the melancholy sound of the windscreen wipers, as they rinse, and return, as they rinse, and reply – as they smear splodges of rain water, and moonlight, and red brakelights, across the laminated glass.

Things are quiet; I am approaching London. Veering off the motorway, into Chiswick, I pull my cigarette lighter from the dashboard and ignite a Turkish Filter. Soon its pungent odour fills the car; I open the window a fraction. When I halt at a traffic light I am able to watch the smoke crawl up the pane, and whip, at the last, out the gap.

All is still.

London is dead; I am patrolling empty streets, festive fairylights kick and swing in the wind.

At the corner of Ravenscourt Park, by a telephone box, I spy a girl, a solitary blonde. In the Christmas Day emptiness my sudden headlights startle her; she turns and visors her blinded eyes. From my Spyder's dark interior I watch her, quietly, like a rapist *manqué*. Even at this distance I can see that her face is pretty and that her hair is fancily done. I admire this hair: the way it loops and bounces and corkscrews down the side of her face, like piano trills.

On a whim I take the car up Holland Park Avenue. Normally I would swing left and hit the Westway; tonight the streets are completely nameless, so I might as well go through town. Towards Oxford Street I brake at the Baker Street junction and adjust my seatbelt and turn up the stereo. I am thinking of nothing.

# 22. Finsbury

'What's she like?'

'Beautiful.'

'Really?' I ask. 'Really pretty?'

'Textbook,' he says. 'Total babe. Not jealous, are you?'

I am jealous, and I am also ill: in bed, at home. Evidently, Andy is at work: I can hear the bustle of the dealing rooms behind his telephonic voice. Despite the pressures he is kindly taking time off to tell me about his latest success: 'It was a real seeing-to. *She* didn't walk away with a tear in her eye.'

'Heartless bastard —'

'I know, I know —'

Andy laughs, and shouts something to someone else, away from the receiver. Then he returns: 'So what about you. What's up?'

'Oh, flu . . . Or something. It's a bummer . . .'

'Sure it's not the clap? Shagged any Aussie birds?'

'Nope,' I say, coughing.

Andy makes a whistling sound: 'You do sound pretty duff. You should take a day off. Stay in bed.'

'Thanks. Haven't you got any other news? Tell me about . . .'

'My girlfriend? – great tits, fucks like a witch —'

'I was thinking more of financial news.'

'I know . . .'

He pauses; I say: 'Do you believe in God?'

And this silences him. I can hear him looking at the phone. Mentally, I can see him thinking: you what? Finally he says: 'Sometimes. Last night. When she swallowed. Yeah. Why d'you ask? You dying, or what?'

'Don't know,' I say, although I do. While he digests this, I say: 'I'm sorry, mate. I think I've got to go now. You're starting to depress me.'

'Been a bit lairy, have I?'

'Could say that . . . See you – tomorrow?'

He chuckles, again. 'Right you are, shag.'

Putting the phone down I flop back on the bed and stare at the ceiling, then I reach under the bed for a porn mag. As usual they have been neatly stacked by the cleaning lady; I have to unstack them to get at my favourite.

Unfortunately, such is my keenness to masturbate, as I energetically lean around and under the bed I crick my neck, pulling a muscle. Lying back on the pillows, I try, and fail, to believe this. I simply can't believe it. I have injured myself masturbating. Incredible.

Disconsolately rubbing the pain in my neck I decide that perhaps this is a message from Nature: stop wanking. It makes some sense. The other day I had another, very similar message from Nature. It came with a wet dream; but not a normal wet dream: I actually dreamt I was flicking through a porn mag and masturbating. I had a wet dream about wanking over a new copy of *Fiesta*. God's bollocks, I think: how removed can one get from normal, healthy intercourse?

Allowing the magazine to slide onto the floor, I sigh and tut and pump up my pillows, feeling hugely sorry for myself. My neck hurts; I have wet dreams about porn mags; I am obviously very sick.

*

'She's . . . not getting better. I'm sorry. But that's just what I feel.'

I am still in bed: talking on the telephone to my mother. About Alice. Normally my mother and I shun this topic: we are like two skaters, avoiding the ice at the centre of a suspect lake. This time, for some reason, my being ill has lent me the will, or the flippancy, to broach it. Against expectations my mother doesn't flinch at my brutality. She seems to welcome it.

Keenly she snaps back: 'Don't think I wasn't aware.'

'Sorry?'

'It's obvious, Guy.'

'That I don't reckon she's going to recover?'

My mother affirms, impatiently: 'It's *painfully* apparent you and Simon have given up. I can see the way you two look at her in hospital. It's awful. Don't you think it's just a little premature to abandon hope? Can't you stop and think about your sister, for once? Think about what she's going through?'

'I do, Mum. But I just . . . I just can't pretend. I can't act what I don't feel —'

'I see. And you spend your whole life afflicted by this sincerity, do you?'

Ouch.

'No. I didn't mean that. It's just . . . every time I look at Alice I get a sad and nasty kind of feeling . . . And I can't help showing it. You know?'

'No, I don't. Goodness, it's not as if we don't feel it from time to time. Sometimes I feel the same – do you think I don't feel like running out of that room and crying? And giving up? Sometimes? Of course I do. But we can't. It's our duty not to give up. It's our duty to be positive – for Sarah. Sometimes I wonder if you realise what your sister is going through. She's being incredibly brave. Incredibly brave . . .'

My mother is waiting for me to reply. I don't. I am

188

violining the phone under my chin and lighting a cigarette and exhaling it at the ceiling.

In the absence, Mum goes on: 'And there is another
point – you know, you really have no idea whether
Alice is going to improve or not. No matter how grim
things appear, no matter how bad the doctors in
Winchester say things might be . . . we can't know anything for sure until the second Cat Scan.'

'When's that?'

My mother pauses, consulting a mental diary. 'April.
That's the first time they can get her into Great Ormond
Street. There's some important surgeon there who thinks
. . . well . . . who seems a little more optimistic than
those awful people at The Royal Hampshire. So . . .'

'Right.' I am chastised. 'I'm sorry, Mum. I'll try and
smile and . . . crack a few jokes next time I go down.'

'Not jokes,' she tuts. 'Just appear more hopeful, if
you can. And if you can't, *well*.'

'Sure,' I say. I am thinking: why is my mother so mas-
terful at making me feel guilty? How come she's so good
at the language? Where did she acquire that accent?

I change the subject. I cough, horribly. This has the
desired effect.

'Are you feeling better? That's a nasty cough.' Her
voice has changed, a little; this is more the solicitous,
motherly croon. So I guess I'm pretty good at the language of guilt as well.

'I'm fine, Mum.' I cough again. 'It's a cold. A head
cold, or something.'

'Really? Are you sure you're eating?

'Yes. I had . . . a bit of soup. You know.'

'And you are completely sure it's not a hangover?'

'No it's not,' I smile. 'This could be AIDS, you know.'

She quietly laughs, before saying: 'If I thought you
were really ill I'd be on the next train. You're a big boy
now.'

'Right . . .'

My mother is good; she is a rock; I love my mother. As she goes on about some news from home, about some just-married cousin, I lie back and think of my childhood. Then I listen to the wind as it rattles my window. Then I say goodbye.

Waking up, later, I croak, and spit and rub my aching neck, and look upwards out the window: outside it is four o'clock, a mid-January twilight. The fact that most of the day has already passed depresses me, so I telephone Eva. She is back from Central Art School, she is full of her day. Listening to her happy, girlish babble, I feel nostalgic for her life, for my life, for life. It seems I have been stuck in this fucking bed for weeks; although it has been only three days. So I am lonely. So strikingly lonely: I want to be totally unalone. I want to be in a pub surrounded by all my friends.

Fiercely I demand that Eva comes to see me. I hate being dependent: that's why I do it so badly, so ungraciously.

With goodish grace my girlfriend accedes: she is going to the theatre with her father and brother, who are temporarily in town, but she'll try and stop over, in transit.

I ring off.

In my softer moments I know I am treating Eva badly. I know this. But what else should I do? She keeps sticking around. She keeps taking it on the chin. Normally I treat women so bad they leave; or I get so bored I leave them. Normally, in fact, I regard girls the way I regard tabloid newspapers: at first I use them for a thrill; then I keep them for a laugh; then I bin them.

But Eva and I have lasted: despite all my mistreatment, my infidelity, my cool and nonchalant cruelty, she sticks by me, and what's more I let her stick by me.

190

Why is this? Why can't she just do the sensible thing and leave? Why doesn't she quit on me? It can't be much fun for the poor girl: the nicest of my feelings for her is pity. And you can't base a relationship on pity; just as you can't base a relationship on sex. Apparently. There has to be something else: like love. Lying here in bed it occurs to me that I have never, actually, made love to Eva. Ever. In all the time I have been going out with Eva, I have never made love to her. I've fucked her, I've screwed her, I've taken her savagely over the ceramic hob, but I have never made love to her.

This is not so surprising, perhaps. I have never made love to anyone apart from Nathalie.

For a long time after the thing with Nathalie, after her tearful departure from London City Airport, I managed to avoid Simon. Then I failed. His and my chance meeting happened during the following summer, eight months after The Event. I was, by this time, well down the sliproad to drug addiction: in an attempt to silence the voices of regret and despair and unrequited devotion I had taken up with Josh and his druggy ways, pretty much full time. I was ensconced in the drugs-and-squatting scene.

Somehow in the meantime I had managed to secure a degree. Although my final two terms of University had been spent in a boozed-up stupor, although I had latterly only been to college to score hash and girls and subsidised lager, I had managed to scrape a 2:2 in Philosophy. The night I met Simon was the same day I discovered that I had got a degree. So I thought I was happy. I thought things were looking up. I was certainly drunk.

I was so wiped, that night in the Wag, I didn't recognise Simon – not at first. It had been quite a long time. I had heard rumours that he had changed, but as our paths had long since diverged – he was always in the library, I was never in the library, he was never in the bar, I was always in the bar – his existence and state-of-mind had virtually ceased to concern. Walking into that tacky nightclub, that night, in my Star of David rave top and my ripped-at-the-knee Levi's, the only thing that did concern me was how much Josh Diamond and Jones the Death and Alex K and Hackney Fats and Steve and Joe and Simi and I could drink and smoke, without paying out a cent. We were poor but cool squatters; we knew the world owed us a living, or at least a beer.

In the end Josh and I ran out of benefactors, of pretty girls to buy us double vodkas, and we stumbled to the bar. Swearing and sweating, and jogging on the spot, we leaned over the zinc and winked at the bar girl, and checked out the mirror: immediately I realised I was standing next to my nemesis. Next to my old best friend, Simon Reeves. Turning his head slowly, Simon looked at me. Feeling my crest fall, I looked back. A surreal silence enveloped us. Simon appeared lonely, and balding, and sad . . .

Yet I was the one feeling embarrassed. The last time I had seen Simon was when he was standing in the doorway watching his girlfriend fellate me. Now he was standing here watching me. It was grim. I wanted to hit Simon because of it. I was so wired and embarrassed and uncomfortable, and angry that he was reminding me of Nathalie, something I definitely did not want to be reminded of, I went on the attack.

Loudly, I said: 'Hello Reeves, you hopeless bastard.'

Whistling, Josh reeled back. Others made room. Not a word came from Simon. He just stood there. Doing nothing. Again, I needled him. I sledged him. I even pushed him, physically. With all my heart I wanted him to flip. I needed him to punch me. To react as I would.

To be the same as me. To be as bad as me. But he wasn't. He didn't say I hate you or I loathe you or even sod you. He just got up and went away. And as he left, as he rose from his stool and walked politely past, all I could do was stand there, calling out his name: 'Simon! Simon! Jesus! YOU CUNT! SIMON!!!'

Eva is here. She is bursting through the door in a blaze of youth and health. So much youth and health it makes me feel vaguely resentful. This feeling ebbs when she hands over her gifts: an architecture book, a bag of nectarines, some chocolate, a copy of the *Spectator*, some Beethoven tapes and a hand-held computer game.

'Thanks,' I say. Dextrously I munch a nectarine, while flicking through the architecture book. The book is called *Post Modern Triumphs in London*; it is a rather slim book. This brevity is not, of course, Eva's fault: nevertheless my ungracious resentment now reappears. These presents are all very nice – presents are one of the very best reasons for having a loaded Swiss girl-friend – but they are not what I need. What I *need* is a *blowjob*. But how to broach the topic? The girl is all dolled-up for a night on the tiles: just-so eyeliner, YSL perfume, expensive stockings, lipstick. The last thing she's going to want to do is muss up all that maquillage by getting down on her knees like a scullery maid. This is a delicate matter. I must approach the question with *chivalrie*, with *debonnaireté*, with a suave and gentle-manly *courtoisie*.

'Eva —'

'*Ja?*'

'Suck me.'

Silence. I can hear the trees outside, rustling in the wind. The streets must be pretty deserted, if I can hear this. With a dark flash of anger in her eyes, Eva nods;

193

she has decided to adhere to my wishes. And: well. This easy victory worries me, as much as it pleases me. This victory terrifies and saddens me. I have complete power over this girl, and it is bad. Because it derives from the fact that she is in love with me, and I am not in love with her; and the fact that the more I don't love her, the more she loves me; and the fact that the more she loves me, the less chance there is of my ever loving her. Over the last couple of weeks Eva has become more liberal in bed, certainly more permissive. But she does this because she knows it pleases me, not because it pleases her. Our relationship is now a vicious spiral. Our relationship is a slalom, a downhill race into greater and greater cruelty; every single day I have to stop myself from testing its boundaries, from doing some of the nasty, sexual things I can think of, from enacting some of the ideas that are developing, in the darkroom of my soul.

In the meantime: I might as well let Eva do her thing. She does do it so *well*. As I smoke my cigarette I look down: the sight of her head is faintly ridiculous, as it bobs up and down like a Texan oil-pump, but the feeling is sensational. She really knows how to suck.

Languidly I half-close my eyes and turn and watch the darkened window of my bedroom. I like living at the top of the house, at the top of Islington Hill. It means I can see the world, as now. I am looking levelly across a rainy, moonlit, January-ish London, that stretches from the barrier blocks of Finsbury to the terraces of the Angel, to the arc-lit industrial wastelands of Camley Street. The deep distinguished blue of the cloudless night sky is beautiful tonight. It is a great Gothic vault, arching over the cathedral of evening.

And I am a cockroach, scuttling obliviously across its floor.

# 23. The Princess Louise

Bustling to work in my usual affable-cynical manner, engrossed in the Bach cantata on my Walkman, I start thinking about Alice. As my Tube train judders slowly into Barbican station, I remember that long-suppressed image of her in the hospital bed, with the tubes coming out of her mouth and her nose. As I consider this vision, I suddenly remember what the image recalls, I am about to solve that certain *déjà vu.*

Struggling with my briefcase, I push my way out of the carriage, egressing onto the Eastbound platform of Barbican station. At the end of the concrete ramp I see a man begging: in front of him is a flat cap full of laughably small five pence pieces. Normally I would ignore this everyday sight; this time I can't. Tied around the man's neck is a card with a felt-tipped slogan, saying: I am Cold And I Am Lonely. Rooted to the spot, I think *that's a nice bit of copy-writing* and I stroll over to donate. Before I can reach the man, another realisation occurs. I recognise the man, the beggar. I actually know him: it's an old friend. But who? From where?

Extracting my Walkman earphones, I stand and sieve the possibilities: then the truth dawns. This tube station beggar is an old mate, he's an old acquaintance from my drug-taking days, on the Mozart Estate. Sweet Jesus, I think. Sweet fucking Jesus. Executing a swift about-turn, I make to escape what will clearly be an embarrassing encounter. The beggar-friend spots me.

'Guy!' His voice is reedy. 'Guy!!!'

Shit, too late. Turning towards the man I feign a smile. All the time trying to remember his name. Just in time: 'Toby. Hello . . .'

'Yeah, Guy —' Toby cracks a brown-toothed smile: 'How are you, mate? You doin' all right?'

Seeing as I am dressed in a £600 pinstripe, a hand-painted silk tie, and brand new brogues so shiny I can see Toby's filthy face reflected in them, it is futile to deny that, yes, in comparison to Toby, I am doing pretty well. And yet . . .

I squat down, opposite.

'Things are OK, I guess. I'm making a few quid.'

'Yeah, that right? Whatchew doin' then, 'zackly?'

'Oh, not much . . .' I am trying not to look at the sores on Toby's neck, and the socks I can see through his dilapidated Docs: 'I'm working in the City, actually. Doing a bit of dealing —' It dawns on me what this sounds like. 'I mean – a bit of foreign exchange dealing. What about you, what are you doing now?'

This STUPID remark was not what I intended to say. Kicking myself, I listen to Toby's inevitable reply: 'What am I doin'? Well, I'm like . . .' He frowns. 'I'm like . . . beggin' . . . y'know . . .?'

Jesus, already. I am keen to finish this conversation before it declines further. Extracting my wallet I find a folded tenner. This I slip into Toby's palm, as if I am a gangster sweetening a traffic cop. Staring down at the ten pound note, Toby mumbles, and looks doubly uncomfortable. Fuck it. With a strange, half-swallowed 'see-you-later', I turn and flee up the stairs to the ticket-hall, exiting with relief into the winter sunshine.

All through my morning, and my lunchtime, and my

196

day, I find I cannot shake this encounter out of my head. Even though I enjoy my afternoon's work, I am not happy. The awkward encounter with Toby has got me cogitating, has made me think about fate, about kismet and karma. Why should Toby end up sitting on the tube platform of failure, while I have ended up here in the dealing room of success? Why is this? I was just as bad a junkie as him – why did I survive, and he take a dive?

Don't know. Turning back to my dealing-desk I divert my attentions, focusing on the figures and the Telerate screens; keenly and expertly, I try to get a handle on what's up. Having got a handle, I recommence my efforts to destabilise the Franc.

Until I am interrupted. Distracted, I look and see Andy. He laughs: 'Jesus. Take it easy —'

'What?'

'You look like you're raping somebody —'

Ignoring this fatuity I sit back in my black leather swivel chair, and yawn. I notice that the sky outside is black; the working day has passed. *Already.* With a rush of vigour I begin clearing my desk: binning the day's sweetwrappers and newspapers, and clicking off my Reuters monitor. On my left I can hear Andy faffing around. He is toying with a calculator and doodling on his Tuffs reports. I know this mood of his. It means he has done a good day's work, and is now keen to unwind. To chat. To drink ten pints of lager.

Turning to me, he asks: 'How long?'

'What?' I am still filling some things into a briefcase.

'How long before the ERM blows up again?'

'Ohhh . . .' I gesture vaguely, 'Four months, tops. There's no way the Germans will keep spunking this sort of dosh.' Agreeing, Andy nods; I go on: 'But the Franc will be the last. The Spanish and the Irish will chuck it in first.'

197

Again, Andy agrees: 'Serve 'em right, the spams.' Then he returns to chat with someone to his left, leaving me to complete my briefcasing. But the energy will not subside: I am still bodysurfing on the day's adrenalin; I need to relax. So I try: standing up I walk over to the windows, to where I can smoke a furtive Turkish and gaze out over London. Yes, I think. London, London, London. London is looking unusually noble, tonight. From the floodlit blue-and-silver of the Lloyds building, to the black abstraction where the Thames should be, from the lava flow of brake lights that is London Wall, to the coven of Franciscan monks that is the skyline of Minster House: it looks great. Brave. It occurs to me now that one reason I adore London, despite its substandard skyscrapers and cheapskate mass housing, is because its substandard skyscrapers and cheapskate mass housing are a testament to the city's bravery. They are Prussian duelling scars. London is a battle-scarred veteran. London is a capital city that has stood up to tyrants and bombers and terrorists and airforces, and suffered thereby. Whereas Paris is beautiful like a whore: a trollop who saved her good looks, by going down on her jackbooted conquerors.

My reverie is interrupted: Andrew has joined me. Mirroring my posture he stares out across the unforgivably average skyline of the City of London, and says: 'Fancy a pint?'

We are in the Princess Louise in Holborn. This is a dire pub most of the time: at seven in the evening it is Gin Lane *à go-go*. It is also excellent fun, if you are in a bullish mood. As I am. Tonight I am in the mood to relish the debauchery: to revel in the mayhem, in the couples snogging on the tables, and the boy bankers chucking pints at each other, and the frizzy-blonde office girls singing George Michael songs – not forgetting the few kagoul-wearing tourists who stand in the middle of it all, bewilderedly sipping from half pints of Ruddles as they wonder what happened to English decorum and British reserve.

Amidst the noise, Andy grabs my lapel: 'Tell you what I just did?'

'No.'

'Just bought some blinding Bronson.'

'How much?'

'Shagloads. Wanna line?'

Pausing, I consider. A second later, I decide. 'Try anything once too often.'

And so we crush through the crowd, into the Gents. Once secreted in a cubicle we gigglingly scrape out five lines – one each for Andy and me and for the other three dealers who are drinking with us – and then we snort, and sniff, and wait for the carillons to ring. They do. They *do*. Within minutes I am a ten-year-old in the fairground of life: happily dazzled by the din and the neon and the zaps of the bumper-cars.

After this, the five of us drink another ten pints of Tanglefoot, play the slot-machine trivia quiz, and nearly get into a fight with some no-hoper bank clerks. Then we chink glasses and down our last pints, and somehow end up outside. Shocked by the cold air we turn right onto a traffic-jammed Kingsway and march gleefully if unsteadily up Great Queen Street, striding past the empty Indian restaurants and the packed-out theme pubs, and the janitored ad offices, until we attain the freezing, windswept Piazza of Covent Garden. Here the women are horny as always. One, in particular, catches my eye, partly because her high heels keep skidding sexily on the rainwet cobbles, partly because she is wearing the shortest skirt in the visible universe, but principally because she is a *sort*. With her sixteen-inch waist and her uppity breasts and her crude-oil black hair this girl is swooningly pretty – and she sure as fuck knows it. As I emit a soft croon of desire she turns and gives me a stare that says *stuff*. But who gives. I don't. The girl looks so stunning in the soft white lamplight thrown from the portico of Inigo Jones's Church, for a moment I am simply pleased to simply know that she exists.

Oh, this coke, this coke. I like it. I *need more*. I suggest the same to Andy; Andy nods. Stalled in a dank streetcorner, between the Art Nouveau ironwork of Floral Hall and the Wendy House Doric of new Clifton Nurseries, Andy smiles and says 'Here's one I prepared earlier,' taking out and igniting a largish coke-reefer. We chuckle. Soon the cold winter air between our laughing faces is filled with the decadent smell of smoked cocaine. This makes me laugh, even more, as I watch the red glowing tip of the passed-around cokespliff get longer, and longer. And suddenly it spins. I am out of it. I am over the top. I am laughing and drinking and scowling. Then I am in some bar and I can hardly speak. Then it is another moment and I am in a cab and I am sniffing more coke off a glossy mag cover, as we stall in a nose-to-tail traffic jam on Charing Cross Road.

Finally we are disgorged in a rabble of shouts and handslaps, into another Soho bar, Blacks: where I meet a girl. She is very, very cute. It is now late, about one.

And I have been drinking for a straight seven hours.

My mind is fizzing with the coke and the alcohol. I am sitting on an armchair, absorbing the lazy, languid, basement buzz that is Blacks' bar, at night – and there is this delectable girl sitting on my lap and I am nuzzling her shoulder and laughing. Who is she? I don't know; I like her, anyway. I like the straplessness of her dress. I adore the lack of it; indeed I love all that is -less about women: I love them when they are strapless and bra-less and top-less and crotch-less and knicker-less – and mind-less . . . and name-less. . .

Way to go. Whispering in the mystery of the girl's ear, I suggest we return to my place. Giggling, she nods. She nods! Triumphantly hiccuping I lead her by the hand, out onto the freezing pavements of Dean Street. Here, under the high starry sky, this sky that soars across London, I stand on the pavement and look hard in her eyes and blindly she leans nearer – expecting to be kissed on her wet luscious mouth – but as she does so I halt. Through the beer and the coke and the smoke and the Stoly I have just seen. I have remembered Alice again; now I can place it: that *déjà vu*. The sight of Alice with those tubes coming out of her mouth, and her ears, and her nose, reminds me of photos of Nazi atrocities: of those photos of Red Army soldiers and Free Polish airmen who were experimented on – who were subjected to vacuums, who were injected with typhus and phenol, who had tubes thrust down their throats whereby they were force-fed water and chlorine until they burst open and died.

Turning to the girl, to this sweet, puzzled, soon-to-be-naked young woman, I shrug, and say: 'Let's get a cab.'

# 24. The Mozart Estate

Saturday lunchtime I wake up to find Eva hitting me. She is hitting me around the face and shoulders, insanely: her eyes red with anger.

Heaving her aside, I blurt: 'What the fuck's the matter?'

But she doesn't reply: she just keeps swinging these wild, roundhouse punches, like she is the fat kid at school: teased beyond endurance.

As I hold my naked and infuriated girlfriend at arm's length, I try to recall: to think it through. Last night I arrived here at six in the morning: so this outburst could be part of a general you're-so-selfish-why-didn't-you-ring-me hysteria. And yet, I'm not so sure. Eva doesn't normally freak at my selfishness. What can it be?

'Eves. Tell me . . .'

After shooting me a glare, she subsides, sitting back on her haunches. Then she lifts the duvet, like a forensic scientist at an autopsy, and points at my groin. Alerted, I look. My penis is covered with what appears to be dried blood. Now I stare at Eva: at her tearstreaked face. Is it her period? Did she bleed on me last night? Is this what's the matter?

No: it can't be, because we didn't fuck this morning; I didn't even touch her. So what is it? Tweaking back the duvet I wince at my genitals, again, and it dawns:

the powdery substance on my penis that looks like paprika is not blood; it is old lipstick.

And Eva *hardly ever* wears lipstick.

Ah. Ah-hah. This is a tricky wicket. How do you explain incontrovertible evidence of having had a blowjob last night to a girlfriend who didn't give you a blowjob last night? Hungover, I go through a few possibilities: like . . . like . . .

Without a word I slip out of Eva's bed and struggle into last night's shirt; my silence infuriates Eva further. She starts belabouring me on the back of the head with a pillow. I turn to stop her and as I do so she lands her first half-decent punch. Thock. Right on the number. Fully prepared to congratulate Eva on her aim I turn and smile, and she kicks me neatly in the shin. Crack. This is numbingly painful; now I start hopping about her tiny new Fulham bedsit, one leg halfway down my trousers.

'Speisser, leave it out —'

'Why?' She cries. 'Why? Who were you with last night?'

'I told you. Friends.'

'What friends?'

'The usual . . . Jesus —'

'You mean you were just getting drunk?'

Is this a pun? *Getting drunk*? Probably not. My girlfriend's mastery of the language is not that profound. In turn I shrug, painfully, and ask her if she wants a blow-by-blow account. This *is* a pun. But Eva doesn't get it. Instead she continues wailing.

'You said you were only going out for an hour and you came home at six in the morning —'

'I know. We did a bit of coke, I'm sorry.'

'A bit?'

'Well . . .' I slur. 'The evening just . . . sort of . . . snowballed.'

Another jape; Eva doesn't smirk: 'So what about this?' She is gesturing peniswards. 'What about this . . . lip-stick?'

'Don't know, Eves. I guess it must have been . . . a laddish prank?'

'*Scheiss*! *Scheiss*! Fuck you!' She doesn't believe me . . . 'All the time you sleep with me, and all the time you have lipstick on your —'

'I didn't sleep with you,' I say. 'I was too pissed. Or don't you remember?'

This makes things worse: now Eva starts raining a flurry of slaps onto my scalp, which she follows with a bony teenage knee in the bollocks.

Momentarily, I stand there, squinting in the winter sunshine: then the nauseating pain kicks in. Crumpling to the floor a warm ache pervades, and I feel like I want to throw. The world is nasty, spiteful, bitchy. I feel sour. I hate my girlfriend. Oh yes.

Finally the waters of pain drain away, and I open my eyes and see a still-naked Eva standing there, her arms crossed in triumph. Her face looks beautiful and pretty; her blonde pubic hairs are foxy tufts in the sunlight. Meanwhile I am thinking hard. I am thinking: Why? Why is she allowed to hit me, anyway? When I'm not allowed to hit her back?

Standing up, unsteadily, I say: 'You stupid bitch —' And I pincer my hand around her face, squashing her mouth into a comic pout. She splutters. I ignore her spluttering. Instead I ram her against the wall and feign a karate-chop to the face. Yes! Now Eva yelps, and ducks, and tries to squirm away, but as she wriggles I kick her bare feet from under her, twist her in midair, and push her hard onto the bed. From high above I backslap the side of her face so hard her spit goes flying across the pillowslip. She is crying, now. Real heart-felt sobs. I don't care. Viciously fisting her hair, I hiss in her ear: 'Don't ever hit me again. Don't ever fucking hit me again. I'll stick your tits in the toaster, bitch.'

Then – while she lies there, weeping into the duvet – I finish buttoning my shirt, fix a lazy tie, slip into my suit jacket, and exit.

I hate Fulham. I hate its fucking ugly twattish failed Chelseaness. I also hate the people who live here, who spend their lives gloating over their Conran Shop furniture. Jumping into my car I rev the engine and gravel-spin the back wheels and roar loutishly away, like a drunken yup after a dinner party. Sod them. Sod them all. I am angry today. I am so angry I have to expend my energies. To that end I drive faster and faster and faster up the Fulham Palace Road . . . and I get a sudden craving to be out of it. I want to be drugged: my head is full of the horrors: the horror of this morning's contretemps with Eva, the horror of this afternoon's contretemps with Alice. It's all so very bad. I am expected to do my familial duty at Blue Cedars this lunchtime, as Alice is coming out of hospital for her first unsupervised weekend: and I just don't want to. Jesus . . . What can I do? As I drive towards Hammersmith I slap some Texan rock music on the stereo, but instead of cathartically calming me, its nonchalant Dixieness, its grits 'n' lynched niggers-ness only winds me tighter: my hands are white on the wheel. I simply don't want to do this. I do not want to see Alice again. She frightens me. She makes me dream. All I want to do is turn around and drive to South Peckham and score some fucking drugs. Just like I used to. I can remember how drugs once stopped me thinking about Nathalie; now I want them to stop me thinking about everything.

This is paradoxical. My memories of my drug-taking days, the days before and after my nightclub altercation with Simon, are very bad. Yet I have a perverse nostal-

205

gia for them. They were horrible and squalid, yet they are romantically alluring, in retrospect. It was, certainly, a bizarre era. I was living in Josh Diamond's Albany Street squat: a cornucopia of recreational narcotics. There were drugs in the kitchen, the attic, the garage, the bathroom, the garden. Everywhere, in every ramshackle room of the squat, there were people popping, sniffing, smoking, basing, piping, jacking, spiking, chasing. This variety was neatly matched by the array of different addicts: nice middle-class boys, poor little rich girls, Geography postgraduates, down-at-heel expopstars; we were all at it.

And as I sit here in my Spyder, whizzing down a windy, sunny, remarkably empty M3, it occurs to me that I can paraphrase the Hemingway phrase 'we all had a girlfriend, and her name was nostalgia' – to make it applicable to me and my drug-taking confreres. Viz: *We all had a beautiful girlfriend, and her name was narcotics.* That's it. That explains why I occasionally and paradoxically yearn for my drug addict days: because drugs were like a girlfriend. A bad girlfriend. Drugs were a replacement for Nathalie; another *femme fatale.* Drugs were a girl we all shared: a beautiful bitch who we buggered – who then buggered us back. And how I miss her. How I miss it. How I miss that time of religious indolence, that land of Cockayne, that island of sirens, that Garden of Eden hard by the Mozart Estate.

We are here. Blue Cedars. Slamming the door of my Spyder, I scrunch the ancestral gravel and march into my father's house. In the house the men – Simon and my dad and Simon's younger brother – are gathered around the TV watching the rugby – France versus Scotland. This does not involve England so I am not overly interested. Instead I go through to the kitchen,

206

to the women, where I find my sister fussing over Alice. Going over to my sis I say hi. My sister kisses me. Behind her I notice my mum: my mother is here, too. Pausing, I think how ironic it is that Alice's accident has had the otherwise unachievable effect of bringing my family closer together; the only trouble is they didn't want to be closer together. They were quite happy being far apart.

Stepping round the kitchen table I stealthily approach my tea-making mother, clasp her round the waist and kiss her. She turns and hugs me. We talk. She is making optimistic noises about Alice. About how much better my niece is looking. About how it is so good they've allowed her home. Oh, sure, I think. *Sure.* That's so very true, except that Alice *isn't* home. Alice is at the bottom of the pool, or in the Intensive Care Unit, or in some distant limboland. Anywhere but *home.*

Nonetheless, now that my mother has brought up the subject, I can avoid it no longer. I have to fake some avuncularity. I have to go over to Alice and kiss her and pretend she is normal, that this is normal, that our afflicted family is perfectly normal.

So I try. Alice is propped up on the sofa at the end of the big, winter-sunlit kitchen. She looks like a discarded ventriloquist's doll: her limbs are stiff, her soft hair lank, her head is twisted upwards and to the side, as if she is staring at the ceiling, interestedly. She isn't, of course. What she is doing is making an unpleasant gurgling noise through the tracheotomy in her throat. While I lean and kiss my niece's forehead I sniff. She smells of vomit and Dettol. Stepping back, I take a longer look: at my niece's spasticated little legs and her contorted little neck, and her furiously clenched fists. Absorbing this, I notice that Alice has developed a weird, new, spasmodic tic. Every so often her left arm lifts painstakingly up towards her chin, and then jerks back down. Up, up, up – and down. Up, up, up – and down. My mum checks my bewildered expression.

'That's perfectly normal,' she explains. 'It's called athetosis. The doctor says we should expect it. It's a sign of the tissues, the brain tissues mending. And the drugs, of course.'

Yeah, right. Now I get it. Like it's the drugs *and* the healing process. Bollocks. Going to collect an offered cup of tea, I decide to forget it. To forget it all: to let the weekend drift. And I almost manage it. As the afternoon progresses into the evening we watch telly, and eat, and drink, and chat. And it's not so gruesome. We discuss Simon's job and my car and Simon and Sarah's house; and we also talk, as usual, about my love life. Sensitively my mum enquires why I haven't met a truly suitable girl; equally sensitively I reply that I don't know why I haven't met a truly suitable girl. Shrugging, I admit that I must be unlucky.

My mum frowns: 'What do you mean?'

'Well,' I say. 'Four million women in London – and I can't find one with a nice figure and a pretty face and a fine intellect . . . and a good sense of humour and a curiosity about architecture and an adventurous sexuality and an interesting but not too absorbing career. It's outrageous.'

My mum laughs: 'All right, all right . . .'

Soon I am laughing, as well. I feel . . . sort of . . . OK. Kind of fine. The weekend with Alice is not going too badly. Simon is being truculent and morose, but I've come to expect that of late; my sister is being tearful and dippy, but I've come to expect this of late. All in all things aren't so grim: Alice, who is propped on my sister's lap as we watch TV – sans my father, who has gone out for dinner with my step-mum – is being subdued and invisible. And I can cope with all this, for a few more hours. Just a few more hours . . .

The moment I start to properly relax, it happens. Alice makes a noise. An odder-than-usual noise. We gaze at the TV, attempting not to notice. But Alice will not stop. The noise that is coming from her mouth continues and worsens. It is a weird noise: it sounds like Cockney, or German. Alice appears to be speaking German. Turning my head, involuntarily, I notice that Alice is not only crying, she is coughing and jolting – and then she is puking, horribly puking, down my sister's white blouse —

'She's fitting,' says my sister. 'Simon. I think she's *fitting . . .*'

Instantly we panic: Simon rushes over and starts mopping the puke, but his clumsiness betrays him: he drops the sick-sodden cloth. To calm things my mother joins the throng, struggling with the jerking, spewing child and the consternated parents. Meanwhile I continue looking at the telly. My niece is still making that wretched rasping sound. I don't want to look. But I have to. I can't keep watching *Match of the Day*. Switching off the telly I gaze over: to where this scene of Satanic possession is being enacted: to where my niece's eyeballs are rolling white, as yellow vomit dribbles from between her lips; while my sister fiddles with the tracheotomy tube, saying: 'God, Simon – it's her trachy —'

'No, it isn't!' shouts Simon, and he pushes her away. But as he pushes his wife aside something important dislodges and even from this end of the living room I can hear a ghastly gulp of air. Suddenly my niece is whooping, and yelping; and now my sister screams, too: 'She's coughed the trachy out! I can't get it in! Simon!!!'

And I am trying to look at the floor and I am trying not to think – but I can't help it. My sister is now in floods of mad, helpless tears and Simon is cursing and swearing and lifting Alice over his shoulder. Loudly he commands: 'Out of the way! – I'm going to take her to the hospital!'

And in an instant it is done. They all rush out of the door and into the hall – and as they do, my mum turns and orders me to stay behind, to look after the house. I obey. I have no choice; standing there in the middle of the living room I stare at the wall. Forlornly. In time I hear wheels spinning and the receding sound of accelerating cars, and suddenly all is quiet. I am totally alone.

Opening the French windows I step outside into the moonlit garden, into the wintry evening. It is cold. Buttoning my jacket I walk over the dewy lawn, around the covered-over swimming pool, to where the fields begin. Here I stand by the cedars. There is a full moon in the sky. The cedars look indifferent and serene: their silvery blue boughs are ghostly in the moonlight. Shivering slightly I look up: listening to the wind as it creaks between the branches, while the clouds race silently across the sky. As I stand here I find myself talking to the trees. I am saying: let her die. Let her die. Let her die let her die let her die let her die.

Startled, I swivel. The phone is ringing. I'm not sure how long it has been ringing; I've no idea how long I have been out here. Rushing into the house I clatter the receiver, drop it on the floor, and pick it up by its cord – swinging it like a naff rock star with a microphone, round to my face: 'Yes? Hello?'

Silence. All I can hear is silence. Then my mother.

'She's all right . . . She's alive.'

# 25. Robin Hood Gardens

I am trying to chuck Eva when the bomb goes off.

Attuning, I say: 'That's a bomb.'

We are sitting in a clearing, in the woods of Hampstead Heath. It is a sweet April day; full of sunshine and daffodils and cherry blossom. Eva is under the misapprehension that we have come here to tour Kenwood House and enjoy a picnic. In fact I have brought her here to dump her: I have escorted us to this consolingly charming place with the intention of explaining why it's over; why I think we do not have a future; how I am worried that I might just hurt her, if she doesn't see sense and quit. And now this noise. This weird noise, this *crump*, that sounds loud but far away.

Tapping my girlfriend's knee I say: 'I know that sound. I was at home when the last one went off. It's a bomb!'

Puzzled, Eva frowns, then pivots to her feet. Symmetrically, I do the same; together we walk across the green, past the frisbees and the kites, and the lolloping labradors, to the top of Parliament Hill. Here we stand and take in the famous view of London, that stretches from Archway to the City, to the suburbs and the Surrey Downs.

At least: that is what we should be looking at. Today

211

you can't see much of those famous hills, as a huge plume of smoke is rising between the stumpy towers, occluding the further aspect. Proudly I gesture at the view. I am saying: you see? It *was* a bomb . . .

Resting her head on my shoulder, Eva murmurs: 'I hope no one is dead. It's terrible.'

Naturally, I concur. Then I think: well, I hope they've blown up the Stock Exchange. And the Home Office. And Zen Central. And Knightsbridge Barracks. And the Casey Jones Burger Bar at the front of King's Cross. And most of King's Cross. I can't help it but that's what I think. They could do so much good, the IRA. They could be an antithetical Wren: redesigning London, *improving* London, by knocking large chunks of it down.

So nihilistic are my thoughts, I am about to swivel from the view, and finish it with Eva, here and now, when my girlfriend smiles sweetly and says shall we go and look at the paintings in Kenwood House?

This soothes me. With a last glance at the City's smoke-obscured skyline we turn and climb the various dales of Hampstead Heath, and eventually take a left into the gardens of Kenwood. Here we stop for a breather and the chance to take in the celebrated south aspect of the house. It looks grand today: beneath the buttermilk stucco of the frontage, old women are slothfully sunning themselves; hard by the elaborate Orangery, French children are talking much too loud; here on the immaculate lawns, young couples are winding around each other, in double helices of delight. My heartbeat slows, taking in all this. This is Hampstead. This is April. It is difficult to conceive that five miles away large areas of the City are presently engulfed in flames and smoke and flying glass.

Inside the building I smile at the Gainsboroughs, squint at the Vermeer, and feel disappointed by the

Robert Adam decor of the recently restored library. The room is too ornate, too tweely gold and green. Regretfully I gesture to Eva and together we slip upstairs, to look at an exhibition of eighteenth-century shoe buckles. Half a minute later we move on, to other, better exhibits, of jet and iron and coral jewellery, even some old, yellowing, walrus-tusk jewellery. Eventually I happen upon the last and most curious exhibit. In the corner of the museum is a single case devoted solely to hairwork: to Victorian keepsakes manufactured out of genuine human hair.

These perturb me, greatly. Calling Eva over, I explain what I have seen, and curiously she bends to the glass. Side by side we squint and gawp at these necrophiliac knick-knacks, and as we do I find my mind swimming. Pictures of Alice are invading and horrifying me: visions of my niece with fungus-furred legs and finger-nail-less hands and with knitting needles rammed in her ears. Images of Alice locked in a freezer, and dis-solving in battery acid . . .

Outside the House, in the mild spring air, Eva turns her big Bambi eyes on mine and says: 'You OK?'

'Yes. Why?'

'You look . . . kind of weird.'

'It's nothing,' I say. 'Just the weather. Hay fever.'

'Also.' She smiles, squeezing my hand; placidly we walk arm-in-arm through the alley of pleached limes that leads to the rear garden of the House. I am glad for Eva's presence, today; and again I am sorry for the way I have treated her, for the way I am about to treat her.

Sitting on the southwest lawn Eva unpacks the pic-nic. It is warm and sunny. Shading my eyes I lie back and smoke a fat spliff, as Eva busies herself shelling hardboiled eggs and slicing smiles of melon and measuring out two plastic cups of cold champagne.

213

Spying the drinks, I sit up and accept my plastic cup. Meanwhile Eva continues uncellophaning sandwiches. This is a good picnic, I reflect, as I guzzle some roast beef and horseradish. It has a good diversity: the taste of fruitcake against the dryness of Krug; the juice of Galia melon juxtaposed with Moroccan hashish.

I am happier; slightly calmer. Eva asks me what was wrong back there, and I shrug, admitting I am wrestling with a conundrum.

'You mean?'

'Well . . .' I equivocate. 'It's like – have you ever felt an urge to do something you didn't want to do?'

'I don't understand.'

'Have you ever felt a moral obligation?'

Eva laughs: 'You? Moral obligation?'

'It has been known.'

'No. It hasn't.'

I shrug. 'All right . . . But it's true. I do feel this . . . dilemma.'

'You mean . . .' she says, 'because you do not want to go to work any more?'

'Yeah – that's it.'

'Well. You will get the sack, no? If you keep taking time off?'

'Uh-huh.'

'Then you must expect it.'

'Mm.' I say. 'Gizza kiss?'

Later on we wander through the green, gold, Robert Adam-like oakwoods of West Heath, and the verdant lawns that abut the ancient Vale of Health. Here I marvel at the slumbering tramps somehow still cradling flagons of cider, and the sunbathing Jewesses with shockingly unshaven armpits. I also marvel at a couple of lumberjack-shirted young guys armswinging their way downhill, towards the Vale. The guys intrigue me. Something about their attitude reminds me of something. Over my shoulder, I observe – standing at the very end of the Vale, under a lamppost, is a black-jeaned drug dealer. I don't know how I know he is a dealer but my instincts tell me so; these intimations are confirmed when the two guys approach, pass over a couple of twenties and take a tiny package. The whole transaction lasts no longer than a few seconds: very sweet. As the dealer disappears and the two guys head off towards Rosslyn Hill, I start to envy their success.

Their success, and their drugs.

Leaning languidly against a sunwarmed wall by Hampstead Heath station, I open my eyes wide, and lie. Mendaciously I explain to Eva that I have to go and work; that I have to catch the North London line back to the Caledonian Road, to my home and my home-work. For a second she eyebrows me, sceptically; then she nods and pecks and gets in a cab, and as soon as she is gone I step into the nearest payphone and make a number of phone calls. I am ringing all my old dealers. It is years since I last scored, and these few numbers I keep in my head are my only contacts, my only hope of finding gear.

As I expected half the numbers have been discon-nected; and the other half are answered by unEnglished Asians or inquisitive yuppies. Hopeless. Persistently but despairingly I slot in my silver and tap out the last number I know, and wait. Ten rings later a gruff man answers. It is my man. To my entire surprise, he informs me that not only is he still at his old trade, he is at this very moment in possession! This is unheard of; remarkable; brilliant; serendipitous. Urgently I arrange an afternoon rendezvous, by his flats in Robin Hood Gardens in Canning Town. Then I exit the phone booth and start dancing.

There is no time to dance. Hopping on the

Eastbound North London line I take its rattly route through Gospel Oak, past Barnsbury, and Highbury, and Hackney, whence it emerges into the badlands of Poplar and the Dogs. Pretty soon I am shivering and feeling sick. Staring through the grimy, sunny windows of the train at the industrial outback of East London I get to feel nauseous. I am thinking of the smack I am about to do. My body is experiencing a conditioned, Pavlovian response. It's years since I last did the stuff, and just thinking about doing the stuff is making me feel shivery and sick – is making me think about something other than Alice.

Stepping off the train at Canning Town I breathe the weird smells of the factories drifting across the flatlands from Silvertown. In the distance, on the other side of the river, I can see the green wooded foothills of Blackheath and Greenwich. Quickening my pace up the East India Road I walk towards my appointed place —

And I stop, suddenly. I do not know where I am: the last time I was here was about four years ago and the whole area has changed. I don't recognise a thing. There are new roads and new railways, glamorous offices and gleaming apartment blocks: everywhere. This disused Docklands area was always inhuman and atmospheric – now it must be the surrealest urban landscape in all Europe. On the skyline is the shiny anodised phallus of Canary Wharf Tower, on the left is a windsurfable expanse of mirrorflat water, on my right are hard-to-let council flats next to Dutch-gabled yuppie blocks; and right in front is a flyover that exuberantly loops around those exemplars of late British hi-tech: Nicholas Grimshaw's fastidiously masculine *Financial Times* Printing Works, and Richard Rogers' big, blue Reuters HQ – the latter building squatting

216

amidst the dust and rubble of unfinished Docklands like a car engine on the moon.

The whole effect of this area is at once exhilarating and depressing. And confusing. You can't get there from here, indeed you can't get anywhere from anywhere: I am pacing up the hard shoulder of a motorway en route to Canary Wharf – even though I don't want to go to Canary Wharf. I want to turn right: I can't. The only way I can do it is to shin up a concrete wall, jump down the other side, scramble through an overgrown churchyard, emerging into the backyard of Robin Hood Gardens. Standing here, looking at these buildings, I see the place as I once saw it. Years ago, Simon and I used to have apoplectic arguments about this development, about Robin Hood Gardens. During our university days this housing scheme was the touchstone of our aesthetic opposition: Simon used to claim that Robin Hood Gardens was a clear and coherent expression of contemporary architectural ideas; I used to claim that it was the worst building in the Western world.

What intrigues me now is not that I was wrong, but that I didn't know how right I was. Robin Hood Gardens is just a couple of ten-storey barrier blocks: in size and ambition it is dwarfed by plenty of other council housing developments in this area. And yet it isn't. As I gaze upon its brace of concrete tenements, at its jazzily annoying fenestration, at its pointless grass tumulus, at its brutal grey perimeter wall that resembles the barriers they employ to divide West Belfast, I see that this place is evil. A scheme of unparalleled Evil. Idealism and optimism might have been the architectural parents of this building; the progeny is, nonetheless, an obscenity. Looking at Robin Hood Gardens, at the kids kicking Cola cans in the stairwells, I get an overwhelming sense of outrage. This development looks like a model prison, like a civilised slaughter-house, like a machine for suffering in. Yet it was designed for people, real people, poor people, people who had no choice but to live here. And I want to hurt the architect responsible: I want to kick him in the stomach until the blood comes gargling in his arsehole. I want to stamp on his penis until it looks like a black-ened plantain. I want to burn down his home during the school holidays. All of them. *All* the architects responsible. I want to make them live here. These arro-gant, lefty bastards. These evilly clever people; these horribly caring people; these evil people who cared more about the logic of their theories and the coher-ence of their artform than they could ever care about human beings. I can't help it: this is what I think. They are evil scum. Alice-murdering scum.

Unexpectedly, I see my man. *Waiting.* Shaking my head, unswooning myself, I go over, pay the money, and collect the drugs. I am keen not to think: I don't like what's happening in my mind. Nipping into a Texaco garage I buy a Kit Kat and some matches; then I run down the littery and deserted A13 until I find a Victorian redbrick public toilet. Here I locate a lockable cubicle, go in, shut the door, sit on a lavatory seat and smoke my drug off the Kit Kat foil. For a moment I keep the smoke inside my lungs, trying not to exhale: then the feeling kicks in: the voluptuous languor. A heroin hit is the nearest a man can get to female orgasm: or so I have long felt. The satedness, the repletion, the groaningly gratified ache: they must be similar. Similar enough for me to deceive myself, any-way. Presently, I slump. Within minutes I am slumped uncaringly against a graffiti-covered wall – allowing the sputum to trickle, sluttishly, down my unshaven chin.

*

It is morning. Monday morning.

Groggily I get out of bed, climb into my suit, and climb downstairs. Once in the kitchen I am reminded of what I did at the weekend: heroin. This memory grosses me out; I am appalled that I could throw away three years of clean living, just like that. Going over to yesterday's jacket, carelessly slung over a dining chair, I sort through the pockets until I find the wrap of remaining smack; this I open into the kitchen sink, sprinkling its contents into the plug hole. I have decided I never want to touch the stuff again. Again . . .

On with the day. Sipping some black coffee and snapping at my flatmates I stumble outside into the warm spring sunshine, buy a paper, and hail a cab on the Caledonian Road. Once I am inside the cab, trapped in the back seat, the taxi-driver tries to engage me in chit-chat. This is the last thing I need: by way of giving him the brush-off I open my paper and conspicuously begin reading.

'Jesus Christ!'

We have braked, viciously. Dropping my paper I scan the scene: we are at the end of Houndsditch. A hundred yards away I can see fire engines and police cars, blocking the junction with Bishopsgate. What is this? Climbing out of my cab and tipping the driver I cross to the strips of yellow-and-black police tape that rope off the street, and I look. It is amazing, a heart-stopping sight: the whole of Bishopsgate and St Mary Axe has been wrecked by the weekend's IRA bomb. As far as the eye can see the appalling destruction stretches: every bank and building society, every pub and sandwich bar, every church and office block has had its windows stoved in, its doorways punched through, its floors and walls frayed outwards. From the skyscraping heights of the Commercial Union tower, strips of white window blinds are flying like pennants.

And down at ground level every inch of road is now covered with layers of sparkling, gleaming, bluey-green broken glass, like a rippleless sea of aquamarine, like the coralline waters of a Tahitian lagoon.

# 26. Red Lion Square

'Thanks for this —'

Belinda smiles at my greeting, and rises: 'It's no problem. You sounded pretty . . . urgent on the phone. Shall we go in?'

We are standing outside the Eagle, a trendy café-pub on the busy, filthy, breezy Farringdon Road. Belinda, who is dressed in a neat skirt and jacket, and sensibly fashionable shoes, looks shivery. And awkward. There is a palpable air between us: of difficult history; of indefinable regret.

'OK. Let's go.'

Inside, the place is packed with girl journalists and studenty locals. Once we have squired a table Belinda asks me, briskly, as if to sidestep any other subjects, 'So. How is she?'

'Oh,' I say, not looking across. 'OK . . .'

'She is getting better, then?'

'Well . . . Not really.'

A squint: 'Not at all?'

'I'm not sure, Belinda. I just . . . don't know. She is living at home now.'

'So that's good. Surely?'

'I guess . . . Yes . . .' Even as I speak, my mental processes have been halted. Images are flashing up: of screaming children with masks of wasps, of comatose patients with tubes yanked from their —

Shuddering: 'Actually, I can't say there's been any real improvement.'

'Hm.' Looking away, Belinda leans to thieve a menu from a nearby table; then she returns, and frowns: 'She *is* still in the coma, then?'

'Not exactly. But she's still a *spastic*.' The last word I say with a certain relish. I have come to like saying the word *spastic*. The honest sound of it appeals. I have decided to have no truck with euphemisms, I don't see how they help: why I should protect myself, or others, from the truth?

'That's why I . . . asked you here. I wanted to get a third opinion. An umpteenth opinion.'

She nods, sombrely: 'Guy, I'm afraid there's not much I can tell you. Not much I can say without knowing the facts, the CAT results and the neurologists' reports. Just *seeing* her would help. Without any of that . . .'

Belinda's intelligent face is giving her away: she is mired in confusion. I can tell she must be thinking about the last time we met; about the abortion. She is evidently wondering how to treat me: whether to feel anger or defiance or sadness – or pity, because of Alice.

The better her wins out. In a brave stab at re-assurance, Belinda goes on. While we order lunch, and sip our beers, she tells me of some relevant medical folklore, some miracle recoveries she's heard about. One of these faintly unlikely stories attracts me. It concerns a girl who was under the ice of a New England lake for fifteen minutes, who thereafter made a complete recovery. The idea is nice: suspiciously so. Rather harshly I cross-examine my ex; under pressure she admits that her story doesn't have a direct bearing, doesn't accurately mirror Alice's predicament: 'Icy water slows down the metabolism. Like a kind of instant hibernation, or a cryogenic suspension.'

'So the brain doesn't need so much oxygen?'

'Exactly.' She nods. 'The girl's whole system was on a go slow, so there wasn't a chance for her to get brain damage. Pretty miraculous, really. But ... I presume . . .?'

'The swimming pool was heated,' I say, drily. 'No luck there.'

Silence. Belinda fidgets with her napkin.

'You know, this sort of thing happens all the time. It's one of the main problems with modern medicine. We can save people in situations where maybe before they would have died, but we *never* wonder whether they would have been better off not surviving anyway.' Draping the napkin across her lap, she sighs, uncomfortably: 'We just dump the patients on the parents or the carers. We don't give a fig about the consequences of our actions, or our technology.'

Not replying, I sit back. Above the general babble I can hear plates clattering in the open-range Eagle kitchen. The pub is full of agreeable smells: cigar smoke and rosemary, *pommes frites* and beer. I am trying to concentrate on the good things in life.

'Thank you,' Belinda says, tilting sideways to allow the waitress to place her plate of swordfish steaks. My own meal arrives a moment later: sausages and Borlotti beans: *haute* greasy spoon.

'So how's everything else?' I say, having regained my composure; having displaced any more images of Alice, for the moment.

'Fine.'

'You are OK, then?'

She nods. 'Yes. I'm OK.'

The question of the abortion, of what once happened, hangs between us; a great big mutual thought bubble. Inadvertently, Belinda punctures it.

'Oops, sorry.' She has squirted lemon juice in my pint. Now our eyes meet. Shrugging, she smiles.

'I'm moving into my flat next week. Finally getting out of Queen Mary's.'

'It's near here, yeah?'

'Yes. It's quite expensive. But it's better than QMH. That place was like a school dorm.'

Hungrily she slices into her swordfish steak and scrunches some chips onto a fork. Then she eats; then we drink; then we talk: more. We are beginning to thaw; to rediscover; to remember nice things; to get drunk. This surprises me. I am liking Belinda more than I expected. The things that used to annoy me about her seem, today, to be turning into virtues: her bluntness feels like a refreshing truthfulness and her sarcasm has become a likeable scepticism.

While Belinda and I polish off two more pints of bitter – while she begins to laugh at my jokes – I wonder whether, despite it all, my madcap instinct of those months ago was correct. Perhaps Belinda *was* the right exit, the right junction on the motorway; perhaps she *was* the place where I should have turned off: instead of driving on and on. To Scotland. To Iceland. To the frozen wastes of the North. Ah well, I think. Ah . . . well?

'How's your love life?'

She swallows a last morsel of swordfish, parallels her cutlery, and wipes her lips: 'Brilliant. I met this wonderful man last Christmas. Freelance photographer.'

Images of some leather-jacketed oaf screwing my Belinda swim unwontedly into view.

'His name's Sacha.'

Make that an Armani suit.

'Good-looking, witty, rich . . . and very talented.' I think I am going to throw up; Belinda is going dreamy. 'And his dad's a Lord.' A Lord? 'He's great. Gives me

224

loads of orgasms – last night I actually *fainted*.'

'All right, all right —'

She grins. 'Just teasing. Thought you needed . . . cheering up.' She looks expectantly at her beer glass; while it is replaced by a waiter, she explains things, properly: 'He *is* very nice. Makes me laugh. And he is a bit of a . . . workaholic in bed.'

Finishing my own drink, I smile. Belinda has succeeded in lightening my mood; I sense the angst draining away.

Then she asks: 'How's Simon?'

And the tension returns.

'OK . . . Bearing up.'

'I always liked Simon. He's nice. Kind.'

'Sure.'

'In fact I've always wondered what on *earth* you two had in common.'

'Thanks.'

'No, really, I mean – hasn't it ever struck you? You are rather different.' Sipping her beer, thoughtfully. 'Wasn't there some scene between you two? Over some girl?'

'Yeah. There was a scene.'

'Right. Right . . .' Belinda is nodding. 'Truth be known ... I've been thinking a lot about you and Simon, recently. I'm doing a psychology paper on friendship, you see, and you two were my case history . . .' Her eyes find mine. 'I reckon your friendship is based on the fact that, deep down, you share a similar outlook. Share the same background.'

'I'll order a cab —'

'It's true. Listen to me . . .' She chuckles. 'I know what I'm talking about. His dad died when he was young, didn't he?'

I affirm.

'Well then. And your dad was hardly *there*. He was

225

either making money, or bonking other women, right?'

'True enough. But a lot of peole have single parents, and —'

'Natch. But you both reacted strongly to not having a dad. He's been searching for some system to replace that paternal authority, ever since. That's why he's religious. Right? And why he gets so *dogmatic*. He feels a need to have some authority in his life, some order, some discipline.'

'And me?'

'You've been testing the boundaries. Without anything to guide you, without a dad to show you the way, to impose that moral framework, you've been doing lots of bad things, going off the rails, racing off to the horizon, hoping to run up against some barrier. To provoke the world into punishing you. Therefore you and Simon recognise each other as soulmates, *subconsciously.*'

Belinda's analysis sounds a bit half-baked to me. Half-baked, but not wholly unbaked. Maybe she has a point?

Attracting the waiter, I make a cheque-signing gesture.

'Maybe you're on to something . . . I must admit I've never committed a moral act. Know what I mean? In all my life, I've never done a consciously moral thing. I've never done anything because I see it as *specifically* the moral thing to do.'

Judging by her expression, this has obviously sailed right over Belinda's head. Not surprising, seeing as it sailed right out of mine. I don't know what I am trying to say. While we wind up our conversation, I sign for the bill. Belinda glances at her watch.

'I'm going to be late.'

'We can share a cab.'

In the taxi we talk more; I enquire about the Cancer

Ward. 'Doesn't it ever worry you, all that death?'

'You get used to it,' she says. Then she changes her mind. 'Actually, you *don't*. It's *always* horrible. You *never* get used to it. You just . . . ignore it. You don't even deal with it. Just push it out of your mind.'

'It must be worse, the way they die —'

'Yup.' We are passing the fanciful skyline of the Law Courts, and St Mary le Strand; we are exiting Fleet Street and veering right up the Aldwych.

Again, I wonder: 'Do you ever . . . knowingly assist . . .?'

Matter-of-factly, she responds: 'All the time. Usually they're hooked up to morphine pumps. So if they are *really* suffering, and *definitely* terminal – it's not difficult. You just turn the knob a little. Give them a bit too much. An overdose, I suppose. But you'd know more about that, wouldn't you?'

Too true, too true. Gazing out of the cab window I think about what my ex-girlfriend has said. It is ironic. My fond comparisons of my *own* heroin abuse to a bad love affair are, as I see now, not the whole of it. They could even be regarded as trite and commonplace. Yes, addiction is a fatal attraction: yes, the similarities are striking and obvious: smack *is* a jealous, demanding, expensive, brainwashingly bad girlfriend. But if what Belinda is saying about morphine pumps and geriatrics is correct, smack is also the most faithful of lovers. Heroin, smack, morphine – when all your wives and mistresses have left you, she's still there. She's there, right at the end. *We die in her arms.*

The taxi is taking the corner of High Holborn: we are approximately three hundred yards from Red Lion Square. This is a further irony. Red Lion Square is where I lived, after Albany Street, at the very height of my London-based drug-taking craze. A huge empty flat in a thick-walled Edwardian tenement. In Red Lion

227

Square I adopted gear, properly; as a life choice. With Alex and David and Josh and the rest. Red Lion Square was where I descended the helter skelter of addiction: going from what could still just about be called re-creational abuse, to lying and puking and stealing and sweating and not washing and not eating and not being nice to everyone. In Red Lion Square I reached what I thought was bottom; what I thought was the very edge of self-destruction.

'Have you got a library at Queen Mary's?'

'Sorry?'

'I was wondering if I could borrow some books, about anoxia. I want to do some research on Alice's condition.'

Frowning, Belinda thinks; then she nods: 'There is a library. You'll need a card. But I could give you mine. Shouldn't be a problem.'

'Great.'

When we reach Paddington, Belinda guides me out of the cab, into the hospital, and down innumerable corridors. At the door to the library, Belinda relinquishes me with a kiss.

'Good luck.'

'Thank you.'

Checking myself through the turnstile, I go into the reading room. Here I spend ten minutes ogling all the nurses. Then I spend an hour locating the relevant shelf. Eventually I transport five large medical text-books to a desk: *Paediatric Neurology, Infantile Rehabilitation, An Introduction to Paediatric Neurology, Brain Disorders in the Newborn*, and another *Paediatric Neurology*. These books must weigh twenty kilos: about as much as a two-year-old child: *dead weight*.

Spreading the books across the desk I begin to read.

It is soon apparent that I have chosen the wrong volumes: none of the books properly discuss head injuries or drowning, nor do they address the ramifications of anoxia; still, I cannot stop. As I skim the pages, I am gripped. This material is unacceptably riveting; like a snuff movie, or bestiality porn, or a Holocaust documentary. The horror is at once banal and transfixing. Cornelia de Lange; Amsterdam Dwarf; Muscular Dystrophy. The diseases are bizarre and morbidly interesting: worse, there is an addictively deadpan humour to the terms that describe them. Cocktail party syndrome. Bird-headed dwarfism. Kinky hair disease. Some of the nastier childhood neuropathies are also described in strange detail – in a kind of sardonic detail —

*Dystonia musculoram deformans*
This inherited trait is characterised by slow spasmodic twisting and turning of the spine and limbs. Changes in brain structure have been noted but the cause is unknown. The initial symptoms are always the same, with languid and distressing writhing movements of a foot, a hand, the neck, or the trunk. The duration and frequency of the movements gradually increases until ultimately the abnormal postures are fixed. Frequently patients are diagnosed as having an hysterical illness, partly because of the bizarre postures, and because of the absence of objective neurological signs . . .

Abruptly laying the volume aside, I open another; it has the same dry tone, the same laconic voice.

*Lesch Nyhan's syndrome*
Lesch Nyhan's affects male children only. Typically it is characterised by a disorder of purine

metabolism due to enzyme deficiency; this syndrome has been called 'the cruellest of the neurodegenerative disorders'. It is manifested by cerebral palsy, choreo-athetosis, mental retardation, and gout, but its most unequivocal symptom is a tendency to self-mutilation: the patient will gnaw at his own hands and feet, and the lining of his cheeks, until he bleeds, often to death . . .

# 27. Richmond Bridge

Another dour, dull, overcast Saturday lunchtime. Sarah and Simon and I are pushing Alice around the pathways of Chiswick House. Despite the substandard May weather, the avenues and pathways, the *pattes d'oie* and *pointes de vue* of Lord Burlington's Gardens are clogged with people, with locals and couples and yappy dogs and duffel-coated children and the odd architectural student taking snaps of the Villa.

Sarah is in despair: 'I hate it, I can't stand it – it's horrid.'

'Come on —'

'But everybody's staring!'

'No they're not.'

'Yes. They are. They *are*. They're all having a good look at Alice. It's so completely unfair . . .'

She is right. It is horrid and unfair: the way everybody is trying not to look at my poor little niece, as she fits and starts in her sad little pushchair. It is so gruelling and horrible it makes a surge of pity wave through me: for myself. I am the one that has to endure the embarrassment of being seen with my sister and Simon and their spastic child. And I can't hack it: despite my best attempts to be a good person, I can't deny that a deep dark part of me loathes being associated with the Reeveses. I don't want people to think I have any genetic relationship with this distraught woman and her badly dressed husband and their pitiful corpse of a daughter.

This is why I am walking about three yards in front of the trio: just enough to create a sense of separation, not enough to insult Simon and Sarah: I hope.

My aspirations are dashed when Simon goes to buy a paper and Sarah asks me to assist. To cover my awkwardness, I pretend to be avuncular and nice: leaning over Alice's pushchair I fuss and croon and rearrange her rugs. Then I gag: there are still flecks of blood and orange vomit on Alice's bib: evidence of this morning's attempt at breakfast.

Standing erect, I pretend not to care, not to be thrown; nonchalantly I glance at the tourists and the roller-bladers and the happier families; as I do so a man catches my glance. Immediately the man snaps his head away. Obviously he was staring at Alice; now he appears to be intently interested in the ornamental lake.

Jesus on speed. Swaying in the wind, here on the north side of the Villa, I feel an urge to run up and punch the man in the face. I also feel an urgent need to explain to him: '*It wasn't our bloody fault. She fell in a pool. Don't you understand? She wasn't always like this. Do you see? Don't you get it?*'

But I do not. Instead, as we stand beneath the hexastyle portico of Lord Burlington's diminutive mansion, I attempt a conversation with Simon. This is difficult. Getting a feedback from Simon these days is like trying to crack a lobster claw: the result never seems worth the sweat. But I have to try. Winding the conversational gramophone, I aver.

'It's a bit bloody small, don't you reckon?'

I am deliberately dissing Chiswick House, in an attempt to get Simon going. Normally such remarks would suffice to start some conversation; perhaps on the relative merits of English Palladianism, perhaps on the triumphs of totalitarian neo-classicism, perhaps on the England football manager. Not this time. Turning to look at Inigo Jones's gateway, Simon shrugs.

Slowly we move on. Very slowly. The crush is worsening. To escape these madding crowds we opt to inspect the interior of the house. This isn't so easy: right inside the porch a young Orthodox Jewish guy is arguing with the check-in girl; as the man raises his voice and shakes his angry head, his black tassels swing. He is blocking the way. For a moment we wait. The man doesn't move. He is happy for us to languish, while he finishes his argument. Alongside, I see that Simon is beginning to get angry: he is staring at the unseeing Jewish man, giving him a malevolent scowl. This gets worse when the Jewish guy concludes his tirade, and shoves past.

Shoving back, Simon hisses: 'Think about someone else . . . Yiddo.'

All I can hear is distant breezes, distant shouts. The Jewish guy turns and stares, and says: 'I'm sorry, what did you say?'

The man has a puzzled but intelligent face. Instantly I feel sorry for him, as well as hugely embarrassed. I nudge Simon: but instead of shutting up, Simon goes further.

'You obviously don't give a toss if we freeze in the queue. Do you? You're all the same – *kikes* ——'

This is terrible. I am appalled. I am appalled that this outburst has privately excited me. Roughly I tug my brother-in-law by the lapel of his raincoat: dragging him through the mobs of old women and Japanese teenagers, right down the garden, as far as the Great Chertsey Road gate. Sarah follows, clumsily trundling the pushchair across the gravel. To drown the oily

233

squeals of the pushchair, and the noise of Alice making her German sounds, I shout: 'What the hell did he do to you, Simon?'

Giving me the shrug, Simon says nothing. Forcefully, I repeat the question.

He replies: 'Beware the Jew who laughs in your midst . . .'

This strange reply chucks me. I simply don't get this. I don't have time to: Sarah is wailing.

'What's wrong, Simon? Please tell me. Please?? Simon?'

Methodically turning his head, like he has a crick in his neck, Simon stares at his wife. His expression is inexpressibly chilling. Now I try to say something, but I can't. A few seconds later Simon ends the debate by just walking away: leaving me with Sarah and the half-dead child and a distant view of a disappearing husband.

Resting her forehead in her hand, Sarah wails: 'I don't know what we can do any more, Guy . . . He is so . . . not there. Just so . . . not there.'

'Of course,' I say. 'I know . . . Shall we . . . uh . . .'

Shall we what? *Shall we what?* I don't know what we shall, what we might, what we could, or should, or will, or can. Maybe there are no more verbs for action: maybe we should just give up. Maybe Alice has got the right idea, just sitting there dribbling and puking, just sitting there in her pushchair, quoting Goethe and Rilke.

All right. Taking Sarah by the hand I say: 'Let's go and look at the house. We might as well.'

Obediently she follows. Approaching the ground floor door we pay our dues and step inside. Once within we find the newel stairs and wind our way upwards to the reception rooms, the dining rooms and saloons that comprise the principal glory of the

234

Chiswick House interior. These interlocking rooms are lovely. Wandering around the halls and corridors, I spin into a kind of synaesthetic daze. Sarah is pretending she doesn't mind, that she doesn't particularly care that her husband has deserted her; she is chatting to me about Alice's future, about next week's CAT Scan and what it means and how it's all going to be OK and how the doctors will deliver a vote of confidence; but I am not following her desperate rambling. I am regarding the red velvet wallhangings and the William Kent ceiling and the paintings by Ricci, and I am thinking: Oh Fucking Hell I Wish I Was In Love. God. Yes. I want it now: I want the whole caboodle, I want to feel the rain on my face, to experience all the pain and trauma. I want to be loved and hated, to be possessed, imprisoned, tattooed: to have another's name carved deep into the crystal of my soul.

I am alone. The ageing couple who were talking too loudly have disappeared into the octagonal saloon; my sister has disappeared to the Ladies with Alice. Standing in the Red Velvet Room, surveying the *rond points* through the wide Venetian windows, I relish the solitariness, the momentary sense of ownership, before turning to my guidebook to gen up on the place.

For some reason I am thinking back, to Bangkok, to those years of drug addiction that ended in Thailand. For some reason my mind is full of Bangkok and Nathalie and Josh and heroin – and everything else that kills me, still.

I decided to go to Bangkok the moment I was bailed from Vine Street Police Station. I had been banged up for possession of a mercifully minuscule amount of heroin, following a police search of Red Lion Square. This ordeal shook me up. As soon as I emerged into the doleful, rainy, litter-strewn streets of West London I thought about how all my friends were doing well, how they all had jobs, how it looked like I was going to be the one who swam out too far – and I decided: I'm off. Crossing the road I phoned Josh and told him it was time for us to run away to sea. Only thus, I explained, would we be able to escape the cruel vortex, the spiralling whirlpool of dealers and dope and dangerous friends.

Naturally, Josh agreed. He thought it was a brilliant idea: to escape our debts and addictions so easily and neatly and quickly and unbravely. Once Josh had concurred, I rang up my father and won a few hundred pounds for the air fare: on the premise that this was the only surefire means of curing my drug problem – short of my signing myself into a very expensive drug clinic. Despairingly, my long-suffering, still-guilty father paid out. As did Josh's trust fund. Three days later we caught the first plane out of Gatwick.

The plane was going to Bangkok. This seemed the obvious choice: it was fun, sunny, cheap and trendy. We didn't stop to think what else was in Bangkok. Or maybe we knew all along, and that's precisely why we went. The moment we landed in the Thai capital we caught a cab to the Khaosan Road: this being the notorious hippie hang-out near the Royal Palace: a hot, dusty, noisy street of cafés and Thai curry-stalls and cambios and cheap hotels; a street where hippies and dopeheads sold bootleg tapes and batik shirts alongside Siamese babushkas hawking plastic bags of pineapple chunks and plastic bowls full of fishball soup.

Right at the end of this tumult we located a slummy, slimy, fetid little alley. Down the end of the laundry-lined alley we found the sad, pretty, teak-stilted hotel: the VS Guest House. This was our chosen destination; our understanding was that you could score the best grass right here. Once we had checked in we walked out onto the wooden VS roof terrace. Here it began to go wrong. Despite our grapevine information that the VS sold great grass, we still weren't expecting the sight that awaited. The entire roof-terrace area was full of half-dressed Italians munching bananas and lounging in sun-hammocks and reading old copies of *La Stampa*. Every single one of them was also *scratching*; a behaviourism we knew all too well. Quizzically Josh squinted in my direction: from me he got no argument. All my best intentions, all my best mental defences, were trashed in a second by the seductive exoticism of the scenario. There was evidently plenty of heroin available here. And not just any old smack, either: given the locale, the chances were these Italians were strung out on Golden Triangle heroin. China white heroin. The *best* heroin. *Fait accompli*. All Josh and I had to do was come up with a suitable excuse for indulging. Our excuse went thus – if we did heroin here it would be more like a holiday romance, like a meaningless one-nighter, like a simple, uncomplicated, casual fling, than the sordid and destructive love affair we'd known at home – wouldn't it?

No question. Crouching beside one smacked-out Genoan, we enquired as to where we could find.

Lazily, the Genoan looked us over, scratching his shoulder as he did so: 'You mean – you donna know?'

'No. We only just arrived. Can we get it round here?'

'You can geddit downastair. Juss ask for . . . number four.'

After tossing a coin, to see who should do the deed, I sidled downstairs and went up to the wizened old Chinaman who ran the hotel, and before I could even ask he leered at me, and said: 'Allo Pee-ah. You wan' number four?'

*

It is now late afternoon. I am standing by the river, at Richmond. Miraculously, the sun has come out and it is warm – and I am no longer with Sarah and Simon and Alice. Consequently I am happy. I have wandered here from Chiswick House, over Richmond Bridge, through Mortlake and Sheen, and now I am standing on the riverbank of Old Palace Lane. The sun is dappling on the surface of the sweetly placid Thames and I feel a profound sense of contentment steal across me. Like a happy shiver after a swim.

Richmond always does this to me; it's one of those places – like St Ives or the Pantheon – that never fails. Its combination of hills and greenery and elegant shops sends me into a happy reverie. It is fine and light. It is sublime. Not least because of Quinlan Terry's Richmond Riverside Development.

Even as I stand here now, surveying the enfilade of Terry's effort, I can see why the more anally retentive of modern architects hate Richmond Riverside. It is so popular. For all its supposed illogicality, its so-called degeneracy, its contrary mix of old with new-old, of Georgian with neo-Georgian, it is a hit with the citizens. This selfsame afternoon, while I stroll along the Thames corniche, it is apparent how people enjoy being near this building: teenage boys are ragging each other and necking cold beers, little children are nagging their parents and begging for lollies, old women are halting by the gangways and turning blindly smiling faces to the sun. Several strolling couples have even stopped to kiss each other – by the pier and the steps and the Italianate east tower – so inspired are they by the *unauthenticity* of Terry's design.

Then again, maybe I am letting sentimentality get the better of me. As the sun fails, and I return north, towards central London, I decide I require more time, more time to think. To this end I take the long route

238

home: the looping riverside path that curves from Richmond Lock, around Old Deer Park and Kew Gardens to Kew Bridge and the station. This really is a long route: before I am halfway home the sun is completely gone and it starts getting chilly. A distance away I can hear dogs barking; and car-alarms wailing; and footballers shouting for lost balls in the gloom. On my left, across the tidal Thames, the tourist coaches are departing from Syon House; beyond that, on the Great West Road and the Chiswick flyovers, tired children are staring sleepily at the dazzling lights of the Gillette Tower, and Hoover Factory, and Vantage West.

It is night.

I am approaching Kew Bridge. Even though it is dark I know that I am close to Kew because, across the width of the bronze-black river, I can see six tall, slim, light-spangled tower blocks. These towers represent the vertical aspect of one of the most degrading and dehumanising housing estates in London: the Haverfield.

Standing here on the south side of the Thames, looking at these anorexic pillars of light, I realise, with a start, that from a distance the Haverfield Estate is completely beautiful.

# 28. Gunnersbury

'You twonk.'
  'It's true —'
  'Sure.'
  'It is. She looks just like Nathalie. Same tits.'
  'Pointing at the sky, right?'
  'Right. Same peachy arse as well.'
  'In your dreams!'
  'Just turn the page, Mackay —'
Andrew and I are in Osaka Bank, whiling away the
afternoon by flicking through a copy of *Vogue*. We are
comparing notes on what models remind us of which
ex-girlfriends: which explains why for half an hour I
have been banging on about sex and love – in particular, how love is like Sony Walkmans, in that it lasts for
eighteen months, and then always goes wrong . . .
Laying the magazine down, I sigh, and yearn: the
boss's copy of *Vogue* has fallen open at a different
page, at a spread of Kate Moss, the teenage superwaif.
In this set of pictures the model has been maquillated
to look like she has been recently beaten up. Her tenderly highboned cheeks have been made up to look
like she is savagely bruised.
  Seeing my interest, Andy snorts: 'Give me a break.'
  'Sorry?'
  'The Belsen babe?'

I drawl. 'She appeals to my . . . protective instinct.'

'More like your paedophile instinct. Gizzit 'ere.'

Tossing the mag over I watch as he expertly sweeps through the glossy pages.

'You're right, you know, she's got a certain nothing. She looks like a Cambodian on smack. Is she wearing knickers, or what?'

My friend is lost. He is in raptures. The conversation is over. Swivelling in my chair, I determine to stay frivolous. Idly picking up a pencil I drum it on my desk; then I locate a disposable chopstick in the bin, and use the two to paradiddle. But it is no good; my good form, so reminiscent of my old cheery self, cannot last. The weight of recent reality is overwhelming. Soon I am on that lonely track . . .

I have to think about it: *Alice*. At 6pm yesterday evening the results of the second CAT Scan came through: and they were not good. They were exceptionally grim. They confirmed what the first Scan inferred: massive damage to both hemispheres of Alice's brain. Or, as the Great Ormond Street neurologist put it: 'If she gets an infection, perhaps . . .'

What the consultant meant by this unfinished locution was that if – at some point in the future – my niece looks like dying we should not strive officiously to keep her alive. We should allow her to die with dignity. In saying this, however, the good doctor was ignoring the fact that Alice may not oblige. She was and is a remarkably robust child: otherwise she wouldn't have survived the principal trauma. And this is the nastiest rub of the lot: over the last weeks it has become apparent that my niece could carry on just about existing for decades: there's no guarantee she ever will get pneumonia or pleurisy or anything suitably terminal.

And as I sit here staring at my Bloomberg screen, I wonder, anyway: supposing Alice *did* succumb to

241

some viral infection, how could my sister ever be expected to look at her precious daughter, turn complacently to the nurses, and say: *OK, that's the lot. Let her die?*

The situation is dire. It appears my sister and Simon are doomed to spend their years manacled to a living corpse. For the rest of the decade, and beyond, the forces that rule the Reeves family will be perniciously centripetal. The Reeves family will hereafter resemble one of those doomed distant galaxies that spin around – and into – an annihilating Black Hole.

Picking up some Tuffs reports I scan some guff about Japanese interest rates and dollar futures and Clinton's healthcare reforms, and the last named's effect on Cable. But then I despair: how can I keep on doing this? How can I keep at my job? I like my job but it doesn't seem overly relevant to what is happening in my mind.

'Phone call,' says Andy, handing me the receiver.

I clear my throat: 'Guy Simpson.'

'Guy —' It's my mother. She sounds panicked.

'What's wrong?'

'It's Simon. I'm at the house. At their house —'

'And?'

'It's bad news. I have to tell you he's beaten her up.'

'Sorry?'

Slowly, my mum repeats: 'Simon's . . . beaten Sarah up, rather badly. I think you should come down, Guy.'

I am already out the door; I am already down on the ground and climbing on the Tube. When I reach Chiswick I march around the street corner to Upham Park Road where I find my mother standing in the middle of the Reeves's humble living room, trying not to cry.

'Where's Sarah?' I say.

She carries on nearly weeping.

242

'Where is she, Mum?'

'In hospital.'

'Hospital? How bad is it?'

Pulling a handkerchief from the sleeve of her cardigan, my mother dabs at her rheumy eyes.

'They say . . .' She swallows. 'They said . . . she's going to be all right. She's got some nasty cuts and bruises, but it's not anything life-threatening . . .' My mother's voice is wobbling, as she says: 'You know, Guy, I simply don't understand this any more. When does it end? What did we ever do to deserve this?'

Awkwardly, I shrug: 'I don't know, Mum . . . I just don't know.' I have no idea what to say. 'Where's Simon, anyway?'

'At the police station.'

'How ——?'

'It was a neighbour who heard them . . . She rang me at Great Ormond Street.'

'But – did anyone say *why*? Why the hell he did it?'

There is a pause. Shuffling over to the window, as if she is awaiting visitors, my mother mumbles at the curtains: 'He just went insane, it seems. Sarah was too shocked to really tell me. But . . .' Another sigh. 'It's all down to the accident. He's never really let it out, has he? Neither of them. They've never had the chance to mourn, never the option.' Delicately dabbing another tear, my mother continues: 'To think . . . How it must have been building up. And then he heard the result of the Scan . . .'

Going over, I stand alongside my mother and together we gaze out at the semi-detached houses. Now I say: 'He's always blamed Sarah, deep down, hasn't he?'

Not looking at me, my mother nods: 'Oh yes . . . Oh yes, I think so.'

*

243

After this I go into the kitchen and make a series of phone calls – to the hospital, to get a report on Sarah, and then to the local police stations, in the hope of locating Simon. It turns out Simon is banged up in Gunnersbury nick, and that the police want me to come and get him; the difficulty is that Simon doesn't want to be conditionally released: he wants the police to lock him up and lose the key.

The police station is a ten-minute walk. Ambling past the redbrick Edwardian terraces I wonder at what has brought us here, to this particular suburban turn-around, this karmic cul de sac; I wonder why our lives, his and mine, are so curiously intertwined.

The second time I saw Simon after Nathalie, I was nearly dead: I was desperately ill. I had been living in the VS guest house in Bangkok for exactly six months. Those months had been characterised by debt, despair, self-doubt and doom. Soon after arriving in Thailand Josh and I had built up a handsomely destructive drug habit, a habit that, despite the cheapness of drugs in Bangkok, was financially insupportable. Thus our main problem was working out ways of supporting it. We spent most of those days sitting under the languid fan of our VS hotel room, doing heroin off cigarette-foil while dreaming up ruses, new scams for swindling our friends and our families in England. It was appalling, it was sad. We were worse than the Italians; we were the worst junkies on the Khaosan Road. We were such bad news, we were even known to the British Embassy: not least because we'd already swindled a Repatriation Loan out of the Consul, and spent the Repatriation Loan on drugs.

One morning: things changed. I woke up, bleary-eyed, dusty, aching, mosquito-bitten, already sweating – and found a note for me on Josh's empty bed. Two

244

days before Josh had taken a taxi through the crazy Bangkok traffic to the Amex office on the Sukhumvit Road, to collect yet another, absolutely final this-is-the-last-time dollar wad wired over by his father in London; yesterday he'd obviously been down to one of the Indian bucketshops on the Khaosan Road and spent the sum on a plane ticket home: when I yawningly opened the letter it said, simply: *Sorry. I had to take the chance. See you soon?*

Reading this letter, I couldn't find it in me to blame my friend for baling out. For the long months prior to this moment we had been two drowning men drowning each other. And now Josh had broken the loop: he'd done the strong, sensible thing and used the last wad of cash for its intended purpose. I respected him for this: even though it threw into ever starker relief my own predicament. Truly was I fucked: three days previous my own cash cows in England had finally dried: my father and mother, and what friends I had left, had all refused my desperate collect calls. They had dumped me; and the very same afternoon I had been forced to pawn my possessions to the VS hotel-owner in lieu of rent: even my passport, even my *Walkman.*

And three days on I was still sitting in a filthy wooden hotel room in Bangkok: still lolling in the humidity, still lying on a filthy bed, still listening to the sing-song accents of the Siamese workmen outside, still smelling the lunchtime smells of lemon grass and coconut and frying chilli, still lazily watching the smoke wind through the slats of my shutters from all the streetside woks and *tom yam* stalls.

In a different mood, at a different time, this ambience of foreignness would have solaced and enlivened me; instead it revolted me. Rising from my sweat-soaked winding sheet I went downstairs and approached the wizened Chinaman. Tapping the side of my nose I

245

winked: giving him the acknowledged signal. Obediently the hotel-owner disappeared, and reappeared with a clear plastic straw full of white heroin. Handing over my very last baht with a languid *Sawadi-ka* I took the straw and padded back to my room. And for the next two days I did nothing but heroin – I smoked and puffed and coughed and puked – until the last grain of powder turned into the last wisp of smoke, whereafter I put my foil down, exhaled agreeably, lay back on the bed, wiped the sweat off my nose – and considered suicide. It seemed a neat way out. I was now penniless and friendless and passportless and Walkmanless and pretty soon I was going to be homeless. So why not? Lying on the bed I stared at the ceiling-fan and thought about utilising the light-flex, when – almost too neatly – there came a knock on the door.

'Pee-ah? Pee-ah?'

Blocking my ears, I tried to ignore the interruption. It could only be the hotel manager, hassling for rent, or my immediate removal. The banging went on: 'Pee-ah? Pee-ah?'

This second assault was closely followed by another voice, by a different voice, saying: 'Guy, Guy, it's me. Open the door.'

No. No way. I couldn't believe it. I wasn't sure I wanted to believe it. Getting up I groped for the door handle and opened the door and saw: Simon. On the threshold was a flushed, smiling, eager, Hawaiian-shirted Simon Reeves. Flopping back onto the bed, I stared up at him. Standing in the doorway he stared down at me, and said: 'I must say, I've seen you looking healthier.'

Thus was it done: thereby was I saved. After ordering a couple of Cokes, Simon sat me down amongst the banana peels and reefer-stubs that littered the sunny roof terrace, and got me to explain what had happened in the last three years. Then, after listening to the edited highlights of my lowlife, he explained that he was here to bring me back; to bring me back home. I was speechless with gratitude and with embarrassment. Virtually the very last time I had seen Simon was when he'd caught me being fellated by our first love. I had to confront this thorny problem. Sipping my Coca-Cola I attempted an apology.

'Look, Simon – about Nathalie . . .'

And that was as far as I got: at the mention of her name Simon flapped an impatient hand. Enough said, it seemed; or rather: nothing to be said. Thereafter the subject was never raised. He didn't want a grovelling apology. He only wanted me to return to London. He also wanted to tell me about my sister.

'My sister? *Sarah?*'

'We're getting married,' he smiled. 'She's pregnant.'

This was unexpected: as I sat there on the terrace, I dimly remembered that my sister had once been vaguely sweet on Simon; and I also recalled his once mentioning a penchant for her; nevertheless this turn of events was still a nice surprise. The two people I had most feared would never find happiness were Simon and Sarah. Now they had found it together – and I was coming home. I broke into a broader smile: sorted.

The following day Simon bought me some new clothes, some food, some toiletries, a haircut, my old passport, and a pair of Aeroflot tickets to London Heathrow. The day after that we flew home; to sweet England, to my homeland, to my beloved London, to *la vita nuova* . . .

Gunnersbury Police Station. I am here. Going in I check with the duty sergeant; he leads me to a cell and opens a steel door and inside I see Simon in classic prison pose: slumped forward, head in hands.

Sitting down alongside him, on the hard horsehair mattress, I say: 'I understand, you know.'

He says nothing.

'I really do. It's OK.'

He lifts his eyes. These eyes are hollow, and red from crying. Blinking wearily, as if he can't be bothered to focus, Simon says: 'I've lost it. I've lost it, Guy.'

'Come on —'

He slumps further. 'I have . . . O Me of Little Faith.'

'What . . .?'

'When I got back from the hospital, I lost it. I just thought . . . I just thought bugger it, I can't be bothered to believe, I can't be buggered to believe in God any more. Not any more.'

I nod, autistically. He sighs.

'It's . . . difficult to say this. But I have to say it. I have to tell you. I do.' I keep silent; he goes on. 'When I saw Alice, this morning, in hospital, I thought . . . I just wished . . . Christ. I just wanted her to be dead. To get it all over and done with. Do you see? I wished she was dead. My own daughter. I wanted her to die. Because if she doesn't die this is just going to go on and on and on, do you see? . . . the pain's going to get worse. Not better. She's always going to be there, dribbling, in that bloody wheelchair, sitting in that chair, accusingly. Her existence will always be an accusation. Making us feel guilty. Making us hate each other. Each other, and her. And God. God . . . I mean . . .' Simon is gazing fixedly at the yellow-painted wall.

'That's what I felt at the hospital, you see . . . And then when I got home and Sarah walked in the room and started shouting at me, started the whole argument off again, about whose fault it was, about why I shouldn't have been asleep, I just . . . just . . . you know . . .'

'I know.' I say. 'I know.' And I do, sort of. Maybe.

248

The cell is silent. Simon is silently crying. This is embarrassing and upsetting, and touching. I do not know what to do. I am remembering Bangkok. I am remembering when he came to me. I am remembering how once Simon swallowed his pride and his anger and his feelings of vengeance to rescue me from myself, to save my life; and I am thinking, therefore, that I must try and help him now. But how? How can I help him? There must be something I can do; must be something, something . . .

Whatever it is, I can't think. All I can do is sit here and put my arms around my friend's shoulders in an awkward, I'm-a-man-but-I-do-sort-of-love-you sort of way.

Jesus, what next?

# 29. Pitzhanger

Grief is an aquifer, an underground river, a cool blue subterranean lagoon into which I can dive without leaving a ripple. I could drown in this pool and no one would know; I could descend unto its siftless, sandy bed, and thereafter swim on and on: under a sump, through an aperture, into grottoes and chambers as big as cathedrals, into vast limestone caverns never seen by the sun.

Watching Eva do the washing-up I attempt to prevent myself. Diving into the cool blue pool of grief . . . can only lead to madness. So I shall help to dry, instead: picking up a Tube map tea towel from the draining board, I say: 'Here, let me help —'

She gives me a wry look.

'Too kind.'

Eva and I are in Blue Cedars to help look after Alice, to help out with the housework, and other things, while the mess that is my sister and my brother-in-law is sorted: until Simon is bailed and my sister comes out of hospital. Observing my girlfriend, as she attacks a roasting dish with a Brillo pad, I consider how it is quite useful that she and I are still going out: her compassionate, caring, girly nature has come in quite handy during these afflicted days. Nonetheless I really wish we weren't going out any more, I wish I had had the guts to finish it in Hampstead, as I planned; I am beginning to feel overwhelmingly trapped in this relationship. Like an animal imprisoned in a thorn bush, every move I make seems to hurt, leads to pain: every attempt I make to change the unhappy nature of Eva's and my relationship turns inexorably to squabbles, to arguments, to stand-up rows about our appalling sex life, about her lack of orgasms, about my general selfishness.

Tapping Eva's bottom, I say: 'Any chance of a shag?'

'What?'

'A shag, a tup, a fuck. The sweet commerce of limbs —'

'*Nein*,' she says, wiping her brow with a forearm. 'We must finish the dishes first. OK?'

'Whatever . . .'

Dumping the tea cloth, I take out and ignite another Turkish. Apathetically drawing on this new cigarette I sidle across the expensive kitchen floor to the south-facing windows. Outside it is raining; the rain is pummelling down. Through the curly blue Paisleys of my cigarette smoke, I can see the Forestry Commission conifers of Lexley Wood, marching across the soft, southern English landscape: in the foreground I can see the swimming pool.

Half of me does not want to confront the haunted swimming pool; half of me wants to go out there with bell, book and candle, and exorcise its ghosts. I trust the braver me will win out: if not, the whole world will soon become unliveable. These last few months I have noticed that everywhere is becoming spooked by the past – particularly London. Wherever I go, in town, I come across places where Nathalie and I made love, or where Josh and I took drugs, or where Alex and I got busted. From Pitzhanger Manor to Peckham Station, from Hanging Sword Alley to Hounslow West, the city

251

is becoming horribly resonant, profoundly historical; when I stroll around London, these days, I feel like a Christian scholar walking the streets of Jerusalem.

Maybe the cigarette is making me buzz a bit too much. Grinding it out in a saucer I turn and look at Eva.

'You have finished the drying?' She is pointing at the huge pile of undried dishes.

'Yes,' I say, curtly. It is enough. Crossing the kitchen I stare blankly at Eva, wondering whether to punch her or kiss her. Instead I pick little Eva up. Deftly I put her over my shoulder and carry her through into the hall. The house is empty apart from us and Alice's nurse. And Alice. Making the most of this desertion I hod a struggling, punching, squealing Eva into the downstairs guest bedroom. Throwing her body onto the double bed – like a gamekeeper offloading the carcass of a deer – I bark an order for Eva to strip. Gazing at me with malevolent resentment, Eva starts unbuckling her belt and her shoes; drawing up her tee-shirt she lets her hair tumble, likewise her breasts; then she peels off her knickers and kicks them away.

Now I have to make her come. Having short-sightedly started this process, I must try and bring my girlfriend to orgasm; from grim experience I know this will take an hour, at least. So I had better begin: flexing my fingers I start by manipulating her clitoris; after a few minutes of that I pause; then I finger her clitoris again, until she coughs; then I go down on her and make my jaw ache. For a few minutes I penetrate her and she yawns; then I withdraw and start rubbing her again. Then I stare out of the window and she drinks some water. After that I fuck her again from behind; as I do this I rub her clitoris and bite her shoulder slightly, then I stop and stiffen myself on my straightened arms, and I gaze out of the window at the rain, listening to

252

the wind as it staggers drunkenly about the garden: knocking over plant pots and slamming shed doors. Then I gaze down into the cold, sullen eyes of my girlfriend and I smash her straight across the face.

'Fff —' she says. 'Fff —'

Blood is trickling from her nose, so I slap her again. She gulps and squirms. Grabbing a fistful of her hair, tearing it like grass from earth, I hit her again, and bite her; then I lick her bleeding cheek and the blood tastes like old coins in my mouth. She is saying: 'Hit me – go on then – hit me you *bastard* – fucking *hit me* —'

I hit her. Slapping her face with a loud crack I make her eyes go wide; ignoring her gasp of pain I wallop her across the neck and she makes a gurgling noise. Then I move onto her stomach and I force open her legs and I penetrate her dry vagina, gratingly. As I rasp into her she starts to sob, and sob, and my ears are full of her little bleats of pain as I fuck her and slap her and fuck her, as I lever myself on an arm – and use the other hand to belt her across the chin until she screams: 'Guy —' she says, '. . . Guyyyyyyy —'

She is flooding: she is coming; this is the cactus bloom, blue cedar wood, the stands of black poplars. I have my teeth clenched around Eva's gulping, sobbing throat; I am biting her neck, biting her windpipe between my teeth like a lioness throttling a downed gazelle. I am spinning her, blissing her, sending her —

'Please – *bitte schön* —'

Her cunt is sopping; she is coming, she's saying 'Daddy . . . oh Daddy!' And I can feel it. I have touched it: pierced the permafrost. Biting her neck, I feel the buzz of her orgasm against my teeth: and then I come, too. I am coming. As we climax together I sigh and swallow saliva and then I collapse onto her body, and the Pietà of my nakedness is draped in her maternal lap and I am trying not to bust open into millions of tears, into a million shards of unhappiness.

Stroking my hair, she sighs, she cries, she turns away. The rain is tapping at the window, like a cat that wants to come in. Daffodils are wet and yellow and broken-stemmed in the garden.

Wiping the snot and tears from her nose with the inside of her wrist, Eva says: 'I fucking hate you.'

'I know.'

'It's over. It's all over. I fucking hate you.'

'I know.'

'I don't love you any more.'

'No.'

'I hate you. I hate you. *I hate you I hate you.*'

'I know.'

'Always. It's always like this . . .'

'The parabola of love . . .'

'*Leave me alone!*'

Commanded, I climb off the bed and wrestle myself into my jeans, shirt and shoes; re-belting myself and buttoning my flies I walk out into the hall and cross the parquet floor, and then I mount the stairs.

In Alice's room Sally the nurse is doing some knitting; this looks strangely old – she is only twenty-one. Dropping the needles, the nurse gazes up at me in that keen, sincerely nervous way of hers.

'Hello.'

I smile: 'Hello.'

'Where's . . . Eva?'

'Downstairs. Sleeping off lunch.'

'Oh really. That's nice.' Nodding, satisfied, the nurse picks up her needles again. It occurs to me that I could tell this sweet, dippy girl almost anything, and she would believe it. She is just that kind of girl . . .

'Sally,' I say.

She looks up again, brightly. 'Yes?'

'Could you leave me alone, with Alice, for a while?'

Momentarily, the nurse frowns; then she smiles and rises and leaves. When she has gone I sit myself down in the chair and I look at my niece. Alice is lying in her cot and her faded blue eyes are gazing at me, unseeing. The sweet cloudless blue of her eyes looks like an underground pool: staring into them I feel dizzy, a kind of vertigo. Too much. Taking the seat I cross my legs and pinch the top of my nose between thumb and forefinger to cure my splitting headache. After that I sit in the chair and just stare at Alice staring blindly at me. For hours. For what seems like hours we stare at each other; the only sound in the room is her stertorous breathing, the rattle in her throat, the sound of her tracheotomy filling with phlegm. Her thumbs are still protruding through her fingers; her legs are scissored; her face is still bleakly sad; she looks very tired; Apple Crackles, Numberelli, Toffypops, Ricicles. Reaching over to Alice's cot I button up her Snoopy pyjamas, as far as the small pit of her tracheotomied throat.

Then I begin talking. For some reason I cannot fathom, I start talking to Alice, telling her about her accident.

'You fell in the pool. You see? You fell in my father's pool and you are never going to get better. You used to be happy and alive and then you fell in the pool and you were under the water. That's why you are brain-dead, Alice, you couldn't breathe under the water so your mind went wrong, your brain went wrong. You are never going to walk again, to run, to climb things, to grow up. You are always going to be lying there, you will always be in pain, you will never be real, never be a proper person. You are just going to lie in bed for ever and ever. You are not ill. You cannot get better. You cannot get better. All because you fell in a fucking pool. All because you spent seven minutes at the bottom of a pool.'

During my rant I have risen to my feet. Coming to my senses I look down at my niece and I notice that her head has moved; somehow her head has jerked, as if she is trying to follow me with her eyes; as I near her I see, with a shudder, that she has been weeping. Alice is crying. Tears are streaming soundlessly down her face.

Aware that these tears are reflexive, are meaningless reactions to loud stimuli – such as my impromptu outburst – I still find the pity of it excruciating. Reaching into the cot I extract Alice's body, and then I cradle her stiffness in my arms and press my mouth to her warm temple and I rock us backwards and forwards.

'Alice Alice Alice Alice Alice Alice . . .'

# 30. The Huntingdon Arms

I am sitting on a bar stool in my local pub and I am finishing my fifth pint of cold lager. Downing the empty glass on the fake marble bar top I do a chilly burp and wink at the Serbian bar girl; giving me a weary smile she comes across and takes my empty. This she tips to the beer nozzle until it is full.

'That's six,' she says, handing me my new pint.

'I know,' I say, slurring.

It is three in the afternoon and the spring sunshine is trying to break through the clouds and I am the last person left in the pub. My intention is to drink straight through. I want to drink to forget. I want to drink to remember. I want to remember the day we went to Baldhu . . .

It was a warm, dank, overcast day. I was in Cornwall, with Nathalie, showing her the sights of my mother's home county. Simon was safely – and ignorantly – ensconced in Somerset. Skidding the car aimlessly along some leafy Cornish B-roads, near my mother's home in Truro, we saw a sign saying BALDHU, ½ MILE. The name intrigued. With little else to do, we swung a right, and a left, down a long, muddy track, passing a school and a field and a couple of rundown stone cottages.

257

Right at the end we found the church. It was derelict: the doors and windows were boarded up; the gutters had been turned to swallows' nests. Climbing out of the car we decided to investigate anyway. From the roadside the graveyard looked baroquely interesting: it was. Surrounding the shell of the church was a wealth of magnificent Victorian statuary, a field of marble gravestones and granite crosses, all wreathed with green ivy and dripping briars and rotting wild roses. Absorbed, I started reading the epitaphs and the architecture; Nathalie, more easily bored, wandered off to talk to a horse in a nearby field.

At the far side of the church I noticed another wooden door; it had been covered with graffiti. Stepping nearer I stooped to make out the scratched writing. It said *Christ is dead.* And it said *Light and shadow by turns, but always love.* And right at the bottom it read *Suffer the little child that comes unto me.*

I never mentioned this to Nathalie, at the time. I didn't see why. But for a long time it reverberated. I kept on wanting to go back to Baldhu church; to read the graffiti again. To break into the church itself. To shout into the cracked and nettle-sprouting tombs. Much later on I asked my mother about the church, about Baldhu. I asked her what the name meant.

'Black mine,' she said.

The Serbian bar girl is switching the CD: she is putting on 'Tubular Bells'. I haven't heard this in years but somehow it fits. The pub is ambient this afternoon: it is full of that deliciously indolent mid-afternoon feeling when there's nothing to do but sit round and drink. Which is what I intend to do. Today it's just me and the bar girl and the bar girl's nail file, and the nail file seems to interest the bar girl most. She is sitting on a black and metal stool by the CD player, her legs tightly

258

crossed, as she slightly sticks out her tongue and minutely files her unvarnished nails. Her distance agrees. It leaves me alone to get drunk.

Drunker. Outside I can see a crocodile of school-children heading up the Hemingford Road. The kids are holding hands and laughing in the sunshine. Seeing these happy children I realise with a frisson that these selfsame infants are racist thugs. Fascist hoodlums. Potential Klansmen. Witnessing Simon's anti-Semitic outburst at Chiswick House the other day made me realise this: we are all racists *manqués*. Whenever I see a black British sportsman doing well, a negro sprinter winning a gold, an Antiguan-born bowler skittling the Aussies, I get a puff of slightly patronising pride and warm fellow-feeling. And yet, and yet: whenever I am cut up in my car by a boy-racer in Brixton, or a West Indian bus driver, I don't think you stupid bastard. I think: you stupid black bastard. Fucking nigger. Fuck you.

The CD player has switched from Mike Oldfield to Don Henley. My Serbian bar girl obviously has *retardataire* tastes in pop music. But I do not mind. It is nice to wallow in nostalgia. In nostalgia for a time when I wasn't aware of moral precepts, of the categorical imperative . . .

With a defiant belch, I rise from my stool and slouch into the Gents and I unroll myself and urinate and sigh and burp again. Then I go back into the bar and re-situate myself atop my bar stool. Slumping forward I stare at the silvery streams of chainy bubbles arising from the bottom of my lager. I think about drink. And I think about drugs. Why did I do them? What am I so afraid of observing? What am I scared of seeing if I stall long enough to look in the mirror?

Raising my glass, here and now, I toast myself in the mirror, then I neck the rest of my Tennants and I slam the empty glass down on the bar top. The slanting sunlight is making laddery shadows through the window blinds. Squinting between the slats of sun, the Serbian bar girl looks up, and smiles, and says: 'Seven?'

'Seven.'

Consequently she takes my glass and beertaps it to the brim with fizzy gold lager, and then returns the resultant pint glass to my particular beer mat.

'Thanks,' I say, adding a slurred 'Spasibo!', in an attempt to be Slavically matey. The girl shakes her head and says: 'Stick to the English, Guy.'

I nod and chuckle and chill the tickle in my throat with another neckful of cold beer. Not sitting down, the Serbian bar girl engages me: 'No work, today?'

'Not today,' I grimace. 'I'm taking the rest of the year off.'

'That bad?'

Shrugging, I fist some peanuts and fill my mouth: talking through the salted crunchiness: 'I've had a bit of bad news. Family stuff, you know. Mind's a bit of a scrambled egg . . .' Taking up my pint, I down it with three or four hungry gulps, and then I sit back on the bar stool and it spins: suddenly I'm watching the room move around me. Shit. I feel ill. I feel like a picked-on child in the schoolyard. The room is shifting on an axis called me. I have drunk way too much: holding on to the bar I close my eyes to get a proprioceptive grip, to stop the roomspin. Then, lifting myself off the bar, I swallow and try to revive myself. But I can't. With a shiver I realise that I am beginning to blur: I am beginning to confuse things. My mind is fucked. Even now, I can blearily see the Serbian bar girl staring at me from across the pub and I cannot tell if her expression is one of shock, or curiosity, or casual friendliness. Am I that drunk? That gone? How come?

Stumbling down the bar to the cigarette machine – in

an attempt to be normal and sensible, to be just a guy who smokes, just a guy who's buying some fags – I bend to the machine and I squint myopically at the instructions. *Insert two pound coins*, it says. *And a 50p piece*. Reaching in my pocket I try to steal some change from myself but it is no good: with a sudden snap of my head I lift my eyes and I look out the window at a sunlit Hemingford Road. The road is being used by cars, slowly negotiating the speedbumps. There is a man gardening, and another man whitewashing. All looks normal, but then so does Ulster. And now I know where I live. I live in Northern Ireland: on the Shankill, or The Falls. I am living in a place where normality and horror are blurred, where memories are synonymous with nightmares – where history comes mixed with despair. My life is the site of a sectarian war: and I do not know which is the right side. I cannot. All I can know is that atrocities are taking place, that bombs and mortars are going off, that shops are being gutted and that people are being kneecapped – and that I do not know which side is responsible, or whether or not they are justified.

I also accept, as I sit unsteadily back on my bar stool and order another beer, that if life, my life, has become subject to civil insurgency, blighted by Troubles, morally blurred by terrorist violence: then when an atrocity is committed there is only one way to respond.

# 31. Pucci Pizza

I am thinking . . .

   I am trying not to think about . . .

   I am thinking about . . .

   I am trying to focus on the scene outside my father's wide kitchen windows, on the skyscape of evening, on the early summer sun that is melting into a horizon of colourful clouds – into ochre, and yellow, and beaujolais . . .

   It is late in May. It is late in the day. It is late, it is late, it is late.

   I have been daydreaming. I have been daydreaming about laughing children with machete wounds. About seeing a girl I once loved with no mouth. About my mother standing alone, in a car park . . . My mind is fried. Sitting here in my father's big Sixties kitchen I try to unfry it: invoking some kinder images, some nicer memories. Sipping some wine from my lonely glass I think about toys I once loved: translucent red plastic water-pistols and chunky Dinky dumper-trucks and a big see-through ray gun that sparked when I squeezed the trigger. Considering these things makes me cheerier; makes me fond with nostalgia. The contemporary world is so unchildlike, so old and serious: it sends me. Surely things didn't use to be like this? I can recall when everything was miraculously frivolous, gorgeously pointless.

Yes. Sitting here in Blue Cedars' pinewood kitchen, staring at the trees and the lawns and the serenely roseate sky, I wonder about the way it has all panned out. About the weather systems of life. Did she have to fall in the pool? If Simon hadn't been asleep, if Sarah hadn't been map-reading, if my father hadn't made coffee – and if the weather hadn't been so good that they kept the pool open – would my sister now be lying in a hospital, contemplating suicide, and would my best friend be sitting in a bedsit, contemplating suicide, and would I really be sitting here in my father's kitchen, contemplating —

'Hi.'

The voice belongs to Sally, Alice's nurse. She is timidly nosing through the kitchen door. Twisting in my chair, I gaze over, and I smile. During the last couple of days I have come to know the nurse, properly: she is genuinely sweet-natured and likeable, if a bit shy.

'Where is everyone?'

'Gone out.'

'Your mum and dad?'

'I think you mean my stepmother . . .'

'Sorry. Yes.' She smiles nervously. 'Where have they gone?'

'Just for a meal, they'll be back about ten . . .' I pick up the wine bottle, and chuckle: 'Don't suppose you fancy a glass, do you? There's no way I'll get through it alone . . .'

Uncertainly smoothing her blue cotton dress, Sally approaches the table.

'Well, I suppose . . . Alice's alarm is switched on. But only one glass.' Her bottom lip trembles. 'Really.'

Nonchalantly grinning, I rise and hand the girl an already filled wine glass. Ten minutes previous, I filled this glass with Rioja and Diazepam: the red Spanish

263

wine is spiked with a whacking great slug of Alice's liquified tranquilliser.

Accepting the adulterated drink Sally moves away from the table: she crosses the kitchen, and chooses to lean against the draining board. From this vantage point she glances flickeringly at the telephone and me, and the ceiling, and the sunsetting sky through the wide picture windows. Finally she sips at the red liquid and makes a sudden face.

'Euchhh . . . I mean . . . golly. Is this wine . . . all right?'

Her drinking hand is poised above the sink, as if she is about to up-end the glass over the plug hole. This is not what I want. Cruelly I play upon the girl's ignorance: 'It's meant to taste like that.' I say. 'It's vintage.'

Sally blushes. 'Oh . . . right.' She anxiously chuckles. 'Never was much of an expert.'

And obediently she drinks, in hasty gulps. Rapt, I watch her do this; she is disconcerted by my steady gaze. Stammering, she covers her mouth with a hand.

'Is there – something on my face?'

That was clumsy. Chastising myself for being so obvious, I mollify the girl with good humour. Spinning a line about my father's retarded taste in furniture, I offer her a curved wooden chair at the other side of the table. Sally accepts. Once she has sat down I am able to relax, a little: from here I can observe the girl's alertness without appearing too interested.

Sipping the last of her poisoned wine, Sally smiles and accepts another inch from the bottle, and asks me about Alice's parents. Candidly I shrug and tell her the whole long horrible story: about the accident and the coma and the horrific sequelae. The girl nods sombrely and sympathetically. She is, I think, beginning to get a little woozy. The Diazepam must be beginning to kick in. Continuing my story, I inform the nurse about Simon's violence, and his breakdown, and about

Sarah's hospitalisation, and suicide threats – and the looming certainty of a divorce. In other words I tell the nurse exactly how Alice's near destruction is destroying all our lives. Nodding quietly, the nurse sips the last of her wine, and suddenly yawns.

'God . . .' she says. 'I just . . . God, I'm sorry. I just feel . . . a bit tired . . .'

Concerned, I lean across the table. 'Are you OK?'

The nurse is yawning, massively.

'I don't know . . . I think . . .' She tries to smile at me, but fails. Her lips are twitching, her eyelids drooping. 'I must go and see . . .

Seconds pass while Sally blinks and swallows and stares at me with a slightly panicked expression. She is really losing it. Widening her eyes she goes to talk – then she changes her mind and scrapes back the chair and makes to rise, but as she does so she suddenly wobbles on her feet and stumbles into the table; now her speech is totally incoherent.

Going round the table I catch Sally about the waist, and help her to sit down again. As soon as she is seated and released, her head slumps forward onto the table; she is gone.

OK. After positioning Sally so she will be comfortable and less likely to wake, I cross the room to the hall, turn, and climb the stairs to Alice's bedroom. From behind Alice's bedroom door there issues an almost chimp-like chatter of noises: my niece, sleeping in her uniquely tortured way. Creaking the door open I go inside and scan. The room is pretty dark. Attached to the nearest wall is the baby-alarm: taking out the alarm's batteries I replace the cells with some dead batteries from my Walkman, thus disabling the device. Then I go over to the cot, and stare into Alice's ineffably sad, ineffably pathetic, ineffably weary face.

*

Once I returned from Bangkok with Simon, my life swiftly readjusted to normality. This was largely due to my attendance at Narcotics Anonymous meetings. For the first few months of that first new year in London, I diligently made a daily trek down the Kings Road to the corner of Pelham Street, to a smoke-filled basement room around the corner from Pucci Pizza. In this dingy basement was the HQ of the Chelsea branch of Narcotics Anonymous. Here I changed my life: by talking about my smack-taking experiences with other smack-takers, and ex-smack-takers, and recovered smack-takers: a freemasonry of fucked-up young people. The only problem with NA, as I found, was the philosophy of drug-taking as illness. I didn't mind many of the other objectionable aspects of the NA system – the slightly naff New Ageishness, the hugging and the handholding, the sessions of dubious praying. These were OK: they were a small price to pay for the chance of meeting a regular supply of new off-the-street junkies. Those poor, sad, still-using bastards were important: they were what kept me off drugs: they were the ones that served to regularly remind me of just how insidious and horrible heroin abuse was: how it was an AIDS of the soul, a Karposi's Sarcoma of the psyche: uglifying everything and everyone it touched.

What truly unsettled me about NA was its insistence that heroin abuse was a disease. That we addicts were sufferers of a peculiarly cruel affliction. That we were all victims. This was, I felt, bollocks. What kind of victim was I? It was me that bought the smack. It was me that held the foil. It was me that puffed away. Apart from the sadness of Nathalie, I had no real excuse, no mitigating difficulty, no particularly horrible parents or nasty adolescent scars or stupidly over-privileged background: mine wasn't the kind of psyche in which the bacillus of drug addiction should ever have flourished;

yet it did. Because I wanted it to. I did it. *I* did it. I went out there and thought, fuck it. It was me that made the phone calls, it was me that went to Peckham, it was me that crouched in pub toilets, it was me that stole and lied and fled to Bangkok and got more addicted. It was *me*. It was also me that cleaned up, found a job with Osaka Bank, sorted out my emotions and generally got a life. That was a noble achievement, as I saw it, and I wanted credit for it: more than the credit one gets for surviving an illness.

So I quit.

Standing in Alice's bedroom, gazing into Alice's cot, I try to work out how to remove her tracheotomy tube. It is difficult to concentrate on this: everything in this room – like Alice's Snoopy pyjamas, and Alice's expensive stuffed leopard, and Alice's Asterix duvet cover – is screaming at me: go away. You never thought about it. Go back downstairs. Concentrating on Alice's sad, softly staring eyes, I bring my mind into focus. These blue eyes remind me of my duty: the way they stare listlessly into the middle distance, like she is a caged monkey, like she is a sad circus animal. These eyes seem to be yearning for a distant place, for a place where painlessness and tranquillity reside.

So.

Fumbling with the plastic sticky tape that keeps the tracheotomy tube attached to Alice's flesh, I gingerly begin peeling. It proves difficult. My hands are sweating so much the tape won't give: I can't unpick the corners. To compound the hassle, Alice has begun to stir: she is moving into that strange pseudo-consciousness she knows for waking. This means I must be quick. But I can't. All my overrides are telling me, are directing me, are *demanding* that I pick up my niece and kiss her on her frightened brow, and croon into the

267

downy hair by her ear . . . *Jesus,* Jesus. Steadying myself I focus on the glazed eyes and the contorted hands and the adducted legs, so tightly scissored under the Asterix duvet cover.

After gripping a corner of sticky tape, again, I unpeel it from Alice's neck, following it with another bit of tape, and another; finally the whole arrangement begins to loosen from the flesh and I start to pull – No. *No!* A noise has frozen me. What is it? A car? Is it my dad and stepmother, coming back? Standing here in the half-light of Alice's bedroom I listen, rigid, as a car stops outside the house. Cold sweat is running down my back. I feel giddy. Then the car moves away – and I swallow drily, like I have been saved from a fatal fall. Once more I look down at my niece. Alice hasn't moved; she is now making more noises. She is making those noises. She is moving her left arm in that androidy way and gargling those unsettling words, those German poems.

Finding the tracheotomy tube, I begin to pull, and then I halt: once more paralysed by the hugeness of what I am doing. The sweat is beading on my forehead, and sliding down my face, and down my neck, and into the small of my back and under the elastic belt of my shorts. I can feel the pain points of adrenalin breaking out on my chest, and inside the crotch of my armpits. The adrenalin is telling me to flee: my duty is to stay.

LIGHT!

The line of light from the half-open door has suddenly widened; standing here I close my eyes hard and suppress the tension from my face and I turn to face the nurse with any kind of explanation. Opening my eyes I look and breathe and see —

A cat. Stood beneath me is the family cat, purring between my legs and cocking a croziered tail and showing a neat little arsehole. She wants to be stroked. Picking up the cat I kiss her soft neck, sinking my face into her perfumed fur, all the time attuning my ears to the sounds from the cot: 'Sh . . . shpiel – shnn . . .'

Dropping the cat, I gather all the willpower I possess: all the strength I have ever had. Shutting my mind, I reach down into the cot and I tackle the tube, properly: hooking it with a forefinger, pressing down the print of my thumb on the curved steel outer tube. Slightly jostled, Alice speaks: 'Glattere – luff . . .'

I hold.

'Glattere —'

I am tugging the tube.

'Glat . . .'

Grasping the tube I begin to edge the whole steel and plastic contraption out of the flesh hole in Alice's neck, out of the neat, surgical vagina in her neck. A bubble of blood appears.

'Schon.'

It is extracted. Looking down I see that blood is now beginning to dribble out of the hole in Alice's neck; a minor overflow of crimson ink. For a minute I sway there, silently, tube in hand – then Alice begins to gabble. She widens her eyes, her arm spasms upwards and the blood begins to gurgle. She is fighting for air, for life: and I am holding her tube in my hand and I am watching her drown. I am watching as I drown my niece, as I finish doing what God started. That's all I'm doing. Just holding Alice's head under water, for a further thirty seconds, for those extra crucial thirty seconds. But it's taking longer than thirty seconds. Much longer. Alice is managing to breath through the frothy hole in her neck. She is fighting for life. Her arm is jerking, up and down, up and down. Her eyelids are fluttering. Her mouth is mouthing words as she contorts and spits and moves her arm. The sweat is stinging under the elastic belt of my shorts and my neck is hurting, and I can hear the blood and vomit rattling in Alice's gullet, like the rattling sound inside a shaken spraypaint can.

'Glückliche! Glückliche!'

The room is tiny, is huge. Clutching Alice's blood-striped tracheotomy tube I close my eyes and try not to listen. Instead I am imagining smart red-and-black pencils, and shiny old Swiss watches, and draws full of keys and foreign coins and golden thumbtacks and paint-flaked screws and pink-and-white gingham-checked pincushions; I am considering the black of the beautiful night sky through Alice's window, through the bedroom window where the trees are slightly bending in the evening breeze; in the soft, cedar-scented breeze —

Please! Just drown! Please!?

Completely panicked, I am fiercely calm. With the tube in my hand, I gaze down into the cot and see. After another gargle of blood, and another contra-flexion of her neck, Alice jerks, and begins to sing. She is singing. Singing something. As she sings she twists and contorts, heartrendingly, and then she widens her gaze. This is unbearable. My eyes are teary with sweat, and I can barely see: yet I can see. I can see Snoopy and Asterix and a gold-and-black leopard and I am holding the tube so hard its metal edges are slicing into the heel of my thumb.

Now Alice's head grates to the right and she stares accusingly at me and the ceiling and as she does this her mouth gapes wide, and she says:

'. . . schrecklich.'

# 32. The Angel, Islington

A year has passed.

It is June.

I am sitting in Andy Mackay's new Wapping flat having lunch with him and his fiancée Janine, with Josh and his fiancée Georgia, and with another couple called Teddy and Emma. The girl Janine is exceptionally pretty; gazing across the table at her delicate face I find it a struggle to stop. The only way I can do this is by distracting myself with the view that fills the windows, beyond. Without moving from my stained-oak dining chair I can see yellow-sailed windsurfers in New Shadwell Basin, the complex baroque spire of Hawksmoor's St George, and the high-rise estates of Whitechapel and Ratcliff.

Andy is asking me whether I am in love.

I say: 'I wish.'

Pouring some Pouilly Fuissé, Josh exhorts: 'If you really wanted to fall in love, you know, you could. You just don't want to. You don't want to let yourself . . . Whatever happened to the Swissie, anyway?'

'Sorry?'

'Spicerack . . . Eva.'

'Eva Speisser . . . Chucked her, months ago.'

'You what? But she was tidy, man. I wouldn't have minded using her one slice toaster – Ouch!'

Josh's Sloaney girlfriend has kicked him under the table: moaning dramatically, Josh amends: 'What I meant was – she looked like she was very sensitive and clever, and expert in Pre-Raphaelite paintings . . . or something.' Deadpan, he turns to his other half: 'All right?'

Georgia grimaces: 'Creep.' But she does not mean it; stretching across the lunch plates she kisses her boyfriend on his unshaven chin. This is altogether a poignant scene. As I sit here in this expensive warehouse conversion, looking at the Modern British paintings arrayed along the chic exposed brickwork, I feel the piquancy: I feel a pang of jealousy. But it is only a pang: not like the angst I would once have suffered. I no longer have such a yearning to be hitched like Andy. In the last months I have stopped waiting at the luggage carousel of love; I have ceased waiting for the Louis Vuitton to arrive. I think I have come to accept I am one of life's Hand-Luggage-Onlys.

Someone speaks. Looking up I see Janine standing by my side in her flimsy white cotton shirt, offering me some trifle from a large bowl. As she leans, the sunlight silhouettes the happy curve of her breast.

'More trifle . . . let's see . . . do I want more trifle . . . hmmm . . .'

Not waiting for a proper answer, Janine dollops a splodge of cream and cold custard and marsala-soaked sponge into my pudding bowl. This I consume enthusiastically, while the lunchtime conversation continues around me, hopscotching from marriage, to children, to schools-in-the-area. Sitting here, spoon in hand, I cannot credit this conversational theme. I never thought the day would come when I would be listening to my old friend Mackay – muffinman Mackay, *snatch-merchant* Mackay – discoursing interestedly and intelligently on weddings and mortgages, and all that.

'How's the architecture going?' Andy has noticed that I have been excluded by the couply chit-chat.

'Oh, you know,' I say. 'Fine. Bit of a shock, being a student again.'

'Guess you're a bit povvy, living on a grant?'

'Could say that. But it is pretty interesting. I'm designing a bicycle shed for a school in South Dorset at the moment.'

'Sounds ace.'

'Yeah . . . I think I might try and use some modernist principles. The glorious interplay of bicycles in light.'

Janine interrupts: 'I'm sorry?'

I turn to her: 'It's a quote.'

'I know that. It's a paraphrase of Le Corbusier. Yes?'

'Sort of . . .' I smile. 'Are you interested in architecture?'

Wrinkling her pretty nose, Janine says: 'Not exactly. It annoys me, I'm afraid.'

'Why?'

'Because of architects . . . Because they are the rudest, smuggest, nastiest —'

'Sure —' I raise a hand. 'Understand. But that doesn't mean architecture is annoying, does it? Just architects.' I give her a glance. 'What do you do, anyway?'

Twisting her engagement ring, Janine confesses: 'I work for the Church of England.'

'The Church of England. *The Church of England*?'

'I do the PR for the Archbishop of Canterbury.'

'That's a toughie.'

'You think so?'

'Definitely.' I shake my head. 'I hope you don't mind me saying this but the Church of England as presently Established and Constituted, is . . . shite, isn't it?' She looks up, I expand: 'Don't you think so? Certainly seems that way. You've only got to look at the new liturgy – it's fatuous and crass and ugly, not to mention vulgar and —'

Janine retorts: 'You're one of those Cranmer Queens, right?'

'Maybe,' I demur. 'But you can't tell me the new revised stuff is anything but total bollocks. I can't see how anybody who cares about God or the language could think otherwise. You know, I went to a C of E church the other day and everybody was calling God You, and She. You? She? *Unbelievable*. It was like they thought God was some caring social worker from the council.' I tut, loudly. 'It was like they actually believed if we called God You and She and Her we could make Him less frightening, less upsetting for the children. Like a wimpy headmaster who wants the kids to call him by his first name. It's *crap*. If God exists He is definitely a big, nasty Father. A big, frightening, cruel, stern, daunting, drunken, heartless bastard of an absent father.' I burp. 'In fact, if you ask me, they should get the Child Support Agency on to God. Ask Him a few *questions*.'

In my inebriation I have gone further than I intended. Across the table Janine is staring at me in a strange way. Her eyes flickering, she says: 'Well . . . I don't know what church you visited, but there aren't many using the feminine pronoun.' She sips at her wine. 'You still haven't told me . . . do you actually personally believe?'

'Don't know.'

'You mean you're agnostic?'

'No. I mean, I doubt my own doubt.'

'Right.' She smiles. 'That's rather neat.'

'It's Graham Greene,' I say. 'And it's not what I really think, anyway. If I really had to formulate my belief . . . I'd say . . . the best way of putting it is: I love God, even though He doesn't exist.'

A pause. Janine laughs: 'That's very theological.'

'You think so? Mmmm . . .' Drawing breath, I wonder

274

whether to continue the debate. 'Actually, I might not be sure about God, but I know I *despise* atheists.'

'What?'

'Atheists. I despise them. Because they are so bloody stupid. They're like people who go to a cinema and sit there grumbling and poking you in the ribs and whining all the way through, saying "it's only a film" ' I can sense myself beginning to rant, again. But I don't care. 'It's *idiotic*. Talk about missing the point. It doesn't make any *odds* whether the film is true or not. It's whether it's beautiful, or funny, or moving . . .' Looking around at my audience, I shrug. 'And that's why I despise atheists, because they're so dim, so vegetarian . . .'

My outburst has provoked another silence. I hear Andy scraping his pudding bowl; this doesn't bother me. Let the silence continue; let them sit there in puzzlement, let what I said sink in. And it *has* sunk in. While I sit back, and torch another Turkish, I notice that Janine, having got over her initial surprise at my peroration, has started giving me that gaze again. That naughty gaze. Staring at her I find my mind wandering – I am suddenly starting to consider what bits of her body I'd like to suck.

Dangerous, dangerous. I should try and stop this. Shouldn't I? Maybe *not*. Maybe instead I should simply accept: that I'll always fancy my best friends' girlfriends, that it's just me, that this is the way I am made. Simply the way my father made me.

Sensing a frisson, Andy intercedes. Referring to today's election, for the European Parliament, he asks: 'You voted yet?'

'Not yet,' I admit, swivelling to face him. 'Not sure I can be arsed. Not unless there's a Blow Up Brussels Party.'

He chuckles: 'Still on your soap-box?'

275

'Yep. The whole thing is a Franco-German conspiracy to subvert our ancient Anglo-Saxon freedoms. And it sucks.'

'Margaret Thatcher's still the man, isn't she?'

'Too right,' I say. 'Too bloody right.'

Despite or because of my concurrence, I am un-interested in a Euro debate. For the last few weeks I have been arguing about Europe with anyone who will take me on; now I am bored with it. I opt to change the subject: 'How's Osaka, anyway – how's the old place?'

Andy shrugs: 'It's OK. The market's pretty bad. Rattled by the revelation that Major hasn't got any testicles.'

'I can imagine —'

'But we're still making a quid.'

'Kash Anderson?'

He laughs. 'She says she misses you. Misses your happy wit and your cheery laugh and the way you would stare at her tits all day.'

'They were pretty ace. No pints.'

'No pints at all.'

Clocking my watch, I see that the afternoon is run-ning on. The lunch party is beginning to get a bit *fin de siècle*: the table is looking decadent. While the girls bustle about emptying ashtrays, and picking up nap-kins, and clearing pudding bowls, the men chat, desul-torily, about sex and rugby. On the hunt for a last hit of wine I nip into the kitchen and find Janine and the girls starting on the dishes. The sight of Janine sinking her arms up to her elbows in greasy water, standing barefoot on the lino, washing up my dirty plates, gives me a sudden but definite erection. I feel like a medieval baron pleasurably appraising the backsides of his dairy-maids . . .

Not informing Janine of my precise train of thought,

I say: 'I hope I wasn't too offensive in there, about your job.'

'Don't worry,' she replies, positioning a sudsy saucer in the dishrack. 'We were actually just mentioning . . .' She looks around at the other girls, who are drying, and putting away. 'We were just wondering whether your unusual beliefs are because of . . . of what happened to your niece?'

Unflinching, I say: 'What do you mean?'

'Well . . . we just wondered whether . . . she fell in a pool, yes? And then she . . . died a few months ago?'

'Yeah.'

'I am sorry.' She looks seriously into the washing-up bowl. 'Andrew told me. I'm so sorry. It must have been terrible. How are . . . Simon and your sister? Are they all right now . . . are he and she . . .?'

'They're OK. Ish. Who knows what's going to happen in the future . . .'

Anxiously, Janine smudges her nose with the side of a washing-up-gloved hand. 'Your sister . . . She's pregnant, again, is that correct?'

'Uh-huh. Let's hope this one has a bit more luck.'

Wincing, Janine returns to her bowl. From the other side of the kitchen, Georgia wonders: 'By the way, whatever happened to the nurse . . .?'

'The nurse?'

'The nurse at the scene. I've forgotten what Josh told me. Wasn't she . . . prosecuted?'

'No.' I shake my head, soberly. 'They decided not to in the end. It was pretty obvious the coroner thought she was in some way culpable. But he decided to draw a veil. Rather sensible of him, I think.'

'Right . . . Right.' The girls nod at each other; Janine nods at Georgia; Georgia nods at Emma; we are all nodding: yes, draw a veil, forget it, move on, life continues.

Turning from the fridge, Emma pipes up: 'Anyone for coffee?'

Lunch is done. It is four in the afternoon. I am outside Andy's Shadwell Wharf warehouse-block, heading home. Around me the streets are full of Bangladeshi children and Sudanese teens and hard cockney kids doing wheelies on trailbikes. Across the road, in a complex of council maisonettes, shirtless men are hosing down their gleaming cars, while pinkly sunburnt housewives peg out white washing. Humming a happy tune, I stroll over the weighbridge that leads into Wapping proper. There I stop: my nonchalant homeward progress has been halted by the name of a pub: The Jolly Sailor.

Disconcertingly, I know this place. Ten years ago I lived near here, in Wapping, in a hard-to-let council flat, with two friends who were attending City Poly: what stumps me now is that The Jolly Sailor is the only place I recognise from that era. The area has been transformed. A decade back everything was wharves and warehouses and derelict tenements. Now, as I stroll the lanes, I can say E1 has become *beautiful*. The once ruinous warehouses have been graciously restored. The noble stockbrick arches of Gun Wharf and Prospect Place are clean and freshly pointed: Cinnamon Street and Monza Road are lined with fancy shops and brasseries.

And all about, where once was the shouts of bummarees, or the warbling of winos, now resounds that quintessential noise of contemporary London: the rippling purr of a BMW accelerating over old Docklands cobbles.

Ambling past Mayflower Gardens and the nettlesome, dockleafy graveyard of St Johns, and the twin riverside terraces of Wapping Head Pier, I come to the end of Docklands. Beyond this point tourist London begins: here, at the end of the road, the crowds thicken. As I crush through the people I hear nothing but shameless foreign languages: French and Italian and German and Japanese. These crowds bug me; I don't want to know. Instead I start marching, around St Katherine's Wharf, past the river police boats and the Panamanian yachts, striding as far as the terrace of the Tower Hotel: a small flagstoned plaza that gazes up in adoration of the mighty bascules of Tower Bridge. In this little square I stop to get my bearings. My sudden presence has disturbed a couple of girls who were snogging on a bench. A couple of girls?

Time to go: ducking down the bridgeside path of the World Trade Centre, I traverse the motorway that is East Smithfield, heading for Trinity Square. Here I pause and reconsider my route. Half an hour previous, on leaving Andy's flat, my intention was to join the Circle Line tube at Tower Hill Station, and head for the Angel, and Islington. Now I don't want to go straight home. My extrovert mood of the moment makes me feel like continuing my walk: to this end I hang a left into America Square, mislaying myself in the sunny, silent maze that is the Sunday-afternoon City.

The streets of the City are quite blissfully empty. Apart from the odd janitor's cat, dozing on a car bonnet, all is quiet. The desertion of the streets underlines the oddness of a noise coming from the direction of Bishopsgate.

As I head towards it, the noise grows louder. Whereas the rest of the City is preternaturally quiet, Bishopsgate is a clamorous din. Rounding the corner by Commercial Union I discover why: the place is alive with whistling workmen, with builders and glaziers and sparkies and blue-helmeted foremen, with shirtless brickies rolling wheelbarrows up steeply angled planks.

This area was where the Bishopsgate bomb went off, last year, and now it is all being rebuilt. Totally. Every building around me is being remade or refurbished; every new office block is swathed in green plastic netting; every space of pavement is obstacled by piles of new bricks and skips full of trash and chundering JCB mixers. Like a forest, after a fire; like a Pacific island, following an eruption: the city is phoenixing into life, just like before; just like she always does.